All the
BROKEN
PLACES

All the

BROKEN
PLACES

M. Jean Pike

Black Lyon Publishing, LLC

Our books may be ordered through your local bookstore or by
visiting the publisher:

www.BlackLyonPublishing.com

Black Lyon Publishing, LLC
PO Box 567
Baker City, OR 97814

This is a work of fiction. All of the characters, names, events,
organizations and conversations in this novel are either the products
of the author's vivid imagination or are used in a fictitious way for the
purposes of this story.

ISBN-13:   978-1-934912-87-4
Library of Congress Control Number: 2019943524

Published and printed in
the United States of America.

Black Lyon
Literary Fiction

For Riley,
who is the loveliest thing in my life.

Chapter One

*M*onica Humphrey had almost talked herself out of going to the Stop-N-Shop. Tired from her workday, all she wanted was to go home, relax, and watch a movie—her reward for making it through the week. The drizzling rain had turned into a downpour, coming down in thick, sideways sheets, and she hadn't thought to wear a jacket that morning. She'd be drenched before she crossed the parking lot. The few things she needed weren't worth that.

By the time she turned onto Hartford Avenue, she decided to go home, at least for a while, and wait for the rain to let up. Or go home and stay there, if it didn't. She didn't really need cat food. Ginger had more than enough for the weekend. And she had enough coffee to last until Saturday morning. There was no good reason to get soaked.

But it's Friday night, a little voice whispered as she pulled up to the first red light.

Friday night. Her night to put up her feet and let down her hair. Her night to watch movies while she enjoyed a half-gallon of ice cream. The Stop-N-Shop offered so many delectable flavors. Lemon Meringue. Birthday Bash. Caramel Mocha. Choosing her Friday night flavor was the high point of Monica's week.

At the second red light, her sweet tooth won out and she swung into the parking lot. She sat in her car as the rain pounded on the roof.

"This is crazy," she murmured.

A car pulled in beside her. A woman and a little girl got out and dashed toward the store. With a sigh, Monica stepped from her car.

Her sheer size prevented her from trying to outrun the rain, so she attempted a brisk walk instead. In heavy rains, Hartford Avenue was prone to flooding. Water sloshed over her sandals as she made her way across the parking lot. April showers would bring May flowers. At least there was that.

With no way to avoid the lake-sized puddle in front of the door, she slogged through it and went inside. The woman she'd seen earlier was busy wiping down the handle of her shopping cart with an antiseptic wipe. The little girl was spinning in circles, laughing.

Monica grabbed a shopping cart from the queue and pulled. Stuck, as usual. Irritated, she tugged again, harder this time.

On her third try, her feet lost traction on the slick floor and she tumbled toward the concrete, her hand shooting out to take the brunt of her three-hundred-and-twenty-two pounds. Her wrist snapped. With a sickening crunch, her face slammed into the floor and she felt a crashing inside her head. Someone screamed. Whether it was her or someone else, she couldn't be sure.

She couldn't be sure of anything. The whole world had turned a fuzzy gray.

"Carly, hush child!" The woman knelt at Monica's side, speaking as if through a tunnel. "Are you all right?"

All right? She didn't think so. She wasn't sure of anything in those first few moments as she lay drifting in and out of consciousness, not sure what had happened or even where she was. And then it came, like a tornado, sudden and swift.

Pain, ferocious pain. Pain in her wrist. Her face. It became all of her, all consuming. No, she was definitely not all right. She tried to take stock, moving her tongue around in her mouth, assessing. All of her teeth seemed to be accounted for. That was good. But there was something, some deep, jagged thing wrong with her jaw. Another face appeared then, another voice in the tunnel.

"Oh, God. Someone go get Barry."

Barry. The store manager. Yes, Barry was nice. Capable. He would know how to fix this. Smiling Barry. Balding Barry. It would be better when Barry was there. It wasn't much, nothing much at all, but she clung to it.

Was she going into shock?

"Monica?"

The woman was gone then, and Barry was there at her side. He was there, but it wasn't better. His big, warm hand rested on her shoulder. "You're going to be all right. Can you look at me?"

She tried to move her head but it hurt too much.

"Lo," she croaked.

"Okay. All right then." And then the gentleness left his voice and his tone was that of a man in charge. "Sami, have Joel call for a squad. And bring me a bag of ice." His hand returned to her shoulder and the softness returned to his voice. But it was not her he addressed. "Lord, we trust in you."

She could not look at him, could not move at all, but in her periphery she saw feet all around her—pumps and sandals, flip flops and high tops and she knew that a crowd had gathered. Lord, she hoped no one had their camera out, hoped she was not at this moment going viral on YouTube.

"Everyone go back in the store," Barry said. "Give us some room. Go on." The feet turned and slowly walked away, and for that, she would be eternally grateful to him.

She'd known Barry for two years, since the Stop-N-Shop first opened. It wasn't the biggest or brightest store in town, but it was close to her home on Euclid Drive and the prices were decent. Barry always took a moment to chat with her, always let her know about the weekly specials. She had always thought of him as rather bland, with his white shirt and blue slacks and receding hairline, but now his presence was like a lifeline. His calm was a port in her storm.

He sat beside her, pressing a bag of Happy Ice to her wrist and talking quietly until she saw the red flashing lights of an ambulance pulling up in front of the store. She tried to distract herself from the pain by focusing on the lovely, cool ice and the smooth sound of Barry's voice, let them sweep over her like a cool, sweet river.

Two paramedics rushed through the double doors, wheeling a stretcher. They got right down to business with questions. Name? Age? Weight? She couldn't answer them, couldn't seem to form the words.

Why couldn't she form the words?

"Monica, is it all right if I get in your bag and get out your ID?" Barry asked.

"Esh."

He retrieved her bag from beside her and pulled her license and insurance cards from her wallet.

"Her name is Monica Humphrey. Age thirty-two. She lives at 288 Euclid Drive. Height 5'3". Weight 322 pounds."

She felt the shame of her secrets, all of her ugly secrets being spoken aloud.

One of the paramedics took her vitals and radioed the hospital. The other started an IV, and then did things with her wrist and jaw. Horrible, painful things. Once he had her wrist splinted, he tied a bandage around her jaw and over the top of her head, tucking a cold compress inside to control the swelling. Then, grunting with the effort, they maneuvered her onto the stretcher. By that time the crowd had gathered again.

As the paramedics jacked her stretcher up into the air, she noticed with alarm that her purse lay abandoned on the floor. Wallet, credit cards, cell phone, a hundred dollars in cash. It could be gone in the blink of an eye. Losing her purse was one of Monica's biggest fears.

"Vy furse."

"I've got it, Monica," Barry said.

On the heels of that solved problem came another one. By now Ginger would be wondering about her, waiting and watching out the living room window. She would be wanting scruffings. Wanting food.

"Vy fat. Vy fat."

"What's she saying?" a teenaged boy in a pair of skinny jeans asked.

"I think she's saying she's fat," answered a girl in yoga pants.

"Well yeah, no shiz."

The girl tittered. Monica had taught middle-schoolers for eight years. She'd been insulted and verbally assaulted more times than she could count, and born it with patience. But somehow it had never hurt as badly as now. Tears of frustration and humiliation rolled down her face. "Vy fat," she said, trying to speak clearly. "Shinsher."

"I'll go and get Ginger when I get out of work," Barry told her. "I'll take her back to my house. How will that be?"

He'd figured it out. He knew Monica bought expensive cat food and a cart full of premium litter every week. Knew how much Ginger meant to her. They'd talked many times about how Monica had rescued her from a storm drain when she was just five weeks old.

"Hank you."

Her tears of humiliation mingled with tears of relief. Barry the store manager would take care of Ginger. He would go to Monica's house after work and get her and take her home.

He would see the weeks' worth of dirty dishes piled in the sink, the laundry in the hallway and the fast food bags scattered around the living room. He would see the way she lived and how much she hated herself. He would see it all.

Her last conscious image as the paramedics wheeled her out the door was of Barry the store manager watching after her wistfully from the entryway of the Stop-N-Shop, her red purse dangling from his hand.

•

Her first few hours in the hospital were all about needles and monitors and CT scans and worry. Pain and the absence of pain. Now, she had to wait. Wait to be moved upstairs to a proper bed. Wait for tomorrow. Wait to be made whole.

Humphrey Dumphrey sat on a wall. Humphrey Dumphrey had a great fall …

She'd had a great fall, all right. A colossal fall. Where were the king's horses and the king's men when you needed them? What a strange thing to think about. Her thoughts were scattered all over the place. But the morphine was lovely.

Humphrey Dumphrey. How she'd hated her last name and the cruel way the other kids used it against her. Even her so-called friends had laughed at the rhyme. She'd learned then it didn't pay to trust anyone. Through a haze, Barry's prayer came back to her. *Lord, we trust in you …*

Did she? She used to, completely. She wanted to again, but it was hard. Trust was hard. Life was hard.

She would have to call the school, let Layla know she would be out indefinitely. Thank God she'd hoarded her sick days.

All of this rain would make the grass go crazy. She'd need to mow the lawn.

The doctor called it rigid fixation. They were going to wire her jaws shut in the morning, and put in small plates and screws to stabilize the fractures so they could heal.

But a broken jaw was the least of it.

She had multiple fractures in her wrist. There would be more pins and plates. There would be six weeks of healing, exercises and hand therapy.

How strange life could be. She'd left her house this morning with no plans besides getting through the workday, and then her movie night. No idea she'd end up here, like this.

Tears fell. She felt so alone. She'd always been alone, really, except for her years with the girls. The girls. How she wished they were here now.

Chapter Two

Monica didn't remember much about her childhood in Pittsburgh. There were a few hazy impressions, like blurry snapshots that had faded with the years. A window fan blowing hot air around a red and white kitchen. A park with a swing set and a fountain. Her mother's bed.

The last few weeks of her mother's life, Monica was allowed to sleep in her parents' bed, her mother's arms wrapped tightly around her. Her mother felt so weak she seldom left her room, so her father moved the TV set into the bedroom. After school, Monica and her mother would cuddle together and watch cartoons. Sometimes, if her mother felt stronger, she would tell Monica stories. Mostly she slept.

The only argument Monica remembered her parents ever having was about her. Her father had wanted to take her mother to the hospital and she had refused to go. She wanted to stay with Monica. She wanted to stay in her own home. The last few days of Maureen Humphrey's life were lived in her bed. And then one rainy May afternoon while Monica was in school, she died in it, waiting for a kidney donor who never materialized.

The worst memory Monica had of Pittsburgh was of the day she got off the school bus and her father was not there waiting for her. Their upstairs neighbor, Mrs. Dawson, was there instead. Walking home, she told Monica something astonishing. That her mother had gone away. That she would not be coming back, not ever.

It couldn't be true. Couldn't possibly be true! Wrenching her hand from Mrs. Dawson's, Monica started to run. She burst through the apartment door and raced to her parent's bedroom, knowing her mother would be waiting for her, as she always was. She'd hold open her arms and Monica would snuggle into them, and she'd give her the pretty rainbow she made for her in arts and crafts that day. Instead of Mommy, though, her father was in there, crying. His whole body shook with it, his big hands covering his face. He held her close and stroked her hair. *Baby. My sweet baby girl.*

He cried all the time after that. The deep, racking sobs she heard in the night through her bedroom wall frightened her, as much as it frightened her that her mother wasn't there anymore, and never would be again.

The funeral was another series of blurry photos in her album. The white room with the chandelier, oppressively hot and sickeningly perfumed with flowers. The songs that made everyone cry. The hugging and kissing.

It was a week after the funeral that the girls showed up at the apartment. They swept in carrying boxes of food—homemade jams and pickles, fried chicken and a chocolate cake. She had only met her father's aunts once that she could remember. The summer before, she and her parents had stopped in Baxter on their way home from a Cleveland Indians game her mother had won tickets to on the radio.

Monica had been enthralled with Penny's copper-colored hair and red lipstick, with the farm and the little general store that sat at the end of the driveway. She remembered vividly the oversized candy stick the girls had given her, striped in red, yellow and blue. Sticky sweet, it had gotten stuck in her hair before the family was a mile outside of Baxter.

Stern but kind, Geneva was older, at fifty-two. At thirty-eight, Penny still had a youthful vitality that her slim body could not seem to contain. It spilled out in her laughter and in the way she seemed to love her life and everything in it. They were two hard-working, hard-loving women, both well into middle age, but everyone still called them "the girls."

Having company seemed to make her father happy. He cleared off the kitchen table, even put out her mother's good candles. The fried chicken was greasy and delicious, and it made Monica feel happy for the first time since her mother left.

Somehow, the girls' food took the sadness away. After the food, while Geneva helped her father pack her mother's clothes into boxes, Penny took Monica to the park with the fountain and they played on the swing set and blew the bubbles Penny had brought. Later that evening, she lay with her head in Penny's lap, drowsy with a day in the sun and murmuring voices and the clinking of ice in the sisters' glasses.

"It's getting late. Should I book you girls a motel room for the night?" her father asked. "I'd put you up here, but I don't have the room."

"No, we'll head on home soon," Geneva said, and Monica felt a stab of disappointment. "Will, Penny and I have been talking, and we thought … Why don't you let the child come and stay with us for a while?"

Monica's eyes shot open. She could see by his expression that the words surprised her father as much as they did her.

"What? No. Absolutely not."

"Think about it before you give us your answer."

"I don't want her in Ohio, Geneva. I want her here. She's never even been away from home overnight." His voice cracked. "She's only six years old."

"But what will you do with her while you're out on the road for days at a time?"

Her father looked sad again. She hoped he wouldn't cry. "I don't know."

"A little girl needs fresh air, trees to climb, fields of flowers to pick. We can offer her all of those things at the farm," Geneva said soothingly. "She could even learn to ride Duchess. What little girl wouldn't love to have a pony?"

Monica's breath caught. *A pony?*

"I don't want her riding any horses."

"All right. It was just a thought."

Silence fell, as thick as the frosting on Geneva's chocolate cake. Monica could hear the pounding of her own heart.

"What about …" Her father's voice trailed away. Looking at his hands, he nodded at Penny. "Can she handle the strain of having a little girl underfoot?"

"I'm perfectly capable of speaking for myself, Will. I can handle it. In fact I'm ready, willing and eager to handle it."

He sighed.

"Baxter is only a couple of hours away," Geneva coaxed. "You can come and visit as often as you like."

Her father's glance swept over his daughter. She was awake, her eyes fixed on his. "Come here, baby."

She rose from the couch and settled into his lap. He stroked her long, tangled hair. "Would you like to go and stay with the girls for the summer? Would you like that?"

She was torn. Torn clean in two.

"If you don't like it, I promise I'll bring you right back home," Penny said, her red mouth smiling.

Monica didn't want to leave her daddy. But she so wanted to escape the apartment. The place where her father was so sad, where her mother wasn't and would never be again.

•

That first summer on the farm was magical. Monica had never imagined anything as wonderful as the spacious hundred-year-old farmhouse, cascades of pale pink roses climbing up its sides. She had never seen the likes of the chickens and goats, the kittens, or the soft, caramel-colored pony.

The first morning, out in the chicken coop, Penny told her running the farm and Two Gals General Store was a job and a half. Geneva took care of the bookwork and the ordering, and Penny tended the gardens and the animals. She showed Monica how to collect eggs. When a feisty brown-speckled hen opened her beak wide, Monica shrunk back in horror.

"No, no, don't let her bully you."

"But she's trying to bite me."

"Just tell her not to do it."

Monica stared doubtfully at the hen, who glared back.

"Josephine, don't be an old biddy," Penny said, stroking the bird's feathers. "You have to give your eggs to Monica, the same as me."

Once again, Monica reached for the eggs. This time the hen grudgingly gave them over.

There was so much to do and to learn that every day was an

adventure. She helped Penny milk the goat, and pick the juicy, red strawberries from their garden that would be made into jam for the store. She learned how to snap the tops off of green beans, and to pick tomatoes without bruising them.

Mondays, Tuesdays, and Wednesdays were for baking and working on the little farm.

Thursdays, Fridays and Saturdays, the store was open for business and Monica learned how to bag the customers' items after Geneva rang them up. Baxter was a wrinkle in the road map, population twelve hundred at the last census. An hour from Cleveland, it may as well have been on the other side of the world. It was a half-hour from everywhere else, and the store was as much a gathering place as it was a necessity.

Sundays were for church.

Monica had never seen the inside of a church before she went to live with the girls. She loved the big old Presbyterian Church with its enormous pipe organ and stained glass windows. Geneva and Penny sang in the choir, and they sounded to Monica like the lovely, chirpy robins she heard outside her bedroom window each morning.

Pastor Cuthbert said amazing things she'd never heard before, things about angels and demons and being an ambassador for Christ. After each service, she would ask Penny and Geneva about things she'd heard, and they would explain things to her in a way that made sense. She was pampered and adored, and if she and the girls were a bit on the poor side, she never knew it.

She loved Geneva, but it was Penny she adored.

Penny wore her long, copper curls back in a braid every day, but in the evening, she took down her hair and let Monica brush it. One night, Monica commented on the silver streaks that gleamed at Penny's temples.

"Those come from a life of living, sweetie. Someday you'll have them, too."

"I wish I had them now."

Penny laughed and smoothed Monica's hair. "I'd give them to you if I could. My hair used to be much darker than it is. That's why they call me Penny. Do you want to know a secret?"

Monica leaned in eagerly. "Yes."

"My real name is Beatrice."

"Nu-uh."

"Uh-huh." Penny wrinkled her nose and Monica hugged her tight.

Her father came just twice that summer. Once on the Fourth of July, and then again in mid-August to take her home. He scooped her up in a hug, then stood her at arm's length and studied her.

"She's getting kind of heavy, isn't she?"

"She's healthy, Will. Healthy and happy," Geneva said. "Why don't you let her stay through the school year? See how it goes?"

Monica was stunned. She loved the farm, loved the girls, but to stay forever? She looked anxiously to her father, waiting for him to be sad, or angry. Waiting for him to remind Geneva that she was only six years old. But he didn't do any of those things. He didn't even put up a fight.

As an adult she would remember that moment and psychoanalyze it and wonder if that was part of her problem, her brokenness. That her father had let her go so easily.

The second summer, Monica was given more responsibilities in the store. Instead of just bagging people's items, Geneva taught her how to ring up sales on the cash register, and arrange the canned and baked goods on the shelves. Over the winter, when business was slow, she and Penny scoured the family cookbooks for interesting recipes. She came across a recipe for snickerdoodles and begged Penny to teach her how to make them. After that, Tuesdays became Monica's days to bake snickerdoodles for the store. It made her feel important, like one of the girls. She had even asked Penny if they could change the name of the store to Three Gals, and Penny had laughed her musical laugh and ruffled Monica's curls and said, "Let me think about it."

The store became Monica's classroom, the place where she learned about life, and how human nature worked. Some of the lessons were gentle. Some of them were just plain bizarre.

One morning in early June, a woman barged in the front door before Monica had even had a chance to turn the sign around to the *Open* side.

"What can I do for you, Mildred?" Penny asked cheerfully.

"For starters, you can stay away from my husband!"

"Stan?" Penny's eyebrows shot up and she laughed in surprise. "You've got to be kidding."

The woman's face flushed with anger. "Don't you try and deny it!" she yelled. "People saw you making up to him in the post office yesterday!"

Monica gaped at the old woman, the loaves of bread she was holding frozen in her hands. She remembered the man from the post office. He'd dropped a ten-dollar bill while buying stamps and Penny had been nice enough to pick it up for him. End of story. The man had to be seventy years old, and just as wide as he was tall.

Penny started to giggle.

Mildred dashed across the store, grabbed a fistful of Penny's braid, and yanked on it. The braid came down, stray tendrils tumbling wildly around her face. Penny wrenched free. With a savage yell, she opened a carton of eggs, took one out, and threw it at the other woman. It hit her square in the jaw. Enraged, the woman grabbed a package of Monica's snickerdoodles from a shelf and hurled them at Penny. They hit the wall, burst open, and broke into a thousand sugary pieces.

All at once, things were flying off the shelves and soaring through the air; cans of baking soda, jars of applesauce, a dill pickle. The ruckus brought Geneva hurrying to the front of the store. Her eyes swept over the madness.

"Stop it this minute! What in heavens name is going on?"

"Ask Mildred. She came in here and started throwing things!" Penny shouted.

"She flirted with my husband. Right on Main Street. Right in broad daylight!" Mildred bellowed.

"I don't want your husband, you silly old hen." Penny started to laugh hysterically.

"You're crazy!"

Geneva spoke softly, but firmly. "Millie, I think it would be best if you left now, before we have to get the Sheriff involved."

Mildred planted her hands on her generous hips. "You're not right, Penny Humphrey. You're crazy as a loon and there's not a person in this town who doesn't know it. Just see that you stay away from Stanley, you hear?"

She slammed the door so hard a package of muffins fell from the shelf. Geneva turned to Penny. "What on earth was that all about?"

Penny leaned against the counter, doubled over with laughter. "She thinks I'm after Stanley. Can you imagine?"

Geneva's hidden smile belied her stern tone of voice. "We'd better get this place cleaned up and ready to open. Monica, honey, go and get the broom."

Monica retrieved the broom from the closet out back and began to sweep up the snickerdoodles, trying to picture lovely Penny with fat old Stanley Bates.

Crazy as a loon. She rolled the words around on her tongue.

Later that night, as she brushed Penny's hair, she asked her what a loon was. Penny explained that a loon was a lovely water bird, sort of like a duck. Its song was beautiful and haunting, and when it sang in the night, in the dark, it sounded like a crazy person howling.

"But your singing is so pretty, Penny. Not like howling at all. It was mean of that lady to say that."

Penny smiled and hugged her tight. "Yes, it was."

It would be years before Monica understood what Mildred Bates had meant.

Chapter Three

*I*n four short days her entire life had changed.

She'd gone from being an independent, self-sufficient woman to needing help going to the bathroom. She couldn't even feed herself, if you could call beef broth and liquid gelatin food. Her right hand was useless, and with her left, she could not fill the plastic syringes, let alone maneuver them to her mouth. The nurses told her that in a day or two she would graduate to a sippy cup. Not that it mattered. For the first time in her memory, she wasn't hungry.

She sat in a chair beside the window, looking out at the traffic moving along East A Street and trying not to feel sorry for herself. That never helped. Self-pity only made things worse and she was in bad enough shape as it was.

The surgeon said the procedure went well. Her wrist was repaired and now the healing process could begin. Same with her jaw. Pins and plates and screws, and a mouthful of wire. She didn't feel repaired at all. She felt like Frankenstein.

"Monica?"

She hadn't heard him come in, and the sound of Barry's voice in the quiet room startled her. She did not want to see Barry the store manager—didn't want him to see her, looking like this, her face bruised and swollen to twice its size, fat, even for her. He approached uncertainly, cradling a Stop-N-Shop bag close to his chest.

"Hi."

The surgeon had urged her to talk, had given her lip exercises to do, to try and regain mobility. But her mouth was numb, and it was hard, so hard to talk through clenched teeth.

"Hi," she grunted.

"I came by yesterday but you were still in recovery from your surgery. Long haul, huh?"

She nodded.

"How are you feeling?"

She lifted her left hand in a small, hopeless gesture.

"I thought you might be worried about Ginger. I want you to know that she's doing just fine."

Relief pooled in her belly. Ginger was fine. Ginger, the only living thing who loved her.

"Zshe ..." She stopped, sucked in a breath of air, tried again. "Ish she eating?"

He smiled. "Like a little horse."

"Sgood."

"I called your school yesterday and explained things to them."

She looked at him in utter surprise. "You did?"

"I spoke with a lady named Layla. She said not to worry about a thing. They'll bring in a sub for you. Just get well."

Tears of relief filled her eyes and she blinked them back. Two things, two huge things checked off her to-do list. Worry about Ginger. Worry about job. Check. Check.

"Tank you."

He gestured toward the other chair. "Can I sit for a minute?"

She'd thought she didn't want company, didn't want to speak or be spoken to, but Barry's presence seemed like a breath of fresh air in the stale room. She nodded and he settled himself into the chair opposite her.

"So how long will you be in here?"

She shrugged. "Few days."

"I'll keep Ginger for as long as you need me to. You were right; she sure is good company."

Ginger. How she missed her.

"I've been stopping by for your mail. I've got it here with me." He opened the Stop-N-Shop bag and retrieved a thin stack of mail, which he'd neatly paper clipped together. It was humbling, that he would do all this for her. She could see what made him an excellent store manager. He paid attention to the details. She clumsily slid off the paper clip and flipped through the stack. It was mostly junk mail, except for her car insurance bill.

"Dish will have to be paid."

"I've got your purse here. Can you pay it by phone?"

He set her purse in her lap and she fumbled for her cell phone. There were no missed calls, not a single text. She tried twice to undo the clasp on her wallet. Failing miserably, she threw it down in frustration.

"Would you like me to do it?"

She nodded.

He opened the wallet and removed her debit card from its slot, then opened the insurance bill and called the automated payment number. Moments later, he ended the call.

"You're all set. Oh, and I took your car back to your house. It's in the driveway."

He was being so nice, showing so much more kindness than she could remember anyone showing her in a very long time. But why?

"Why are you doing all dis for me?"

"We're friends, aren't we?"

Her suspicious nature reared its ugly head.

"I'm not going to shue the shtore, if that's what they shent you to find out."

As soon as she said it, she wished she hadn't. It was rotten of her, when he was doing so much to be helpful. He'd probably leave and never come back. But Barry only smiled.

"I'll be sure to let them know that."

Ashamed, she was trying to think of an appropriate response when he stood. "Well, I'm on my lunch break, so I'd better get back to work. Is there anything else I can do, anything you need from home?"

"No."

"Can I come by again?"

"Please."

"Okay. I'll see you soon." With another smile and a gentle squeeze of her shoulder, he turned and left the room. She put her wallet back in her purse, along with her cell phone. Four days, and not a single message.

She watched out the window for Barry's car leaving the

lot, hoping for one last glimpse of him. Silly of her, since she had no idea what kind of car he drove. She hoped he would come to see her again. The realization hit her then, and it was like a ray of light shining in the deep, dark, loneliness that had overtaken her soul.

She had a friend.

To avoid disappointment, she told herself she didn't care whether he returned or not, but when he poked his head in her room two days later, she felt a flush of pleasure and let out a breath she hadn't realized she was holding.

"Let's get you outside of this room," he said.

"And go where?"

"I found something special, something wonderful. Come see."

He led her down the corridor, into the elevator, and down another long hallway. Then he opened an outside door and they stepped into a healing garden—a lovely paradise filled with plots of tulips in deep pinks and purples, sunny yellow daffodils and baskets of delphinium. Marble statues stood sentinel beneath newly budding magnolia trees, and wooden benches with oversized cushions were scattered along the brick paths. Its domed glass roof created a greenhouse effect, and though it was only early April, all of the spring flowers were in full bloom. The fresh air and the sheer beauty of the garden had done much to improve her spirits.

He visited every day after that, and it scared her how much she looked forward to those visits.

•

At two weeks post-op, Mimi the hand specialist was not impressed with her progress. By now, Mimi said, she should be able to at least wiggle her fingers.

"Are you doing the range of motion exercises I gave you?"

"Shum."

"I know it's painful, and I know it's easier to let your left hand do all the work, but you've got to get that hand moving, Monica." She handed her the tennis ball they used for therapy. "Work on gripping this. Lightly. And do those exercises I showed you. At our next session I want to see you pick up a full glass of water."

She shuffled back to her room, defeated. Would she ever be able to live a normal life again?

When Barry came that evening, she asked him to bring her laptop from home.

"Sure, I can do that."

She dug her key ring out of her purse and handed it to him. "It should be on da table. You might have to look around for da cord."

"I'll find it. I imagine your email is probably stacking up."

"I don't care about dat. I want to play Candy Crush."

"Candy Crush?" He grinned. "Don't tell me you're an addict?"

"Mimi shays I'm not working hard enough. Maybe da movement would be good for my hand."

"Makes sense. I'll bring it next time I come. It's a beautiful evening. Are you ready to head to the garden?"

On their way out, they stopped at the hospital snack shop for coffee. She was able to drink comfortably through a straw now. Dietary was even offering her bulky liquids, like pureed pasta and turkey. She'd ordered it just once, and the sight of it made her ill. On top of that, she'd developed an irrational fear of choking, so she stuck to thin liquids—her broth and her gelatin. And her nightly cappuccino. She always ordered the small cup, and rarely drank more than half of it, but the pleasure it brought her was worth every penny of the four-dollar price tag. She'd come to look forward to it as much she used to her Friday night ice cream.

When they'd settled themselves onto a bench, she told him her news. "I'm getting shprung on Monday."

"Really? That's wonderful news."

"I'm not going home yet. Dey think I need more rehab before I can take care of myshelf. I'm being transferred to St. Cecilia's for a couple of weeks."

"Over on Washington Street?"

"Yeah."

"Are you all right with that?"

Actually, she was. She'd been relieved when the hospital's

service coordinator had suggested it. She'd been choked with fear since learning she was to be released from the hospital. She could barely use her hand. How would she puree her foods or even dress herself? She couldn't even drive. How would she get to her therapy appointments? And she still couldn't speak clearly. What if something happened and she needed to call for help? The thought of staying at St. Cecilia's for two weeks allayed all of her fears. At least for the time being.

"I'm all right with it."

"Well good then. That's good."

They drank their coffee, not speaking for long moments. Then Barry asked, "What do they call those flowers over there, those tall, deep burgundy ones?"

"Those are shtargazers."

"I wonder if they're hard to grow. I'd like to have those around my lamppost."

"Any kind of lily is easy to grow." She gestured toward the plot of pale peach daylilies that surrounded a gently flowing angel fountain. "I'd like those in front of my porch."

She had loved flowers since her childhood days on the girls' farm, loved the columbine and the foxgloves and the riotous patch of lilies Penny grew behind the vegetable garden.

The vegetable garden is our bread and butter, Monica. But the flowers. The flowers are for the soul.

She'd often thought about putting some shrubs and flowers, even a couple of flowering trees, in front of her house. The landlord had encouraged it. But she didn't have the energy for flowers any more. She didn't have the energy for anything.

"What made you smile, just now?" Barry was watching her intently.

"I was thinking about the flower gardens we had where I grew up. The girls could grow anything."

"What girls?"

"My father's aunts. In Baxter. They raised me."

"You grew up in Baxter? I never knew that."

She shrugged. "It never came up."

"How did you end up in the big town of Risingville?"

"I came here for college. Then I got offered the job at the Middle School. Risingville had more to offer than Baxter, so I took the job. And here I am."

He smiled. "I'm glad it worked out that way. Do you see them often? The girls?"

"The girls aren't alive anymore. I go to visit their graves shometimes, though."

"I'd like to go with you, sometime."

She studied his profile in the dusky evening. "Why?"

He shrugged. "I'd like to see where you grew up."

She let her gaze slip away from him then, away to the plots of lilies and the gently flowing fountain. She sipped the last of her cappuccino and wondered why he cared.

Chapter Four

*I*t was a cool, lovely morning and she and Geneva were out in the flower garden, gathering an arrangement for the altar.

"How come we're doing this, instead of Penny?" she asked.

"Penny went out last night," Geneva told her, her mouth dipping into a frown. "She hasn't come home yet, and I don't want us to be late to church, today of all days."

As Geneva busily cut long stems of zinnias, coneflowers, and baby's breath, Monica wandered to the vegetable garden. She scrutinized the tomato plants and the rows of corn, then gently lifted the leaves that covered the new butternut squash.

"That should do it," Geneva said, straightening. "What's so interesting over there?"

"I'm looking for the bread and butter."

Geneva's eyebrows shot up. "In the garden?"

"Penny said the vegetable garden is our bread and butter, and the flowers are food for the soul. I've watched all summer and I haven't seen the first slice of bread. Or any butter, either."

Geneva threw back her head and laughed. "Oh, child. You didn't really think we grew bread in the garden, did you? You've seen how we mix the dough, let it rise, and then bake it."

"But Penny said so."

"That's just an expression, Monica. What Penny was saying is that the vegetable garden is what brings money into the store, with the fresh produce and fruit we sell, and all of the things we make from it."

"Oh."

She cupped Monica's face in her free hand. "Let's go inside

and get ready for church. We have our missionaries visiting today and I want you to look your best."

Many thoughts weighed on her as she followed Geneva back to the house. Geneva seemed more mad than worried that Penny had gone out on a date and not come home, but it seemed strange to Monica. Penny had been out on a lot of dates in the last few weeks, but she'd always come home before.

And the knowledge that tomorrow was her last day of freedom before starting the third grade on Tuesday kept crossing her mind like a dark shadow crossing the sun. Last year she'd been one of the biggest kids in her class, bigger than most of the boys, even. When Geneva made her new school dresses she'd commented that Monica had grown like a weed this summer. She hoped the other kids had grown like weeds, too. Not just up, but out and sideways too, like she had.

She was dying of curiosity about the missionaries. The church had been buzzing about their visit for a month, praying for their ministry and their safe travel home from Costa Rica. She had never met a missionary before. What would they be like? She'd found Costa Rica in the encyclopedia, a beautiful, exotic country of rain forests and clear blue lakes, where black-haired women in brightly colored skirts did amazing folk dances. She hoped their missionaries would look like those women.

Penny came flying into the house just as they were leaving. "Good. I'm glad you haven't left yet," she said breathlessly. "Just give me two minutes to change my clothes."

"We don't really have time to spare, Penny," Geneva said tightly. "I wanted to arrive a little early today. You knew that."

"Two minutes," she said, racing up the stairs to her room.

•

When they arrived at church at 9:00, the choir was already practicing. Geneva arranged the flowers she'd cut on the altar and the sisters took their places in the front row. Monica loved those Sunday mornings in the church before everyone else arrived. She loved to sit in the red velvet pew and listen to the choir sing, as if just for her.

At 9:45, people started filing in. More than usual, Monica noticed. Nearly every seat was filled.

Pastor Cuthbert and a man and woman she didn't recognize strode up to the altar and sat down. Monica studied them, hoping they were not the missionaries. They were regular people, disappointing in their ordinariness. They were plainly dressed, no exotic costumes like the dancing women in the encyclopedia. The man was bald in the front and wearing wire framed glasses. The woman wore a plain blue dress and had short blonde hair. They were not what she had expected at all. After the choir sang the morning hymns and returned to their seats, Pastor greeted everyone and offered up the morning prayers.

"We're just thrilled to have Don and Susan with us today. I know we're all eager to hear about their ministry," he said. "So without further ado, I'm going to turn the service over to them."

The bald man, Don, stood and walked to the podium. "Good morning!"

"Good morning!"

"Firstly, let me say how blessed we feel to have such a dedicated church family at home that supports our mission. Believe me, we couldn't do it without you. To update you on where your missionary dollars are going, we've just built our third church."

The congregation applauded, and Monica joined them.

"All of our churches have local pastors, and dedicated discipleship groups. We're growing, folks."

Everyone applauded again.

"As you know, Susan leads a women's group. They give out roughly two hundred meals a month. She's teaching impoverished women how to sew and earn a decent living. As a result, prostitution is now almost nonexistent in our village." More applause. This time Monica didn't join in. Her hands were getting sore. She made a mental note to ask Penny later what prostitution meant.

"We have a slide presentation to show you, but first, I see our daughter Lydia finally decided to join us," he said, smiling. "She tells me she has a special song to share with you."

Everyone turned to watch the girl walk down the aisle. Monica's breath caught. Lydia was beautiful, with golden blonde hair, sparkly silver sandals, and a white dress that looked like an angel's robe. Smiling, she walked up to the altar, kissed her parents, and took up a guitar that was perched beside a stool.

"Good morning, everyone."

"Good morning, Lydia," the congregation said.

She gently strummed the guitar. "I was eight years old when my parents decided to go on the mission field to Costa Rica. I'll admit I didn't want to go, at first. I wanted to stay here, where everything was familiar and safe. I wanted to stay in the town I'd always lived in, where all my relatives and friends lived. But once I got there and saw how beautiful it is, how warm and genuine the people are, I guess you could say I fell in love with Costa Rica at first sight. What I want to say to you today is, don't ever think you're too young or too old, too rich or too poor, too awkward or too anything, to be a tool in the hands of God. Believe me—no one is clumsier than me."

Everyone laughed. Monica inched to the edge of her seat, mesmerized.

"I was nine years old when I started serving in our community food kitchen. At age twelve I helped build a church. I have a learning disability called dyslexia, but even so, I just finished my first year at Risingville College. I'm going to get my teaching degree, and go back to Costa Rica and teach the missionary children. Because with God there are no disabilities. There's only grace and opportunities to watch him work. If God can use me, He can use anyone. He can use you." When the applause stopped, Lydia sang a beautiful Spanish hymn. Monica couldn't understand a word of it, but even so, she was captivated. That's what she was going to do. She was going to go to Costa Rica and serve soup and build churches. She was going to teach missionary children, just like Lydia.

For the next week, she talked of nothing but becoming a missionary. Geneva took her to the library and she checked out a thick picture book about Costa Rica and another called *Conversational Spanish for Children*. On the evenings when Penny was home, she would quiz Monica. When Penny was out, Monica quizzed herself. By the end of the week she had learned all of her colors.

If not for school, her life would have been perfect. Her fears came true on her first day back at Lester H. Philips Elementary. Still the biggest kid in her class, she was bigger than even the biggest boys. When the other kids called her names, she buried her nose deeper in her Spanish book and told herself she didn't care. She had been called by God. She was special.

At recess, while the boys played dodge ball, and the girls separated into their gossipy little clusters, Monica took her book to a shady tree and sat down to study her numbers.

"One. Uno. Two. Dos. Three—"

"What's that?"

She glanced up and saw Kenny Peters standing in front of her. She didn't like many of the kids in her class, and she liked Kenny least of all. Ignoring him, she turned back to her book.

"Spanish? Hey everyone, Humphrey Dumphrey is learning how to speak Spanish!"

He tore the book out of her hand and glanced at the page. "Uno, dos, tres, quat—"

She jumped to her feet. "Give it back!"

"Why don't you go and get it, seen-your-eat-a." He threw the book across the playground. It landed with a thud in the weeds. Another boy, Marvin Conrad, picked it up and flipped through its pages.

"Let me see. How do you say fat-so in Spanish?"

Angry tears poured down her face. "Please give it back. It's a library book."

"Don't cry, Humphrey Dumphrey. Here." He held the book out to her. Cautiously, she reached for it. But as she'd known he would, Marvin threw it over her head.

The bell rang and everyone herded inside. She picked her book up from the ground and wiped off the dirt. The cover was scuffed and the bottom corner, torn. She hoped she wouldn't lose her library privileges.

•

The thirty-five minute bus ride from Boswell Center to

Baxter lasted forever that day. Within the first five miles, the boys grew tired of taunting her and their talk turned to their latest obsession, The Mighty Morphin Power Rangers. Still, she couldn't stop hearing the hateful words they said.

How do you say fat-so in Spanish?

She cried behind her book, wishing she could disappear. When the bus finally pulled up to her driveway, she wiped her tears with her sleeve and trudged toward the house.

Penny was in the kitchen, singing loudly to a country music station and baking cookies for the store. The kitchen was an explosion of flour and sugar, trays of cookies and turnovers crammed into every available space. Penny was so strange lately, staying up all night baking and talking on the telephone. Where would they put these things, Monica wondered. The freezer was already stuffed full of Penny's baked goods. Enough to last Two Gals General Store a month.

"You're just in time. I just now took the first tray of snickerdoodles out of the oven," Penny said, peeling an oven mitt from her hand.

"No, thank you."

She whirled to face her. "What's wrong?"

Monica shrugged and hurried to the stairway.

"Monica Humphrey. You sit down right this minute and tell me what's going on. Did something happen in school?"

The pain that had been building since recess exploded out of her. "Everybody hates me!" she cried.

Penny guided her to the table. "I'm sure that's not true."

Between sobs, she gulped mouthfuls of air. "It is true! They called me fatso and made fun of me for learning Spanish. They ruined my library book."

Penny examined the book, her eyes glittering with anger. "Why, those brats." Her hand caressed the cover. "Those hateful, rotten little brats."

Fresh tears sprouted. "I don't want to go back to school. Not ever."

"No, I'm sure you don't." An idea came to Penny and she grasped Monica's hand. "You know what we're going to do? We're going to get you a makeover!"

"What's a makeover?"

"How about you don't go to school tomorrow? How about we run up to Cleveland instead? We'll go to The Avenue, get you a nice haircut and some cute new dresses. I'll even treat you to lunch. Anyplace you want to go!"

"Can you really do that?" she sniffled. "Not go to school on a school day?"

"Who's going to stop us?"

"Well … What will Geneva say?"

"Geneva won't have anything to say about it. My mind's made up."

•

Cleveland was wonderful and frightening and overwhelming with its people and traffic and noise. Monica had never seen anything as wonderful as The Avenue in Tower City with its glass ceilings and escalators and chandeliers. A complete shopping mall built inside the restored historic Cleveland Union Terminal, it was intimidating with its sheer number of stores, restaurants and salons. Penny seemed to feed off the energy, laughing as they flitted from store to store.

"Do you like this?" She held up a denim dress, its skirt layers of ruffled tiers that reminded her of the folk dancers in Costa Rica.

"I love it."

"Let's see if we can find it in your size." She rifled through the rack. "This one should fit. Here, take this vest, too."

She'd never been inside a fitting room before. It was awful, taking off her clothes in front of the full-length mirrors. But once she had the dress on, Monica felt transformed. She twirled first one way and then the other, loving the way the ruffles fell around her knees, loving the short white vest, its collar studded with rhinestones. Penny also found her a pastel tie dyed T-shirt and a matching pair of pink pants. A lavender poncho with fringe. In another store there were shoes. Red leather clogs with white flowers appliquéed on the sides and a spanking white pair of tennis shoes.

Monica knew how careful the girls usually were about spending money and was amazed at the nonchalant way in which Penny flicked her credit card down on the counter.

After the department store, Penny hustled her into a salon, another unfamiliar experience. A lady with hair so blonde it was white and shoes so tall they looked like skyscrapers draped a cape around Monica and went to work. When she finally turned her to face the mirror, Monica was amazed. The short layers had released Monica's natural curl and her blonde hair fell in ringlets to her shoulders. She couldn't believe the girl in the mirror was actually her. Again, Penny pulled out her credit card and laid it on the counter with a flourish.

"Thank you, Penny," she said. "For all of it."

"You deserve it, baby. Now … where would you like to have lunch?"

Over cheeseburgers and French fries, Monica told Penny about school. How at the end of last year the boys had started teasing her, the girls all ignoring her, even Sarah, whom she'd thought was her friend.

"Well, I'm sorry Sarah would do that. But you don't need people like that in your life, Monica. You'll learn that, sooner or later. It's better to be by yourself than with people who don't really care about you. I learned that the hard way. But remember," she covered Monica's hand with hers. "You can always count on me."

"Okay."

"Now, what would you like to do next? See a movie?"

"Shouldn't we go back home? We told Geneva we wouldn't be late."

Penny smiled. "You're such a good girl. Yes, we'll go home now."

But they didn't. On the way out of the mall, Penny stopped to buy herself a black dress and two pairs of shoes and a beautiful, red lace nightgown and a pair of high heeled slippers. Driving out of the city, she wove in and out of traffic, making Monica feel sick to her stomach. When they passed a car dealership, she abruptly slammed on the brakes.

"Did you see that?"

"See what?"

She made a U-turn in the middle of the street and circled back amid blaring horns. She drove through the lot and pulled up behind a gleaming red car.

"A Camaro," she told Monica. "Candy apple red. And look, it even has a sun roof. It's perfect."

"For what?" Monica asked, alarmed.

"For me, silly."

"You're going to buy it?"

"I'm going to take it out for a test drive first. But yes, I probably will buy it."

Two hours later they left the car lot. If Penny's driving had scared her in the old gray Chrysler, it terrorized her in the red Camaro. She flew down the highway, her hair whipping in the wind from the sun roof. "I love this! Don't you love this?"

Monica nodded, afraid to speak—afraid her cheeseburger would come up and ruin the black leather seat.

After a hair-raising hour's drive, they finally pulled into the driveway. Geneva, who had been sitting on the porch, stood and walked toward them. She didn't look happy.

"Like it?" Penny asked.

"Penny, how much did this car cost?"

"It cost my old, beat-up Chrysler."

"That and how much more?"

"Nothing more. Today. Just my signature on the dotted line." Penny laughed as if she'd made the best joke in the world. Monica's eyes shifted nervously to Geneva.

"Penny, how did you—"

"Hey, look at our gorgeous girl."

"You look very nice." Geneva glanced at her, but Monica could tell she barely saw her. "Monica, honey, take your new things upstairs. I want to talk to Penny for a minute."

She got as far as the porch when the girls' raised voices rooted her to the floor boards.

"Are we really going to go down this road again?" Geneva asked.

"I don't know what you're talking about."

"When was the last time you took your medicine?"

"That's really not any of your business."

"It's not? It took me months to pull us out of the financial pit you dug last time. We almost lost the store."

"Why do you always have to throw that up in my face?"

"Because you do foolish things like this!" Geneva pointed at the car. "We can't afford this, Penny."

"Maybe, maybe not. But I can't go on driving an old woman's car. It was embarrassing."

"At least it was paid for."

"Life is passing us by, Geneva, while we sit out here like a couple of old hens. I want some excitement. I want some fun!"

"You're sick again."

"I am not sick."

"I'm going to make an appointment with Doctor Stevens in the morning."

"Make it for yourself. I'm leaving!" Monica watched, stunned, as Penny climbed into her Camaro and thundered away, leaving Geneva in the dust.

•

For the next two weeks, Monica watched out the window every day, hoping and praying the red car would pull back in the driveway. She helped Geneva in the store the best she could, and never bothered her aunt with her problems at school. She could tell Geneva was as sad and worried as she was, and she didn't want to make her feel worse.

A month later, Penny returned. But she no longer seemed like Penny. It was as if someone had sucked all the life out of her, leaving only a shell. For days she stayed in her room, coming out only to use the bathroom. She would not talk to any of the men who called on the phone, and barely talked to Monica. She could hear her crying at night through her bedroom wall. It reminded her of her father in Pittsburgh, just before she came to live with the girls. She was terrified that the girls would send her away, like her father had. She never saw the little red car again, but was afraid to ask what had happened to it.

One day when she arrived home from school, Geneva sat her down at the table with a chocolate chip cookie and a cold glass of milk.

"Monica, I want to talk to you about Penny," she said gently. "She's gone away for a while."

Her stomach clenched. "Where did she go?"

"She had to go into the hospital for a little while."

The hospital. Tears sprang to her eyes at the words. She knew what the hospital meant. She scrubbed at her tears with her hands, trying to be brave. "Does she need a new kidney?"

Geneva stared at her, clearly puzzled. Then realization dawned. "No, child. It's nothing like that. She just needs some rest. She'll come home eventually."

"For really?"

"Yes, for really. I promise. She'll be home in a few weeks. And then she'll be all right again."

Chapter Five

$\mathcal{S}$t. Cecilia's Convalescent Facility sat in the third block of Washington Street, a decorous Grande dame in a neighborhood of battered blue collar ladies. Formerly The Cambridge Hotel, the structure had enjoyed four decades of wealth and respectability before falling into disrepair in the late 1960s. Ten years later, it was rescued by a non-profit Catholic organization and lovingly restored as a place for retired nuns to live out their last days. Twenty years after that, it was opened to the general public.

On Monday morning Monica sat in a hospital van, looking out at the building through a light, misting rain. She'd seen the facility many times, but this was the first time she'd ever really seen it. The three-story, white-brick center was the heart of the former hotel. With its enormous columns and floor to ceiling windows, the three tiers of porches on the front of the building reminded her of a southern mansion. Two smaller nondescript wings extending from the sides had been added much later, and Monica supposed she would be staying in one of them. Barry had promised to come by and see her that evening. He'd promised to bring cappuccino. She scanned what she could see of the yard, hoping there was a garden somewhere on the grounds.

The attendant opened her door, ready with a wheelchair. "Here you are, Ma'am."

"Dis is silly. Dere's nothing wrong with my legs."

"It's hospital policy, Ma'am. I've got to hand-deliver you safely to the front door."

With a sigh, she allowed him to wheel her up the ramp and

onto the porch.

The front doors opened to a lovely room with oyster-colored silk curtains, Chippendale-style sofas and potted ferns. She was admiring the intricate detail on the crown molding when a side door opened and a woman appeared.

"You must be Monica. Welcome. Your room is almost ready. I'm Barb, the intake coordinator here."

"Hello, Barb." Monica stood and shook Barb's outstretched hand while the hospital attendant whisked the wheelchair away.

"Why don't we get your information while we're waiting, and then I'll give you a tour?" She led Monica past a discreet reception area and into a back office. "I think you'll be happy here. We offer activities most every day. Or if you prefer time alone, we also have a nice library with Wi-Fi, a small fitness room, a chapel, and a garden in the courtyard."

Good.

"Step on the scales, hon."

She noticed a regular doctor's scales in the corner, but Barb indicated the larger set that sat on the floor. It looked like a cattle scale. Sighing, she set down her purse and bag and stepped on. She looked at the facility's framed credentials on the wall, pointedly ignoring the digital readout.

"Okay, it looks like ... three hundred and four pounds," Barb said, making a note.

Monica's heart jolted. She glanced at the screen. Sure enough, it read three hundred and four.

"Dat can't be right, can it?"

"The scales don't lie, hon," Barb told her, a sympathetic edge to her voice.

Monica smiled as best her mouthful of wire would allow. "I've losht eighteen pounds."

Barb's sympathetic expression vanished as a smile took its place. "Well, that's wonderful, then! Good for you!"

After she'd taken Monica's vitals and recorded all of her information, Barb led her on a tour of the facility. It was a beautiful old building, but she was still too happily stunned to appreciate the original bead board or the hardwood floors. She hadn't weighed less than three hundred and twenty pounds since college. Eighteen pounds! That was a pound for every day since her accident, an eighteen pound ray of sun shining in the gloom of all that had happened to her. Maybe before she left St. Cecilia's she could lose another five pounds. Maybe more.

A half hour later she settled into her room. Small, but lovely, it looked more like a country inn than a rehab center. The walls were white with a subtle hint of rose. The hospital bed was concealed by a white eyelet spread and a vase of pale pink lilacs sat on a round white table beside it. She stowed her clothes and purse in the dresser and set her laptop on the writing desk in the corner. All that was left to do was wait for Barry. It was strange, how important his visits had become. They'd become her way of measuring time.

She ate dinner an hour before Barry's visit. Went to bed two hours after Barry's visit. The days he had to work late and couldn't come see her seemed aimless. Pointless. She told him about her setbacks and progresses, gauged her feelings by his reactions to them. She shared more about herself with him than she'd disclosed to anyone in years.

She wouldn't tell Barry about the weight loss, though. She wouldn't tell anyone. She'd wait until she lost enough that it would be noticeable. She ran a finger beneath the waistband of her pants and wondered what the magic number would be for that.

•

Barry arrived at seven o'clock, carrying two cups of cappuccino.

"This is nice, Monica. Sure is a big improvement from where you've been hanging out."

"Dat's for sure." Any misgivings she might have had about coming to St. Cecilia's were instantly put to rest. "Wanna know da best part? Dey have a garden in the courtyard."

"Lead the way."

Though smaller than the Healing Garden at City Hospital, the courtyard garden was much more charming. Cobbled pathways wound through plots of pachysandra and periwinkle, widening sporadically to accommodate glass topped tables, wrought iron benches, and a lovely wooden swing beneath a wisteria-laden pergola. In the center of the garden was a goldfish pond stocked with a rainbow of coy fish, fairy statues peeking out from the greenery. They sat on the swing, rocking gently in the evening breeze.

"Would you mind bringing me a few more things from home, some closhe?" Now that she was out of hospital gowns, she'd need more than the two outfits he'd already brought her.

"Sure. Anything in particular?"

"Maybe a couple of dreshes from da bedroom closhet. It's getting too warm for pants." The pair she had on was actually roomy! It had been years since her pants were anything but snug.

"What are you smiling about?"

She'd made up her mind not to tell him, but suddenly she found herself blurting it out. "I lost some weight in da hoshpital. Eighteen pounds."

"Monica, that's excellent. I'm proud of you." He dropped an arm around her shoulder and squeezed.

She glowed at his praise. "Don't be. It's only because my mouth is wired shut."

"Still, though. Eighteen pounds, that's a lot."

"This is da least I've weighed in ten years, since college." She dropped her gaze to her hands. "It's got me thinking a crazy thing.'

"Uh-oh." He smiled. "Care to share your crazy thoughts with me?"

"It's shilly."

"Tell it to me anyway."

She'd never told anyone, not the whole story, and couldn't imagine why she would do so now, but having started, there was no going back.

"When I was a little girl, some missionaries came to our church. Dey were serving in Costa Rica. I've wanted to go ever since, be a part of a mission team."

He watched her intently.

"I built my whole life around dat dream. I went to college, got my teaching degree, I even minored in Shpanish."

She stopped. This was the hard part.

"Changed your mind, or…?"

"Not exactly."

He waited, sipping his drink. That was what she liked most about Barry. He never rushed her. He let her reveal herself at her own pace, as if he had all the time in the world.

"After I graduated from Risingville I contacted the mission. Dey were very open to having me join up, said they had a shortage of workers, especially teachers. I took the classes they recommended, and I took all of the tests. I scored amazingly high. Dey gave me an appointment for a physical. After that, all that was left was to wait for my assignment."

The shame of that day welled up inside her, the pain as sharp as if it had been a week ago. "I didn't pass the physical."

"No?"

"I was too fat."

"They didn't say that to you, did they?"

"Not in sho many words. They talked about the physical expectations, the hardships, and the poverty. They suggested I get in better shape, try again in a year. I knew that meant lose weight. A lot of it. The thing was, I was so depressed, I ate even more, and by the time a year had passed, I was twenty pounds heavier than I'd been."

He reached for her hand and gently stroked it.

"Sho I took the first job I was offered. And I've been there ever since."

A chipmunk scampered up the path, its cheeks bulging. Seeing them, it dove into the pachysandra.

"Is it something you'd still like to do?" he asked. "Go to Costa Rica?"

She looked at him. "Yeah."

He squeezed her hand. "Then let's do it."

"What do you mean?"

"Let's get you ready. You've already made a good start, let's go the rest of the way."

"We're talking about a hundred pounds, Barry. Or more."

"So we'll take baby steps. We'll start out walking, slow and steady. And then we'll run."

She laughed. "I haven't run in years."

"Neither have I, but I'm going to start. I could stand to lose a couple of pounds, myself."

"You're as thin as a rail!"

"I wouldn't say that." He patted his belly. "I wouldn't say that by a darn sight."

•

She went to bed that night feeling lighter in more ways than one. She'd tried dozens—hundreds—of diets over the years and failed. Maybe she could do it this time, even after the wires were removed from her jaws and life returned to normal. Somehow Barry's faith in her gave her faith in herself. Faith that this time it would be different. She'd once believed that God had called her to a life of service in Costa Rica. She'd let him down. She'd let herself down. But maybe it wasn't too late. Maybe her dream could still come true. She owed it to them both to try.

Chapter Six

$\mathscr{M}$imi the hand specialist said she needed to work on her grip. Monica was encouraged that she was able to tolerate the wrist deviation and isometric exercises this time. She could even pick up a full cup of water; however, Mimi said there was still much work to be done.

All in all, her first week at St. Cecilia's had been a positive one. At yesterday's weigh in, she discovered she'd lost three more pounds, which caused the facility's dietary supervisor, Meg Keenan, to get involved.

"It's wonderful that you're working on your weight, Monica, and seeing such good results. But you need a plan you can incorporate into your everyday life once you leave here. You can't survive forever on broth and gelatin."

She'd offered suggestions for low-cal meals: fruit smoothies and pureed vegetables, soups with creamed chicken and turkey. Monica was determined to make the changes Meg suggested. She wanted desperately to lose the rest of the weight. Twenty-one down, a hundred and one to go. Despite the constant ache in her wrist and jaw, she felt better than she had in years.

She told Barry all of this on their nightly walk.

"It'sh hard to believe twenty-one pounds could make such a big differenshe," she said.

"Think about it. Twenty-one pounds. That's more than four bags of potatoes you've set down."

"Good analogy." She sighed. "I just hope I can set down about twenty more bags."

He chuckled. "You'll get there. We'll keep walking even

after you leave St. Cecilia's. I was thinking that when your wrist is stronger maybe you'd like to come and walk dogs with me."

"What dogs?'

"I volunteer at West Avenue Animal Shelter two Saturdays a month, walking dogs. I think I told you about it once."

She remembered the conversation. She was in the pet foods aisle at the Stop-N-Shop and Barry was rearranging a display of dog food. "Yes, I guess you did."

"You told me you didn't like dogs."

"I like dogs just fine. I just didn't like to walk."

But now she looked forward to it. The first night they'd started with a fifteen minute stroll. Down Washington Street, a right on Bailey, two blocks to Eastwood, a right onto Ridgeview, and then back to Washington. After only a week they were up to a half-hour, and had progressed into a neighborhood where the houses became steadily nicer and the yards, more manicured.

"I can't help wondering about da people who live in these houses," Monica said, her wistful gaze taking in a tidy Cape Cod, complete with a picket fence and a pink flowering crab tree. "With deir nice cars and pretty lawns, I wonder if dey're really any happier dan the people who live a few blocksh over."

"I don't think happiness comes in a house or a neighborhood. Sometimes more money just means more things to argue about. Like Solomon said, better is a dry morsel and quietness with it than a house full of feasting with strife."

"You mean Solomon as in King David's son?"

"Very good."

She thought about the proverb for a moment, and about the fact that Barry could quote it off the top of his head. She liked his quiet wisdom, and the way he often took her by surprise with the things he said. She'd known him in passing for two years, had known him well for three weeks, and still, she didn't know a thing about him.

"Tell me about yourshelf, Barry."

"There's nothing to tell. I'm just an ordinary, standard-issue guy. "

"Well, other than that you manage the Stop-N- Shop I don't know anyting about you. I don't even know your last name or where you live."

"Goodrich and Grandview."

"And you've lived in Risingville all your life?"

"Every bit of it."

"Which is how many years?"

"Thirty-seven."

"How come you never got married?"

"I did get married."

"Oh, I'm sorry. I jusht assumed—"

"I got married, and then I got divorced. End of story."

The revelation silenced her and he reached for her hand, squeezed it gently, and held on. She glanced at him in surprise. "I thought you might like to work on your grip," he said, smiling.

They strolled along Park Street, past a father grilling hot dogs and a wife spreading mulch in a flower bed. Past children playing kickball and an old woman reading the newspaper on her porch swing. Monica commented on nothing. She no longer wanted to talk. She only wanted to savor the curious sensation of Barry Goodrich's warm hand in hers.

•

The days were long without her job to fill them. In the middle of her second week at St. Cecilia's, Monica wandered into the rec room. It was empty, as usual. A TV played loudly in the corner for no one, some sort of game show. She wandered to a cabinet full of jigsaw puzzles. Sorting through the stack, she found a puzzle of a cat that bore a striking resemblance to Ginger and carried it to the card table. She'd just sorted all of the edge pieces when a woman entered the room. She wandered to the TV and watched for a moment, then made a slow circuit around the room before drifting to the card table.

"Hello," Monica said.

Not answering, the woman picked up the box and gazed at the cat. "Ttt."

The woman obviously had dementia. Not sure what more

to say, Monica turned back to her puzzle. To her surprise, the woman pulled out the chair across from her and sat down.

Monica continued to sort the puzzle pieces, the woman watching intently.

"My name is Monica. What's yours?"

No response.

"Do you like puzzles?"

The woman stared at her.

"I've never done dem too much," Monica said. "But I thought the movement might be good for my hand."

The woman gazed at the puzzle pieces scattered across the table.

It was disconcerting, the way the woman sat there in silence. Monica got up and turned down the volume on the TV, then scrolled through the channels until she found an oldies music station. The woman swayed to Frank Sinatra, humming softly. It was better than her silence, Monica thought, returning to her puzzle.

They sat for a while, not speaking, until Janna, the two-to-ten shift RN walked in.

"Well here you are, Miss Patricia. I've been looking for you. It's time for your supper." She glanced at the puzzle. "Kitten, huh? Cute."

Monica turned back to her puzzle. Gossipy and overbearing, Janna wasn't her favorite among the nurses at St. Cecilia's. It seemed she always seemed ready with a complaint. It was too hot or too rainy. Her workdays were too long. Life was too short. She spoke to the residents as if they were naughty children, these former school teachers, accountants, and mothers.

"Come on now, Miss Patricia. Come, come."

Janna all but clapped her hands, and Patricia reluctantly rose and followed her.

•

The next afternoon, Patricia appeared in the rec room again.

"Hello, Patricia. I'm making progressh, see?" Monica proudly pointed at the nearly finished picture.

"Ttt."

She tuned the TV to the music station and Patricia sat down and watched her, as she had the day before.

She told Patricia about her teaching job, her accident, and about her plans to try and go to Costa Rica. The afternoon crawled by as she worked painstakingly on the puzzle, though Patricia's silence no longer made her uncomfortable.

"You know, dis was kind of fun." Monica said, fitting the last piece in place. "It'sh got my confidence up. Next time I might try a thousand piece—"

Abruptly, Patricia rose from her chair and moved around to Monica's side of the table. She cried out softly, stretched out trembling fingers and stroked the picture of the cat. "Ttt."

A nurse's aide appeared in the doorway.

"It's suppertime, Pat. We're having chicken and noodles." She approached the table. "What have you got here?"

"Ttt." Patricia ran her hand lovingly over the puzzle and the aide looked at her in surprise.

"Do you like kittens, Patty?"

"Tt."

"Well, we'll leave the puzzle up for a while so you can enjoy it. Let's head to the dining room now, before your supper gets cold." She stretched out her hand and Patricia took it, tearing herself away from the puzzle.

"This is amazing," the aide said. "She's been here six months and this puzzle's the first thing she's shown even a sliver of an interest in."

"I don't think it'sh the puzzle," Monica said. "I think it's the cat. I have a tabby at home that looks just like this. Ginger is very gentle and loving. Do you think it would be possible for her to come for a visit? Short of like a therapy cat?"

"I don't see why not. As long as she's all up to date on her shots. We've had people bring dogs in before. Just check with Janna first."

•

The next evening Barry arrived with Ginger in a cat carrier. "This was a great idea, Monica. I don't know why we didn't think of it sooner."

"Come here, baby." Monica gently lifted Ginger out. The cat pressed against her, its motor running. "Have you missed me? Have you been a good girl for Barry?"

Ginger mewed softly.

Monica buried her face in Ginger's fur. "I missed you sho much. I see Barry's been feeding you well."

He grinned. "I might have spoiled her just a little."

Barry had tucked Ginger's sock doll into the crate. They played with her for a while, laughing at her antics, until Janna appeared in the room.

"Oh, good, you brought the cat. Are you ready to take her around? I saw Patricia go in the rec room a while ago. Why don't you start there?"

Ginger purred incessantly as Monica carried her down the hallway to the rec room. The puzzle had been taken down, and Patricia sat at the card table, gazing out the window.

"Patricia?" Monica said softly.

The old woman turned. Seeing the cat, she gasped softly and reached out her hands.

"Tabby?"

Her voice was thin, rusty with disuse. Monica and Barry exchanged glances, and then Monica set Ginger gently in the old woman's lap. The cat purred loudly, her tail swishing back and forth as her paws kneaded the old woman's lap.

"Oh, Tabby, where have you been all this time?"

Ginger met her gaze and gently placed her paw on Patricia's cheek.

The old woman's eyes filled with tears. "Oh, Tabby."

She cradled the cat, weeping, stroking her soft fur. The scene was beautiful and touching and Barry squeezed Monica's hand, a gesture that Monica knew had little to do with working on her grip.

They stayed with Patricia for an hour, until her eyes became heavy and her head drooped to her chest. Once she was asleep, Monica gathered Ginger up and took her back to her room.

"I don't suppose we'd better leave her in the carrier and go for our walk," Barry said.

"She'd probably howl da whole time. We'll probably have

to skip it tonight. It was worth it, though."

"We'll walk extra-far tomorrow."

"Did you see the look in that woman's eyes? It meant everything to her. Thanks for bringing Ginger, Barry."

"Of course."

As Barry was leaving, Janna stopped him at the door. "Thank you for this. It did Patricia a world of good."

"I'm happy to do it."

She gazed at Barry quizzically. "Didn't you used to be the manager at the Busy Mart?"

"That was a lot of years ago."

"I thought you looked familiar."

She continued to study him, and Monica sensed him becoming ill at ease. "I have that kind of face, I guess."

"Didn't you used to play in a band?"

"That was a lot of years ago, too."

"It was a jazz band, right? You used to play at that club out on Woodcliff Avenue."

He turned abruptly to Monica. "I'll see you tomorrow night, all right? We'll try for an hour's walk."

She watched after him as he stepped out the door and into the evening, Ginger's carrier swinging gently at his hip. Janna came and stood beside her. She opened her mouth and with a sentence, everything Monica thought she knew was shattered.

"Is his name Bill Goodrich?"

"Barry."

"That's right, Barry. Barry Goodrich. I knew he seemed familiar. He's the one that killed that girl."

Chapter Seven

The worst thing about living in a town the size of Baxter was the gossip. Reports of deaths, arrests, cheating spouses—things that destroyed their neighbors' lives—were passed across the tables at Joe and Sue's Good Times Diner, like bottomless cups of coffee the townspeople could not get enough of. The gossip was one of the things that broke Monica the most. That and the mean girls.

Up until sixth grade it had mostly been the boys who made her life miserable. They put peas on her chair in the lunchroom, and then laughed at the ugly green stains on her slacks. They wrote her name with Magic marker on a giant-sized pair of ladies underpants and ran it up the flag pole. They were relentless in their chanting: Humphrey Dumphrey sat on a pea.

She'd hoped middle school would be different. That a different building, different classes, would make the kids somehow different, too. But the only difference between grade school and middle school was that now the girls joined in the hateful teasing. Worse than the boys, they didn't limit their teasing to just Monica. They went after her family, too.

It started in the lunchroom, in the middle of her first week as a seventh grader at Boswell Center Middle School. She'd been sitting alone, as usual, when a group of popular girls came and sat at the far end of her table. Among them, Sarah Scott, who used to be her friend until she got pretty over the summer and joined ranks with the popular girls.

At first they talked about boys and what teachers they had for Social Studies and Math. Then their voices became low murmurs, words Monica couldn't make out. It was Allison Fairchild that started it. Slim, raven haired, beautiful Allison, whose father was the president of the school board.

"Anybody want a snickerdoodle? I've got extras."

"I do," Bridgette Morris, Allison's best-friend-of-the-week, said.

"What are they?" Sarah asked.

"They're cookies my mom got at Two Gals Store."

Monica tensed at the mention of the girls' store, sensing that something bad was coming.

"Are they any good?" Bridgette asked.

"Here, get you one," Allison said, tossing a baggie full of cookies to the other girl. "They're amazing. They're lucky cookies, made by Lucky Penny Humphrey herself."

The other girls snickered. Monica cringed. *Here it comes …*

"Why do you call her Lucky Penny?" Carla Mullins asked. Her words were stilted, as if she were rehearsing for the school play.

"Because every man that takes her out gets lucky. At least that's what my uncle Bert says."

"But she's old. Like forty!"

"I know, right?"

"Eww."

The girls at the table laughed, including Sarah Scott. Sarah, who had sat at their kitchen table on too many Saturday mornings to count and begged Penny to French braid her hair. Monica wasn't sure exactly what Allison's comment meant, but she could guess at the gist of it. She wanted to run and hide, but instead, she sat in stunned embarrassment, her face burning with shame. Penny had a lovely, kind, generous soul. She only ever dated when she was sick. She couldn't help the way she acted. But that didn't matter to the mean girls.

For the rest of that week Monica skipped lunch and sat in the library, reading books about Costa Rica. She couldn't wait to go, couldn't wait to get out of this horrid town with its hateful people.

The mean girls caught up with her the following Monday. Once again, they came and sat at her lunch table.

"So I heard something interesting this weekend," Allison

said.

"What did you hear?" Carla asked, in her play rehearsal voice.

"I heard about these two old maids, they're sisters. Well this one time, the younger one went crazy and went after the older one's boyfriend with a kitchen knife. She ended up getting locked up in a mental ward and nobody would date the older sister after that."

Monica's face grew hot again. Not with shame this time. With fury. She knew Allison was talking about the girls. Telling lies. There was no way Penny would do something like that, even on her craziest day. She leveled her gaze at Sarah Scott. Sarah looked away.

"Shut up," she said quietly.

"What?"

"Shut. Up. Allison."

Allison's eyes narrowed. "What if I don't? What are you going to do about it," her glance skimmed Monica's tray and came to rest on the cookie Geneva had packed in her lunch. "Moonpie?"

Without thinking, Monica picked up her open carton of milk and threw it in Allison's face. And then pandemonium erupted.

Allison shrieked.

Bridgette grabbed a fistful of Monica's hair and pulled. Hard.

Carla grabbed a handful of boiled carrots from her tray and flung them at Monica, which caused Petey Lambert at the next table over to grind his mashed potatoes into Curtiss Willis's face. Curtiss retaliated by throwing his chicken parmesan sandwich at Petey. It hit the wall, leaving an ugly, tomato-red stain.

Later, when the principal demanded to know the reason she'd started a food fight, Monica didn't answer, because what could she say? As punishment, she received out-of-school suspension for two days, which as far as she was concerned, was a blessing.

When Penny and Geneva wanted to know why she would do such a thing, she couldn't tell them, either. She mumbled something about being tired of having pea stains on her dresses and the girls let it go at that.

•

When Penny was well, life on the farm was wonderful. The old house rang with singing and laughter. There were late night games of Monopoly at the kitchen table and early mornings of weeding the garden. The unrestricted, unconditional love Penny and Geneva lavished on their "girl" almost made up for Monica having lost her mother so early.

When Penny was ill, life on the farm was hell. She seemed to cycle every third year. In the weeks leading up to an episode of mania, anxious to the point of being nauseous, Monica would watch carefully for signs that Penny was sick. It always started with the dates and the late night phone calls. It always ended with a month's stay at City Hospital. And then life went on again.

Monica turned thirteen on the second Saturday in June, the summer between her seventh and eighth grade years. The girls had said she could sleep as long as she wanted. She awoke at nine o'clock to the scents of pancakes and bacon. She'd barely opened her eyes when Penny crept into her bedroom and sat down on the bed.

"Happy birthday, sleepyhead," she greeted her, ruffling a handful of her blonde curls. "Geneva and I have a surprise for you in the kitchen."

"Pancakes? With chocolate chips?" she asked hopefully.

"Come and see."

When she appeared in the kitchen, Geneva smiled and set a plate of pancakes in front of her. They oozed chocolate chips and as far as Monica was concerned, the day was already perfect. She ate with gusto, taking a second helping, which Geneva didn't normally allow. As she carried her plate to the sink, she noticed the time. "We're going to be late opening the store," she said, alarmed.

"The store is closed today," Geneva said, smiling again.

"Closed? Why?" She'd never known Two Gals to be closed on a Saturday, no matter how snowy the roads, how sore

Penny's throat, or how much Geneva's back ached.

"Don't look so upset, Monica. Penny and I have a wonderful surprise for you. It's not every day a girl becomes a teenager. So go upstairs and put on one of your nice dresses. Go on, now."

It was then that she noticed Geneva had on her good navy blue dress beneath her apron. Dying of curiosity, she hurried upstairs, grabbed her favorite floral print dress from the closet, and squirmed into it. She brushed her hair and teeth in record time and eagerly returned to the kitchen.

"You look beautiful, sweetheart," Penny said. Penny, who at forty-four looked as lovely as a fashion model in a white sundress, her copper colored hair falling to her waist. "Are you ready to go?"

Cleveland wasn't nearly as frightening to navigate with calm, sensible Geneva at the wheel. She steered her old Buick through the downtown streets without a single horn blare or squawk of tires. They parked in the parking garage on Chester Avenue and walked beneath the covered walkway the rest of the way to Playhouse Square. Even though it was early afternoon, the marquis of the State Theater was fully lit up. Dazzling white lights encircled the enormous sign, whose bold, black letters proclaimed: *La Danza! Costa Rican Folk Dance Company Performance Today!*

She gaped at the girls, utterly speechless. Smiling her wide smile, Penny linked arms with her as they went inside the theater. "You're going to love this!'

Given new life more than a decade before, the old theater was lavish with its red velvet curtains, crystal chandelier, and row upon row of red upholstered seats. Monica had never seen such a place, and felt as reverent as if she were in church. She nearly genuflected when the lights dimmed and the dancers came out onstage.

The dance company, La Danza! , consisted of eight women and eight men and were a pure joy to watch. The dancers performed traditional Costa Rican folk dances, telling sad and beautiful stories with their bodies. Her favorite was the lively Punto Guanacasteco, where the beautiful, dark-haired women two-stepped toward their partners, flirtatiously flipping their bright, swirling skirts as marimbas tapped out a beat.

They danced the La Cajeta, which represented the sweetness of young love, and the Borucan Diablitos, which celebrated the native's flight from the Spanish conquistadors. Monica had read about these folk dances, but to actually see them performed was sheer heaven. She felt like she could sit and watch La Danza! perform for the rest of her life.

After the show, they bought hot dogs and vinegar French fries from a street vendor, and then the girls treated her to an ice cream sundae at an old-time parlor downtown. Driving home, she felt drowsy and contented. Her first day of being a teenager had been the best day of her life. The dancers were amazing, Penny was well, she was loved, and life was good.

That summer, Monica was a frequent visitor at the public library. She devoured Young Adult novels, stories of girls whose teenage years were a magical time of girlfriends and parties and boys. Monica had never been invited to single party. Or even a sleepover. And forget about boys. Boyfriends were for cute, popular girls. Skinny girls, like Allison and Carla. Not for heavy girls like Monica.

Eighth grade was as bad as seventh, but for different reasons. The boys seemed to have forgotten about her in their pursuit of the pretty girls, many of whom had developed breasts over the summer. The mean girls didn't bother with her any more, either. Rather than an object of their ridicule, she seemed to have become invisible. She would watch the other girls laughing together, and the girls and boys who held hands in the hallways, and feel so achingly lonely and inconsequential, so broken she didn't know if she would ever be whole. As eighth grade drew to a close, she realized she'd had enough.

Sitting in the cafeteria, on the second to last Monday of the school year, she listened to the familiar talk about the other girls' eighth grade graduation party plans, the boys they would kiss, their upcoming summer vacations to Pigeon Forge and Virginia Beach. She was surprised when she heard her name spoken.

"What are you doing this summer, Monica?" asked Sarah Scott, her ex-best and only friend, who was being nice to her again because she wanted a summer job at Two Gals General Store. Though Monica did not want her there, she told Sarah she would ask Geneva.

The other girls didn't even bother to look up from their lunches, probably feeling certain that Monica's plans would be completely boring.

She spoke without thinking. "I'm going to go back to Pittsburgh. I'm going to live with my father."

"Really?" Sarah asked.

Brittany looked up from her sandwich. "You're from Pittsburgh?"

"Yep."

"I just love the Steelers," Carla interjected.

"I wish I was going to live in Pittsburgh," Allison sighed. "I'd rather be from anywhere but Baxter."

For a moment it felt good. For a moment, Monica was different from them for a good, interesting reason. But only for a moment.

In the last week of school, the Ohio heat became oppressive and it was torture to sit inside the un-air-conditioned class rooms. At lunch recess, Monica sat beneath a shady Sugar Maple and watched her classmates playing tennis. As usual, she hadn't been invited to play. She'd told Sarah that the girls didn't need any summer help, and that was the end of Sarah being nice to her. As their laughter drifted across the tennis court, the thought returned to Monica with complete clarity.

I've had enough. Enough of being ignored, enough of being an outcast. Enough of Baxter and of Boswell Center. I will go back to Pittsburgh and live with my father.

The thought brought an incredible sense of freedom. She wouldn't live like this any longer. She didn't have to.

It took her until the first of June to work up the nerve to tell the girls. It was evening, and the girls were sitting on the porch in the first cool of day, pulling the stems from the strawberries Monica had picked in the garden that morning. Pulling in a deep breath, she opened the screen door and joined them on the porch.

"So then Sylvie says, and mind you, with a face as straight as a needle, well my dear lady, I certainly would contribute to the missions fund if I could, but you see, I'm on a very limited budget here."

"Can you imagine!" Penny said, chuckling. "With all of the money Walter left her?"

As the girls laughed quietly together, Monica thought she would explode. She had to tell them, but how?

"So, Monica," Geneva said. "Have you given any thought to what you might like for your birthday this year?"

It wasn't the right moment, but she could no longer hold it back.

"I want to go and live with my father. I want to go back to Pittsburgh."

Silence fell, as thick as butter. Then both girls spoke at once.

"Monica, you can't mean that."

"But sweetie … why?"

She shrugged.

"Is it because of me?" Penny asked softly. "If it is, I promise you, it won't happen again. I'll be much more diligent with my medicines. Sweetie, please don't leave us."

The girls looked so sad that for a moment Monica would have given anything not to have said it. But her mind was made up. She had to get out of Baxter.

The next day, Geneva called her nephew to make the necessary arrangements. He no longer lived in the apartment. He'd married Shelly three years before, and his visits went from twice a year to none. He was no longer even really her father, but he was her way out. He owed her that much.

On the extension in her bedroom, Monica listened to the silence that fell when Geneva stopped speaking.

"Oh, well …" her father said. "Well, that's something to think about, isn't it?"

Then, Shelly, who was obviously also listening in on her father's end, exclaimed, "Of course she can come! We'd love to have her, wouldn't we, Will?"

"Yes, of course she can come," her father said, and Monica silently let out her breath.

"How about the end of summer? I'm thinking early August?" Shelly said. "Things are just so busy with the baby and all. I think I can have a room ready for her by then."

And with that, it was decided.

•

On the first Monday in August, she and the girls made the two-hour-and-twenty-minute drive to Pittsburgh, as somber as if they were going to a funeral.

"Here we are then," Geneva said, as they pulled up in front of a red-brick row house. Skirting the toys on the sidewalk out front, they stepped onto the narrow porch. Shelly met them at the door, wearing cutoffs and a white halter top, her white blonde hair clipped on top of her head. Dark gold eyeshadow went clear to her eyebrows, and black eye liner rimmed her eyes, making her look like a cat.

"We're just so excited to have you here, Monica!" she gushed. "Geneva, Penny, welcome to our home. I've got coffee made, ladies, if like to stay a little while."

"Thanks, but no. We have to get back and open the store," Geneva told her. Monica glanced at her in surprise. The store wasn't open on Mondays.

There were hugs and tears, and for a brief moment, Monica wanted to cling to them, tell them she'd made a mistake. But instead she watched them get in the Buick and drive away.

Shelly showed her to her room, which was really a walk-in closet, equipped with a small bed, a night table, and a lamp. A tiny window looked out on the street.

"We'll fix it over cute for you," Shelly promised. "Maybe get a leopard print throw rug and some posters."

The first night, Shelly ordered a pizza for dinner. "Tomorrow we'll start you on a diet," she said. "We'll see about getting you a membership at my gym. It'll be fun!"

Her father said little. It was awkward between them, uncomfortable. Halfway through her second slice of pizza, Monica realized she didn't know this man anymore. Two days later, when he left on one of his long-hauls, she was almost relieved.

That afternoon, Shelly came breezing into her room. "Monica, sweetheart, I have a tiny favor to ask. Some friends of mine want to get together tonight, sort of a girls' night out.

Would you mind watching the baby for a bit? I won't be too late."

"I guess."

She smiled. "Wonderful!"

Over the next few days, Monica's fears that she wouldn't be wanted in her father's house were quickly dispelled. She was wanted. Oh yes, she was wanted. Shelly went out the first night, and the next night, and every night after that, leaving Monica to tend to Juliet, who was three years old and into everything. After an evening of chasing the child around the house, playing dolls and making believe Juliet was a princess, and she was the evil queen, she fell into bed exhausted, wondering why anyone in their right mind would ever have a child.

On the night of her first full week in Pittsburgh, she awoke in the night to the sound of laughter in the kitchen. Shelly's high-pitched giggles mingling with deeper tones. Her father must have come home early. Had she slept so soundly she hadn't heard him come in? The voices drifted up the stairs and to their bedroom, and then the door closed behind them.

Monica lay in the dark, studying the patterns of light the streetlamps made on the walls of her closet. She tried not to think about how hungry she was. Shelly had started her on a diet, which mainly consisted of boiled chicken, tossed salad, cottage cheese, and tuna. For snacks, she was allowed carrot and celery sticks. She remembered seeing a box of chocolate doughnuts in a kitchen cupboard. She tried not to think about them, tried hard. But it seemed the longer she lay there, the more her stomach cramped and her taste buds yearned for them.

When she couldn't stand it any longer, she put on her robe and slipped quietly into the hallway. Taking baby steps, she crept down the stairs. She mustn't wake Shelly and her father. They mustn't know she'd cheated on her diet. She would only have one doughnut, and then go right back to bed. Two, at the most.

She padded softly into the kitchen and nearly cried out in surprise. A man stood at the sink, drinking a glass of water. He wore only his underwear. She could see, even from the back, that it wasn't her father. This man had overgrown blonde hair, and lots of muscles. She backed silently out of kitchen and hurried up the stairs.

She lay in bed, her mind racing.

Shelly was having an affair? No, it couldn't be. But what else could it be?

She was still awake hours later when she heard Shelly's bedroom door open and footsteps on the stairs, and then the front door closed softly. She scrambled to the window and looked out. The man with the muscles, now fully dressed, walked down the sidewalk and disappeared into the darkness.

What should she do? Should she tell her father? Would he even believe her? She wished for Geneva, strong, sensible Geneva, to tell her what was appropriate.

Her father arrived home the next afternoon, tired and grouchy from his long drive. He noticed Shelly's new dress, and then he and Shelly had a fight about money.

Her father and Shelly fought about money every day after that. Their raised voices and the sounds of things breaking through the bedroom walls was worse than the crying had ever been. And much more frightening.

A few days after her father's return, the air conditioning unit broke and the heat inside the row house became stifling and the fighting reached an all-time high. On a Monday evening, exactly two weeks since she'd arrived, Monica walked to the public library to escape the heat and the anger inside the house. She loved the quiet old building, the coolness of it and the smells of books and adventure. She spent hours wandering through the aisles, removing books from shelves, flipping through them, putting them back. When the librarian quietly told her the library would be closing in ten minutes, she grabbed two Sweet Valley High books she hadn't read before and carried them to the check-out desk.

It was dusky by the time she left. Walking out into the evening, she wished she hadn't stayed at the library so long. She hoped she had enough time to get home before it was full dark. She was two blocks from the row house when a car slowed and pulled up beside her. A man in his twenties put down his window.

"Want a ride?"

She put her face down and kept walking.

"Why you gotta be like that, beautiful? When we're trying to be nice." The other man in the car, the driver, laughed.

Heart thudding, she quickened her pace. It seemed she'd read something somewhere about what to do in a case like this, but she hadn't paid it much attention. Walking alone after dark in Baxter was never an issue. There was no place to walk to.

The car followed behind her for a full block, the two men saying things—vulgar, nasty things that made her want to puke. When her father's house came in sight she broke into a run. She dove onto the porch and the men drove off, laughing.

She burst into the front hallway, breathless, nearly hysterical. Juliet sat playing with her dolls in the living room. Upstairs, her father and Shelly were having a fight.

"I did not!"

"Well you most certainly did!"

"So I'm a liar now, right?"

"If the shoe fits, honey, then wear it!"

Gulping for air, she hurried to the kitchen and dialed the girls' phone number. It rang once, twice, three times. Where could they be?

"Maybe you'd like to find a better place to live then, huh?"

"Please," she whispered. "Please answer the phone."

"Hello?"

Thank God. "Penny?"

"Monica, honey is that you?"

Her voice broke. "I want to come home."

"What's wrong? Who is that shouting?"

"I want to come home. Now. Tonight."

"What happened?"

The angry shouts had proceeded into the upstairs hallway, and were now coming down the stairs. Tears filled Monica's eyes. She'd hoped the girls would just come and get her, no questions asked. But of course, it couldn't be that simple.

"Please, Penny. Will you come?"

"Well of course you can come home, but—"

All at once Geneva was on the line. "Monica, we'll get this

all straightened out. Let me talk to your father."

The shouts were in the living room now. If she put her father on the phone when he was like this, his fierce anger would likely turn on her. Feeling like a lone wolf caught up in a snare, Monica hung up the phone.

Chapter Eight

When Barry texted her the next evening, saying something had come up and he couldn't make it for their walk, Monica didn't know whether to be upset or relieved. She didn't know how to act around him now. She didn't know anything at all.

The night before, when Janna had made her preposterous statement, Monica had actually laughed. "What? No. There'sh no way that would have been Barry. I'm sure you're tinking of someone else."

"I'm pretty sure it was him," Janna said. "In fact I'm positive."

Her smug, I-know-something-you-don't-know tone made Monica angry. Whatever Janna's gossipy game was this time, she had no desire to play. "I can't imagine what you're referring to, Janna."

So she'd told her. Every last, gory detail.

Feeling nauseous, Monica went straight to her room and opened her laptop. A ten-minute search brought up the ten-year-old news story. When she'd finished reading, she closed the laptop, feeling as stunned as if she'd been hit by a hammer.

•

All the next day, what she'd learned buzzed around in her brain, like a swarm of troublesome mosquitoes. How should she act toward him now? Thanks to his text message, that wasn't an issue. At least not today. But what about tomorrow, and the day after that?

She went out for her walk alone, to try and think. For once, she didn't pay any attention to the houses or the people or the flower gardens. She couldn't stop seeing Barry's kind smile, couldn't stop trying to make the Barry she knew fit with the Barry she'd learned about last night. One thing was for certain. She had heard Janna's side, which was much more malicious than the newspaper's. Now she wanted to hear Barry's side.

The next day, she received another text message.

Not feeling well. Won't be able to make it tonight either. I'm sorry.

She went out for her walk alone again, more unsure than ever what to think. Why was he avoiding her? And why did she care? She barely knew him.

But she did care. It was upsetting just how much. More than just a friend, Barry Goodrich had become a lifeline of sorts. Lately she'd even dared to think he might like her as more than a friend. The awful events in the newspaper story had occurred more than ten years ago. Surely he was a different man now than he'd been then. Did he think she couldn't see that? Or maybe he wasn't a different man, and she'd been made a fool of.

When he texted again the following afternoon, saying he was sure he had the flu, Monica was concerned. Was he being truthful with her? There was only one way to find out.

Working up her nerve, she called the Stop-N-Shop and asked to speak to the manager. Moments later, Barry's voice came on the line.

"This is Barry, how can I help you?"

She quickly disconnected the call, and just as quickly, her concern turned to anger. She didn't like being lied to. The flu, indeed. She knew that Barry got off work at six o'clock on Fridays. Tonight, she would be waiting for him.

•

When the cab pulled into the supermarket parking lot, at ten minutes to six, she directed the driver to a spot near where Barry's car was parked. She watched out the passenger window, her stomach rolling and her nerves screaming. It was a foolish idea. She should leave. Now. Before he came out. What did any of this have to do with her, anyway? She'd almost made up her mind to ask the cab driver to take her back to St. Cecilia's when the store's front doors swung open and Barry appeared. He walked across the lot, heading towards her.

"Wait here," she told the cabbie. With a deep breath for courage, she opened the car door, got out, and walked toward him.

Barry stopped in mid-stride. "Monica."

For the first time since she'd known him, she didn't know what to say to him.

He sighed. "What are you doing here?"

"I thought you had the flu."

"I don't."

"Then why …?"

"Because I knew that loud-mouthed …" He took a breath, clearly trying to control himself. "I knew Janna would tell you. And I can see by your face that she did."

"Did you think I wouldn't find out about it sooner or later?"

"I wanted to tell you myself."

Her tone softened. "Then why didn't you?"

He ran a hand back through his hair. "Because I didn't want … this."

"I've heard Janna's account of what happened. Now I'd like to hear yours."

"How did you get here?"

She gestured toward the cab. Barry walked over and paid the fare. The cabby drove away, shaking his head.

"Let's get coffee," he said.

They drove to the mini-mart and Barry pulled into a spot out front. He went inside, and later reappeared with two cappuccinos. He drove to the city park and parked the car near an elm-shaded picnic table beside a fish pond. He didn't speak until they were seated.

"How have you been?"

She sipped her cappuccino. "Fine."

He sighed again. Ran a hand back through his hair. "Okay."

"You don't have to tell me. You don't owe me anything."

"I want you to know. Then you can decide."

Decide what?

"If you still want to hang out with me."

Oh.

He stared out at the pond for long moments, then finally said, "I don't know where to start."

"Shtart wherever you feel comfortable."

After another long moment, he began again. "I used to play the saxophone in a jazz band. Small gigs, just here and there. We played for the love of the music, not for the money. After a few years, I was twenty-five by then. I was managing the Busy Mart. It's closed now … Man. This is a mess."

She gave him a small, encouraging smile.

"After a few years, we got a steady gig at this club called The Lazy Dog. That's closed now, too. We played every Saturday night. That's where I met my wife, Mandy. She was one of the bartenders. She moved to Risingville from Buffalo to go to college, but she dropped out halfway through. We dated for a while, not long enough to really know each other, and then we got married on an impulse. We were both lonely, I guess." He gave a small shrug.

"After a while she got a receptionist's job in a doctor's office and gave up bartending. But she used to come on Saturday nights to hear us play. The night … the night of the accident, she didn't come. That was the first thing that went wrong. We'd had a fight, I don't remember about what any more, probably something stupid, and I went without her.

"There was this girl. I'd seen her at the club before, but never paid her too much attention. She was one of those bar fly types. She always came alone, but never left that way. That night, she was drunk out of her mind. Between sets, she kept coming on to me. I ignored her. The things she said to me … I knew it was the alcohol talking. Face it, I'm not a good-looking guy, and besides, I loved Mandy, even if all we did was fight."

He laughed a small, sad laugh.

"At closing time, we started packing up our equipment, and this girl was still hanging around. I was afraid for her, honestly. We didn't always get the best clientele there. I saw the way men were looking at her. I didn't want anything bad to happen to her. I kind of felt sorry for her, I mean, she was so pathetic, strutting around the way she was, so I offered her a ride home. She accepted. That was the second thing that went wrong that night.

We'd only gone a couple of blocks when she started taking off her clothes. She was all over me, trying to get behind the wheel. She was practically in my lap. I pushed her away, but she just wouldn't quit. Finally I shoved her. Hard. And the car swerved onto the sidewalk."

His coffee cup trembled in his hands.

"There was this homeless girl waiting to cross the street. Dressed all in black. All of a sudden she was just … there. I didn't see her, didn't have time to react. I ran her over. I killed her. She was nineteen years old."

"Oh." Monica sucked in a breath.

Tears filled his eyes and he blinked them away. "You can imagine how it looked, me in the car with a half- naked woman. The story around town was that we were fooling around, that I was drunk. But I'd only had two beers. I was well within the legal limits. But that didn't stop the talk.

The judge had a teenaged daughter. I was charged with vehicular homicide. Negligence. I spent six months in jail and lost my license for a year. While I was in jail, Mandy filed for a divorce and went back to Buffalo. One stupid choice cost me everything. My marriage. My job. And almost my life."

"Barry, I'm sho shorry." She reached for his hand. He grasped it, squeezed, held on.

"I was a mess for a really long time. The accident played out in my nightmares over and over. It nearly drove me insane. I spent some time in the hospital, the psych ward. Believe it or not, that's when things started to go right. I met the hospital chaplain. He spent hours and hours talking with me, helping me sort it all out. When I was released he helped me find a new job. But mostly, he led me to the cross. And that's where I finally found peace."

He squeezed her hand again, then let it go.

"And here I am, ten years later, still putting myself back together, one day at a time. I kid myself into thinking people have forgotten. But obviously they haven't."

Her heart ached for him, because Barry, strong, capable

Barry, was just as broken as she was.

"Thank you for telling me."

"I would have, eventually."

She smiled.

"So now that you know, what have you decided? About me?"

"There'sh nothing for me to deshide, Barry. A bad thing happened. You're moving past it, the best you can. I'm not your judge or jury. I'm jusht your friend."

"Thanks."

Dusk began to fall. While they'd talked, the sounds of picnics and children playing had given way to the sounds of crickets and bullfrogs.

"I should take you back to St. Cecilia's."

"We haven't had our walk yet."

They strolled along the paths beneath the gentle glow of gas lanterns, the May evening soft and fragrant.

"This is nice. Maybe we can walk here, shometimes."

"Sure. How much longer are you going to stay at St. Cecilia's?"

"Another week. Maybe two."

They walked on in silence for a moment, and then Barry surprised her by picking up the thread of his earlier conversation. "I know the good Lord forgave me for taking that girl's life. The hard part was forgiving myself."

"You didn't do anything wrong."

"My mind knows that, but my heart hasn't believed it yet. I keep thinking I have to make up for it. To society. To God. To myself." He jammed his hands in his pockets. "People think I'm some Mister Nice Guy, but I'm not, really. I'm just trying to ease my conscience. I try to do all the good I can now. I walk dogs. I shovel snow for old people in the winter."

Monica stopped walking, feeling as if she'd been slapped. "You take walks with fat women."

"No. No, that's not the same thing."

Tears of shame filled her eyes. She'd actually thought he liked her. She should have known. She should have learned by now. She tried to turn away but he took her shoulders and made her face him.

"Monica. I spend time with you because I want to."

"Yeah. Okay."

"Hey." He took her face in his hands. "You're a lovely woman. You're smart. Funny. Caring. I really enjoy your company."

The words tore her heart in two. She so desperately wanted, no, needed to believe them. Her tears fell harder. "If you enjoy my company sho much, why haven't you ever ashked me out?"

He stared at her, his hands falling away. "I never asked you out?"

She sniffled and looked away.

"I never once asked you out?"

"No," she whispered.

He let out a short, incredulous bark of laughter. "I seem to remember that I have. I asked you to walk dogs with me. You said you didn't like dogs. I invited you to a classical music concert, right here in this park. You said you didn't like crowds. I invited you to an antique car show over in Youngstown. You said you weren't interested in old cars. By then I was pretty sure it was me you weren't interested in, so I stopped asking."

She remembered all of those conversations. Casual conversations in the pet foods aisle, and the produce section. But she hadn't realized …

"Those were shupposed to be dates?'

This time he turned away. "I know they were probably not the most interesting or romantic ideas in the world. I stink at this, okay? I just thought they were things we could enjoy together."

Now she felt even more ashamed. "Barry, I'm sho shorry. I didn't realize …"

"I should have thought of roses and candlelight."

"No. I should have opened my eyes and sheen thoshe invitations for what they were. I should have gotten past my lifelong belief that no one could be interested in me."

"Well, you'd better get past it," he said softly. "Because someone is."

Chapter Nine

$\mathcal{K}$enny Peters caused Monica to lose faith in boys back in the third grade. But it was Drake Davenport that destroyed her faith in men. He breezed into her life in her fourteenth summer, and nothing was ever the same again.

Shortly after her return from Pittsburgh, Geneva and Penny called her down to the kitchen one evening. Her glance flicked over the catalogues that were stacked neatly on the table. The start of the school year was just a week away. Monica assumed Geneva wanted her to look through J.C. Penney catalogues, as they did every August, to give her an idea of what kind of dresses Monica might like her to make for her this year.

"Monica, have a seat, child. Penny and I have something we want to discuss with you."

Penny nodded and pushed back a chair for her. The twinkle in Penny's eyes told Monica the discussion was not about clothing.

"We've been talking a lot about this," Geneva said, "and we feel, that is, if it's something you would like, that you might benefit from being homeschooled this year."

"What do you think?" Penny said, nudging her.

Monica didn't know what to think. "You mean not go to school?"

"She means have school right here. Right in the comfort of your own home," Penny said, grinning broadly and indicating the stack of books, which Monica now saw were not catalogues at all, but books of Ninth Grade Curriculum. "A lot of parents are homeschooling their children these days. So we thought, why not us?"

Geneva cleared her throat. "Between the two of us, Penny and I know about as much as anybody. So what do you think? Shall we give it a try?"

Relief washed over her like a tidal wave. She wouldn't have to go to high school after all. Wouldn't have to endure being made fun or, or worse, ignored, for another year, not for another day! She jumped up from the table and ran around to the girls, hugging first Geneva, and then Penny. "Thank you. Oh, thank you both!"

"Good, then," Geneva said. "I'll send in the paperwork tomorrow, and we'll be all set."

•

Her ninth grade literature class would focus on imagery, plot, theme and characters in fiction and poetry, Penny told her. Before the semester was finished, she would be experimenting with poetry and writing creative stories of her own.

"Won't that be fun?" she asked, smiling brightly.

"I guess so," Monica said.

"We're also going to be reading plays and classic literature. Here." She handed Monica a course list of suggested readings. "We have to get through at least six of these books this year. You can decide which one you want us to read first."

She scanned the list, and decided on *Romeo and Juliet*. The next week she and Penny went to the library and checked out the book. On the first day of class, they lounged in the living room, taking turns reading.

They laughed at the complicated verbiage, and Penny had to keep explaining the story to her, but once she caught onto it, it seemed sad and beautiful, despite the awkward phrasing.

The first week of school went well. Penny was very good with words. A longtime lover of history, Geneva knew her way around the Constitution and the Civil War. Monica had always been at the top of her class in Science. But when it came to algebra, all three of them were lost. So Geneva hired a tutor.

"He's a lovely young man, Monica, and he has a teaching degree in Math. I think you'll like him. His name is Drake Davenport, and he's just moved to our area from Georgia.

We want you to have every opportunity to get into a good college, and I feel he will be able to help you with your algebra better than I ever could. He'll come on Thursdays and Fridays starting next week."

•

When Drake Davenport showed up at the farm the following Thursday morning, Monica was dumbfounded. She had expected some boring old man, like Mr. Phillips, her math teacher in middle school. She certainly didn't expect her new tutor to be one hundred and ten per cent gorgeous. He was tall, towering over Geneva as she ushered him into the kitchen. His sun kissed face wore a hint of stubble, and he had short, brownish hair with honey colored streaks. She'd recently come across the word dashing in one of the poetry books she and Penny were reading. He was probably close to thirty years old, but even so, he was dashing. He looked like an older version of JC Chasez from her favorite band, NSYNC.

"This is Monica," Geneva told him. "Your newest student." He smiled at her, and her world spun off its axis. "It's nice to meet you, Monica. Are you ready to get started?"

Oh, yes. She was ready. For anything he wanted to start. She shook the hand he extended, mortified that her palms were slick with sweat. Why was it suddenly so hot in the kitchen? She hoped the antiperspirant Geneva had bought for her wouldn't fail.

"I'll leave you two to your work, then." Geneva headed back to the store with a smile.

Monica took a seat next to Drake at the table. He smelled wonderful—warm and seductive, a combination of spicy cinnamon, pine trees, a hint of patchouli, and very faintly, cigarette smoke.

"I thought we'd start off with some review, some of the things y'all learned last year that this year's math will build on. Does that sound good?"

Everything he said sounded good. His words rolled off his tongue with a sweet Southern drawl that she found fascinating and romantic.

He opened the satchel he'd brought and pulled out a stack of work sheets. "Are you familiar with exponents? These little guys?" He pointed to the figures on the first sheet, the regular sized numbers with the tiny numbers at the top right-hand side of them that had always baffled her.

"Sort of," she said meekly.

"The problem with these little guys is that they're on a power trip," he said. "When you put them next to a number that's bigger in size, they feel threatened and flex their muscles. So this five, with the little guy three beside it actually means five to the third power, which would be five, times five, times five. One-hundred twenty-five. Does that make sense?"

The way he explained it, it did make sense. It was as if he'd turned on a lamp in what had up until then been a very dark room.

By the end of the session, he had re-explained three math concepts in relevant, practical language.

"I'm going to leave a couple of worksheets for y'all to work on tonight. We'll go over them tomorrow, okay?"

Tomorrow. She could hardly wait.

•

The next morning she got up early, brushed her hair to a glossy shine, and put on her prettiest pink top. She wanted to look her best for Mr. Davenport. At the breakfast table, she tried to act nonchalant, not wanting the girls to guess she had a crush on her new teacher. Thankfully, the girls were busy making plans for their day at the store, and didn't seem to notice that she barely touched her toast, or how often her gaze traveled to the clock above the sink. Would ten o'clock never come?

Drake arrived ten minutes early. After greeting her, he opened his satchel and got down to business. The days' agenda included Math Operations and Reasoning, he told her.

"We're going to start with somethin' easy," he said, extracting a worksheet from his stack. "For this one, we'll use the operations plus and minus. Five blank five blank five equals five. You fill in the blanks."

"That's easy," she said, drawing a plus sign in the first blank and a minus sign in the second. "Five plus five, that's ten, minus five, equals five."

"Smart girl."

Her whole body warmed at his praise. She'd never known math could be so rewarding. After what seemed moments, their hour was over and he started to pack up his papers.

"Here are some worksheets for you to do before our session next Thursday. Have you finished the ones from yesterday?"

She handed them to him and he looked them over. "Looks good."

Handing them back, their hands brushed together and she quickly pulled hers away. He smiled and studied her face. "You sure do look pretty today, Monica."

Her face turned the color of the tomatoes in Penny's garden.

"I bet you have a lot of boyfriends," he said softly, and her color went from the red of tomatoes to that of hot chili peppers.

"No."

"Really? A pretty girl like you?"

She stared at the table. "I'm not so pretty."

"Ahhh, but that's where you're wrong, Miss Monica." He reached out and fingered a strand of her hair, then gently tucked it behind her ear. She thought she'd faint.

That weekend, she stayed in her room, doing her math worksheets and playing her NSYNC CD. She listened to *This I Promise You* over and over again, imagining that it was Mr. Davenport, Drake, singing just for her.

•

Over the next two weeks she and Drake reviewed more math concepts. She discovered how to find the surface area of a prism, and how to discover whether a number was rational or irrational.

"You see how this number, when you turn it into a decimal, just goes on and on endlessly?" he asked.

"Yes."

"That's what we call an irrational number. Think of an angry woman at the end of the day. Her husband comes home and they fight. The dude just wants to go to bed, but she nags on and on and on, endlessly, not really making any sense because she's what?"

Monica smiled. "Irrational."

"Good girl."

The next session, he explained the Order of Operations. "Okay, you see this bad boy?"

She stared blankly at the equation: $(53 + 7) \times 4$

"Yes."

"Where do you even start with somethin' like this?"

"I have no idea."

He took out a red marker and wrote the words: *Please Excuse My Dear Aunt Sadie* at the top of the paper. "This is all you need to know in order to figure these out, darlin'."

The endearment went through her like a lightning strike. Flustered, she tried to make sense of what he'd written.

"The first word starts with a P. Please. P also stands for Parenthesis. So when you see a problem like this, you start with whatever is in parenthesis. In this case, it's fifty-three plus seven. Next word, Excuse. Exponents, the little guys, come second. Now the word My. Care to take a guess?"

"Multiplication?"

He rewarded her with a big smile. "You got it! And Dear?"

"Division.'

"Aunt?"

"Addition!"

"Sadie."

"Subtraction!"

"Great! Now figure out the equation."

She went to work, desperate to get it right, to please him. Moments later, she slid her paper toward him."

"Five hundred twenty-eight. The girl is a genius."

To her absolute shock, he planted a kiss on her mouth. His lips were soft and warm, the softest, warmest things she'd ever felt. When the kiss ended, he ruffled her hair. "That's all for today. I'll see you tomorrow morning." And with that, he stood and walked out the door, as if the entire world had not just exploded.

She thought of little else besides the kiss that night, fearfully wondering what the next session would bring. But the next day, he acted as though nothing had happened. He tried to explain the concept of algebra, but how could she concentrate?

"Algebra is nothing more than a variable, which stands for an unknown number. So here, 3T equals 123. How can we figure out what t is?"

She stared dumbly at the numbers, not comprehending.

"Monica, you're not focusin'."

"I'm sorry."

It was a fruitless session with little progress made, and when it ended, the weight of his disappointment sat on her shoulders like a bag of bricks.

"I don't mean to interrupt your lessons," Penny said, breezing into the kitchen. "Geneva and I thought you two might like a couple of cold bottles of lemonade." She set two sweating bottles on the table.

"Well thank you, pretty lady," Drake said, reaching for one of the bottles. He drank it in three gulps. "That sure hit the spot. Hey, do you girls have any homemade bread in your store?"

"Sure do. I baked it myself yesterday."

"I've been hungry for some, lately. We're about done here. Maybe I'll wander over and get a loaf." He started to pack up his papers. Monica glanced at the clock in dismay. They still had ten more minutes together. Even so, Drake stood and followed Penny out the door, leaving her alone with her jealousy.

She thought about him all the time. Evenings, instead of watching her favorite programs, she went over the algebra worksheets he gave her, determined to understand, to make him proud of her again.

In the end, her work paid off, and the rewards were worth every agonizing moment. A kiss. One for each perfect score on her homework.

"You can't tell anyone about this, Monica," he said, stroking her hair. "They wouldn't understand. About us."

He was right. They wouldn't. How could they, when she didn't understand it herself? Because how could a dashing guy like Drake possibly love a heavy girl like her? They were sort of like Romeo and Juliet. Misunderstood. Tragic. Star-Crossed.

By their fourth Friday together, Monica had caught on to integers, fractions and decimals, and factorizing natural numbers. Kiss. Kiss. Kiss.

"So soft," he murmured, stroking her cheek. "So pretty. Next week you'll have your first exam, sweet Monica. And if you do well, I have an extra special reward for you."

"What is it?' she asked, breathless.

But he only smiled. "You'll see."

He packed up his satchel and walked out, and she hurried to the window, wanting to catch every last glimpse of him. He stopped at the gate, where Penny was just coming in, lingering, laughing. Her brow furrowed. What could he and Penny be talking about for so long?

•

The next night, Geneva made chicken and biscuits. The tantalizing smells coming from the crock pot teased Monica all day, and by suppertime her mouth had already been watering for hours. At five o'clock, when the girls came in from the store, she set the table in anticipation.

"It will just be the two of us today," Geneva said, removing her store apron.

"Penny's not eating?"

"She has a date tonight."

Alarm bells started ringing in Monica's ears. "She does?"

"It's fine," Geneva said, sensing her uneasy thoughts. "It's just dinner and a movie with Mr. Davenport."

She almost dropped the plates. It wasn't fine. It wasn't fine at all. Her appetite soundly spoiled, she pushed her food around on her plate, and then finally, scraped it clean in the trash. Washing the supper dishes, she could hear Penny in the bathroom upstairs, getting ready for her date. With Drake Davenport. Monica's boyfriend. Her anger seethed.

When Penny appeared in the kitchen, Monica hurried upstairs and hid in her room. When she heard the doorbell ring, she rushed to the window. Drake looked more gorgeous than ever in a pair of jeans and a white shirt. And of course,

Penny looked amazing in her ankle-length black skirt, her hair falling in loose copper waves to her waist. What little supper she'd eaten rose up and she ran to the bathroom. It all seemed so unfair. Penny going on a date with Drake. And she wasn't even sick this time!

Please excuse my dear aunt Penny.

Never! She'd never forgive Penny in a million years.

•

She went to bed early, her head and stomach aching, and lay staring at the ceiling, trying to understand. She couldn't really blame Penny. Drake had made her promise not to tell the girls about their romance. Of course Penny would want to go on a date with him—who wouldn't? She had no idea she was dating someone else's boyfriend. But that would mean Drake was at fault. And Monica just wasn't ready to accept that right now.

Penny came home much later than Monica expected. It was after one a.m. when she heard their footsteps on the sidewalk, their quiet voices by the gate. She crept to the window and looked out.

They stood for a long time, talking in the moonlight. About what, she could only guess. Finally, it looked like Drake was going to leave. He turned, said a quiet goodnight to Penny. And then it happened. Drake drew Penny into his arms and kissed her. It wasn't like the hurried, secret, reward-kisses he gave Monica. It was a long, slow, drawn out kiss, a sexy kiss, like you saw in the movies. She let out a soft bleat as her whole world crumbled around her. How could he? And how could she?

Please excuse my dear aunt Penny…

Never! Never, Never, Never!

•

On Sunday she stayed in her room, telling Geneva she had a stomachache. Which was not a lie. When the girls left for church, she went to the kitchen and consoled herself with a package of cinnamon rolls. She carried them up to her room, along with a glass of milk, and ate all six of them, one after the other. Then she went back downstairs, retrieved a hammer from Geneva's tool box and smashed her NSYNC CD into a hundred pieces.

On Monday morning, Penny appeared in her room. "Do you feel well enough for class? I thought I'd have you try some writing today."

"No thank you," she said stiffly, turning her face to the wall.

At suppertime, Geneva made her come down to the kitchen. The girls were having goulash. Geneva had set out a bowl of soup and some crackers for Monica. "I know you don't want to, but I think you'll feel better if you eat something," she said. Monica took tiny bites of her crackers, not making eye contact with Penny.

"Oh, hey," Penny said, "I saw a flyer in the city on Saturday night. The festival in Chagrin Falls is coming up next weekend. They're having the haunted maze again this year. Remember how much fun we had last time? Shall we plan to go?"

"No thank you," Monica said, not looking up. She could feel the girls' eyes on her.

"Oh, come on. They're also having archery contests, candle dipping, cookie decorating … and don't forget those amazing sausage sandwiches we got last time."

"I said I don't want to go."

"All right," Penny said, obviously hurt.

"You're not yourself lately." Geneva's level gaze fixed on her. "And I'm not convinced it's altogether about a stomach ache. So why don't you tell me what's really the matter. And I want the truth."

Geneva's tone left no room for argument, and Monica knew not answering was not an option. "Ask her," she said, waving her hand at Penny.

"I have no idea," Penny said. "If I've done something to upset you, then please tell me what it is."

She sat in silence, fighting tears.

"Monica?" Geneva asked.

"I saw you kiss Mr. Davenport."

Penny flushed. "Oh dear. Well, I'm sorry you did. But that shouldn't upset you this much, should it?"

"Well it does!" she shouted.

"But why?"

"Because I know what happens on your dates. I know that you and Mr. Davenport got lucky Saturday night."

Penny's eyebrows raised in surprise. "What?"

Geneva looked angrier than Monica had ever seen her. "Monica Humphrey, you will apologize to Penny this minute!"

"I won't!"

Penny spoke then, very calmly. "Monica, I'm a grown woman. What I do is my own business, and I really don't understand why—"

The secret, their secret, exploded from her lips before she could stop it. "Because Drake is my boyfriend!"

Geneva's voice was stern. "Child, whatever are you saying? Mr. Davenport is not your boyfriend. He's your teacher."

Having gone this far, she couldn't keep the words back. "Then why did he kiss me?"

The girls exchanged shocked glances.

"Drake kissed you?" Penny asked.

"Yes. At least a hundred times."

"What do you mean?" Geneva asked quietly. "Where?"

"Right here in the kitchen."

The girls exchanged another glance, and then Penny asked, "He kissed your cheek? Your hand, or what?"

"My mouth." With the last of her confession out, she burst into tears.

"Monica," Geneva said, barely concealing her rage, "go up to your room for a little while and try to calm down while Penny and I talk."

Upstairs, she fell across her bed and sobbed. It was ruined now. Everything was ruined.

Between sobs, she could hear the girls' voices drifting through the register vent.

"… just had no idea … pedophile … outrageous … something must be done …"

The sky was dark outside her window when Penny opened the door and came in.

"Are you still mad at me?"

She sniffled, not answering.

"I don't blame you if you are. But I'd like to talk to you, if that's all right."

She shrugged and Penny sat down on the bed and turned on the lamp.

"Monica, I'm so sorry this happened. I feel just sick inside."

That made two of them.

She sighed. "Before I say anything else, I have to ask. And I hope you'll tell me the truth. Did Mr. Davenport do anything besides kiss you? Anything Geneva and I should know about?"

She shook her head, thinking of the special reward she was to have earned that week.

"Okay, good." She picked a piece of lint from Monica's bedspread. "I don't know if you'll understand what I'm going to tell you. I've known men like Drake before. He's what you call a philanderer. Do you know what that is?"

"No," she sniffled.

"It's sort of a man who goes around breaking women's hearts. But I'm not going to let him break mine, how about you?"

She shook her head, though it was already too late. Much too late.

Penny moved closer and smoothed back Monica's hair. "Honey, you're too young for Drake. I think you know that. And I'm too old. And the sad thing is he's probably got three or four girls of different ages in between us right now. Looks like we both got taken in by him."

"He didn't really love me, then?"

"Oh sweetheart, no. I'm sorry."

Her broken heart broke again and her body shook with sobs. Penny held her, speaking softly and stroking her hair.

"I promise you, some day you're going to meet a wonderful man. Someone who will treat you with all the love and respect—all of the honesty that you deserve. That's what I want for you. More than anything else."

She hugged Penny tightly. "That's what I want for you too, Penny."

•

The next week, Drake Davenport was replaced by Mrs. Henley, a white-haired, retired teacher from their church. She tried her best to pick up where Drake had left off. But by then, the lessons had already been learned.

Chapter Ten

*H*er jaw had healed.

Six weeks and two days after the accident, Barry drove her back to City Hospital to have the wires removed. He'd taken the morning off from work, had said he wouldn't miss it for the world. Said he was proud of her, as if it were some big accomplishment on her part.

He pulled in the parking garage and drove around until he found a spot. "Are you nervous?"

"Short of."

He squeezed her hand. "You'll do great."

"I hope none of my teeth fall out.'

"Why would they?"

"I did shome reading up on it. It happens."

"Not this time." He said it with confidence, almost making her believe it.

In forty-four days, everything had changed. Three days ago, a soft cast had replaced the heavy plaster cast on her wrist. Tonight, her jaws finally loosed, she would talk without mumbling and eat with a spoon. At last week's weigh-in, she'd used the regular scale, rather than the cattle scale. It had weighed her at two hundred eighty-six. She'd lost thirty-six pounds, total.

In two days, when the swelling had gone down and they were certain there was no danger of infection, she would be leaving St. Cecilia's after four weeks in residence, eighteen pounds lighter than she'd gone in. And she was terrified. Meg Keenan, the dietician, had given her meal plans to follow at home and encouraged her to continue on her weight loss journey. But her fear wasn't about that.

So what was she so afraid of?

In the hospital lobby, she gave her name at the desk and was immediately settled in a wheelchair and taken to pre-op for surgical prep. In the small, white room, Barry squeezed her hand.

"Here goesh nuting," she said.

"Here goes everything," he corrected.

A few moments later, a surgical nurse kicked Barry out, and Monica was given a light sedative. In the operating room, Novocaine was injected into her gums, and that was the last pain she felt.

The surgeon began to cut the wires. She didn't realize he was done until he cupped her lower jaw in his hand and moved it from side to side.

"Looks good," he said. "Now move it just like that, without my help."

It was strange, being able to move her jaws from side to side, it seemed like a miracle. He began again, cutting, pulling, snapping the hated arch bars away.

With the bars removed, he carefully probed each tooth, checking to see if any were loose.

"Your teeth seem to be fine," he said, and relief washed over her. "We'll do an X-ray to make sure there are no wire fragments hanging out in there, and I'll have them set you up with a follow-up appointment in a couple of weeks. Other than that, we're done here."

The jaw would open more in the next few weeks, she was told, as her jaw strength improved. She was given a booklet of exercises to do, and a list of safe, soft foods to eat for the next few weeks. The nurse went over everything with her, explaining that when the Novocaine wore off, she might experience some sensitivity, or even short term numbness.

"That's nothing to worry about," she said. "But if you experience sharp pain, or any sign of infection, be sure to call us right away."

She was wheeled back to the waiting room, and as simply as that, it was over.

Barry set aside the magazine he was reading and stood.

"How'd it go?"

She smiled, exposing her teeth. "Ta-daaa."

He grinned. "Well look at you."

"I can't believe it's over."

"We should celebrate. Feel like coffee?"

"Something cold. Maybe a fruit smoothie."

"You got it."

He drove to a mini mart with a snack bar inside. "What kind do you want? Strawberry?"

"I think I'll go in with you this time. Actually, I'd like to order it."

At the counter, she ordered a strawberry-banana smoothie and a caramel cappuccino. Barry beamed at her, as if she were a child taking her first steps. They drove to the park, where they'd walked the trails every evening for the past two weeks, since Barry's confession, and sat at their usual picnic table beside the pond.

"How long until you can eat regular food again?" he asked.

"I have to stay on soft foods for a few weeks. Mashed potatoes. Yogurt. Pureed chicken."

"So … middle of June, then?"

"I guess so. But I'm actually fine with a liquid diet. I'm kind of used to it by now."

"That's fine for now. But I have something planned."

She gave him a sideways glance. "Oh?"

"I still owe you a candlelight dinner."

She chuckled. "No you don't."

"I want to prove to you that I can be romantic."

"I already know that. You're a romantic devil. A regular romantic fool."

"Gee, thanks." He took her hand. His palm was slightly sweaty. "I was thinking we could go to The Sunset."

"That's the most expensive restaurant in town."

He stared out at the pond. Then back into her face. "You're worth it."

He turned to her, took both of her hands in his. "You're worth it, Monica."

Her heart started to pound as his face came closer. She could smell the caramel on his breath. This. This is what she'd been afraid of. Thirty two years old, and she'd only kissed one man, that fool, Drake Davenport. What if Barry was disappointed?

What if …

"I've wanted to kiss you since the first day I saw you," he said softly. "In the produce aisle. Remember?"

"I knocked over a display of Cuties. They rolled all over the store."

He smiled. "I got on my hands and knees and tried to help you pick them up. Our faces were just about as close as they are right now."

"I remember."

"So … Here goes nothing."

"Here goes everything."

Cupping her head in his hands, he gently pulled her to him. Their lips met at last in a kiss. Soft and warm and shy. His kiss was the most extraordinary thing she'd ever experienced. Blunted by Novocaine, but even so, her world exploded.

Chapter Eleven

$\mathcal{T}$he first thing Monica noticed, on her arrival home Wednesday morning, was that the lawn was freshly cut. The second was the flowers. Pots of cascading yellow petunias and blue lobelia hung from decorative brackets on the front porch. Daylilies in stunning shades of purple and gold lined the sidewalk leading to the front door.

She gaped at them in wonder before turning her gaze on Barry. "You planted lilies?"

He grinned, his shoulder lifting in a shrug. "Just a little homecoming present. Are the colors all right?"

"They're more than all right. They're beautiful. Thank you so much."

"You're welcome."

"Can you come in for a little while?"

"Maybe for a minute or two."

She retrieved her house keys from her purse and unlocked the back door. It had been forty-six days since she'd been inside her house. She shuddered to think what it must look like by now. As she pushed open the door, Ginger mewed and wound around her ankles and Monica eagerly scooped her up.

"How's my baby, huh? Momma's home now." Again, she looked at Barry in surprise. "I didn't know you'd brought her already."

He shrugged again. "I felt like she should be here. For your homecoming."

The house smelled faintly of pine cleaner. Glancing around, she saw that the floor had been mopped, her laundry neatly folded on the dryer, not so much as a single sock on the floor.

Moving to the kitchen, she discovered the floor swept, the dishes washed and stacked beside the sink. The living room was vacuumed and free of dust, not a fast food bag in sight.

"Did you do all of this?" she asked.

"I tidied up a bit. I wanted your first day home to be restful. Oh, and I brought a few things from the store. They're in your fridge. I wasn't sure what you'd want, what you'd be able to eat."

She went to him and gave him a quick hug. "You shop. You clean. You even mow lawns. I might have to keep you around, Barry Goodrich."

He wrapped her in his arms and kissed the top of her head. "I'm kind of counting on that, Monica Humphrey."

"Did you get coffee? Should I make a pot?"

"Yes, I brought coffee, but no, I'd better be getting back to work."

She walked him to the car. "Thank you, Barry. For everything."

"My pleasure."

"Are we walking this evening?"

"We can do that. Or ..."

"Or what?"

"We're having a prayer and share time at my church this evening. We have it the second Wednesday of every month. I thought ... Would you like to go?"

Her first instinct was to say no. It had been a long time since she'd socialized, and even longer since she'd been in a church. But she saw his hopeful expression and was reminded of the other times he'd asked her to go places and she'd said no.

"Wait a minute, is this like, a date?"

He laughed. "It wasn't going to be, but if that will make you say yes, then sure. It's a date."

She sighed. "What time shall I be ready?"

•

The Church of the Cross was not anything like the Presbyterian church she'd grown up in. It wasn't like any church she'd ever been to at all. On the outside, it was a standard-issue little white church, with a tall steeple and a red front door. Three smallish windows were evenly spaced on each side of the building. Baskets of red geraniums lined the steps.

"It's not fancy," Barry said, as they pulled into the lot. "But as of December, we own it free and clear."

Inside the sanctuary, two rows of honey pine pews and a matching cross gleamed in the soft lighting. More red geraniums decorated the altar.

"Good to see you, Barry. And this must be Monica."

Surprised to hear her name, Monica turned and took stock of the forty-something woman who now had Barry wrapped in a hug. Before she could finish her assessment, the woman hugged her, too.

"I'm Phyllis Gleason. Welcome, Monica. We've heard so much about you."

Her husband stepped up. "We're so glad you're here, Monica. I'm Doug. It's nice to finally meet you. We've had you on our prayer list for weeks."

She was taken aback. For a moment she thought she'd cry. They didn't even know her, why would these people care enough to petition God on her behalf?

It didn't take long for Monica to realize that the Church of the Cross was a hands-on congregation. There were twenty-two people at the prayer and share meeting, and it seemed like every one of them hugged her.

"I haven't been hugged this much since my mother's funeral," she commented to Barry, as they slid into a pew.

"I'm sorry," he said, looking stricken.

"No, it's fine. It's just … going to take some getting used to, that's all."

Pastor Ryan, a nice looking man in his early fifties, welcomed everyone and opened the service with a prayer. Then he turned it over to the congregation.

Dough Gleason was the first person to step forward. "A funny thing happened on the way to the prayer meeting," he said.

Everyone laughed.

"Phyllis and I had what you would call a genuine God

sighting."

Monica leaned slightly forward in her pew and listened with interest as Doug told the congregation about the flat tire they'd experienced directly in front of the homeless shelter.

"There was a young gal and two little kids sitting on a bench out front. They seemed tired and sad. Well, after I got the tire changed, I felt like God wanted me to go over and talk to them. As timing would have it, just this afternoon Phyllis cleaned out our son, Matthew's, closet. She thought maybe now that he's in college we could part with some of his toys."

A ripple of laughter passed through the pews.

"She had a whole bagful in the car she was going to drop off at the Goodwill on our way to prayer meeting. God saved us the trip. And the joy in those kids' eyes, well, there was just nothing like it."

There was a round of Amens and Praise Gods from the congregation. Doug said a prayer for the woman and her children, and then returned to his seat.

More people came forward with "God sightings" and requests for prayers. Some read poems they'd written, a few sang songs. It was the most uplifting evening Monica had spent in weeks. A suddenly and scary thought occurred to her and she leaned in close to Barry.

"I don't have to go up, do I?" she whispered.

He squeezed her hand. "Only if you want to."

A woman in her fifties stepped up to the altar. "Ephesians 2:10 says for we are his workmanship, created in Christ Jesus for good works, which God prepared beforehand, that we should walk in them. As you all know, I suffer from CBS—Chronic Busyness Syndrome. For years I've been rushing around, trying to be everything to everyone. I realized something this week. I realized that it's not my job to champion every cause known to man. I'm not called to be Superwoman. I'm only called to be what God made me to be."

"Amen, sister," said a man behind them.

"I'm not saying that doing all the good you can is a bad thing, but I realized that being God's servant is not about that. It's not about what I'm willing to do for God. But about what I'm willing to let him do through me. God already prepared the good works. God put me in this place, at this time, for a reason. It's up to me to be aware of the opportunities he gives me to show his love each day, and then be obedient to his leading, instead of doing what seems good to me and asking for his blessing as an afterthought."

"He is the vine, sister," the man behind them said.

As the woman prayed for guidance for herself, and for the church, Monica felt a strange hush come over the room, a sensation she'd never experienced in her church back home.

When the woman returned to her seat, Barry stood and walked to the alter.

"I'd like to thank God for my friend, Monica. She's been through quite a trial, but the good Lord has brought her out on the other side. I'm thankful that she came through her jaw surgery with no loose teeth, and that today, after six weeks of rehab, she finally got to go home."

Everyone applauded and Monica didn't know whether to be pleased or embarrassed. She didn't know what to think of this peculiar church Barry had brought her to.

As the service ended, they all held hands and prayed. For the nation. For the city. For the church. For Monica. This time, the hush was accompanied by a deep sense of loneliness. Like everywhere else, she didn't fit in here, in this little white church. She'd loved God all her life, but these people had a connection to him that she didn't. Barry had it. Phyllis and Doug Gleason had it. Thinking back, Lydia from Costa Rica had also had it. She'd had it as a child, but somewhere along the way, she'd lost it. She sat with her eyes closed and hands folded in her lap, wondering if it was too late to get it back.

•

The next morning, Monica put in a call to her supervisor, Layla Levee. Next week would be the final week of the school year, and she was feeling up to returning for it. She couldn't drive for another couple of weeks, but the school was within walking distance. It would be nice to get the extra exercise, and she wondered why she had never considered walking to school before.

"Good morning, Layla Levee speaking."

"Hi, Layla. It's Monica Humphrey."

"Monica, so good to hear from you. How are you?"

"I'm well. Actually, I'm home now, and I was thinking I'd like to come in next week."

"Oh …" Layla hesitated a beat longer than necessary, and Monica wondered what she was thinking. "I assumed you'd just take the whole rest of the year off."

Her attitude was surprising, to say the least. It was difficult to find substitutes for middle school anything, let alone English, and the subs they did find didn't usually stay around long.

"I'm able to come in. I'm pretty much back to normal."

"I'm happy to hear that. And I appreciate your dedication." She sighed. "I'm just not sure that would be fair to Darlene."

Darlene?

"When I didn't hear from you, I assumed you wouldn't be back this year so I hired Darlene Dixon to sub in your place for the rest of the year."

It was obvious Layla wanted her to bow out gracefully. She wasn't about to do that. "I had my jaw wired shut and my right arm in a cast. Communication was kind of a challenge all the way around."

"I understand that, Monica." Her tone bordered on hostility. "Well, I'll work something out. Maybe we can set up some tutoring sessions, or something."

Monica ended the call, feeling vaguely uneasy.

•

On Monday morning she walked to school, enjoying the cool breeze on her face, the chirps of birds in the trees, and the way her new skirt swirled around her ankles. Loving that she actually had ankles now. After her conversation with Layla, she'd taken stock of her closet.

She'd lost more than forty pounds so far and everything she owned was too big on her. She'd treated herself to a new skirt and top. The skirt was still big enough to be a circus tent, but it was a full size smaller than anything in her closet. She wondered whether anyone at work would notice.

The walk took less time than she'd expected and she arrived at school twenty minutes early. She went straight to her classroom. Unlocking the door, the first thing she noticed were the colorful posters on the walls.

Excel!
Middle School Rocks!
Keep Calm and Read on!

A potted cactus with a bright orange flower sat on the edge of her desk. Beside it sat a photo of a woman in her early twenties—a cheerleader type, with a year round tan, a blonde shoulder-length bob, and a great big smile. Darlene Dixon, she presumed.

The man beside her, with his arm draped casually around her shoulders, was handsome beyond belief.

Darlene Dixon's lesson plans sat on the desk. Monica picked them up and flipped through them.

Read Aloud: The One and Only Ivan. Group discussion.

The One and Only Ivan? That wasn't even on her suggested reading list.

Synonym BINGO
Weird Places Essays: Share with class.

A neat stack of essays sat beside the lesson plans and Monica scanned their titles.

Why Not Visit Whynot, North Carolina?
I definitely would not want to live in Mosquitoville, Vermont!
Have a frightfully good time in Frankenstein, Missouri.
Money, Mississippi is the place for me!

Scanning the pages, she smiled, amazed at the progress her students had made in just a few short weeks.

Finally the early bell rang and the first of her students shuffled in. Seeing her, they stopped in the doorway as if frozen.

"Where's Miss Dixon?"

Her heart sank. *I missed you, too.* "She's not here."

"Why not?"

"Because I am."

"But we're supposed to have an ice cream party."

"We'll discuss that later. For now, get out your journals."

At first there was a collective groan, and then the sound of whispering.

Five minutes later, the final bell brought a stampede of students, and the same questions. Before she could answer them, the girl from the photograph hurried into the room, wearing a zebra striped skirt that was some ridiculously small size, like 3, a backpack slung over her shoulder. Seeing Monica, she stopped short. "Oh!"

"Miss D!" the students yelled.

"Oh. I thought … You're Monica, right?"

"Right."

In the adolescent chaos that erupted, Monica could barely hear herself think. She glanced around for the hand bell she kept on her desk, but it seemed to have disappeared. Before she could say anything at all, Darlene Dixon began holding up fingers.

"One! Two! Three! Four!"

"We ain't gonna talk no more!" the students chanted in unison.

Dear God. Darlene Dixon had turned her classroom into a pep rally. But to her amazement, the students fell silent.

"Good. Now get out a sheet of paper and start your essays while I talk to Miss Humphrey. Today's topic is Make-A-Wish Monday. And I want your best work."

As Monica stood there, astonished, Layla Levee walked in. "Monica, I thought you'd stop in the office before coming upstairs."

"I …"

"I've set up some tutoring sessions, as we discussed. I thought I'd have you work in the back office."

She could work in the back office? She'd assumed Darlene Dixon would be the one doing the tutoring, and she would teach her classes. Humiliated, she followed Layla to the small, windowless compartment off of the main office.

"Look, I know it's not ideal," Layla said. "But being the last week of school, you know how it is. I don't want to upset the students' apple carts."

What about my apple cart?

As the door closed behind Layla, Monica set down her purse

and tote bag, took a seat at the desk, and waited for her first student to arrive, all the while fighting tears. She was pretty sure there was something in her contract that constituted a grievance, but why push it?

By eleven-thirty not a single student had shown up for tutoring and not a single staff member had stopped in to welcome her back. When the lunch bell rang, she grabbed up her purse and headed outside. She didn't want to face the cafeteria, let alone the faculty room, and she was sure there was nothing here she wanted to eat, anyway. She headed across the street to the gas station, bought a cup of coffee, and carried it to a bench in front of the school. She held her coffee, once again fighting tears. The day, which had started out so full of promise, was completely ruined.

Her phone alerted her to a text message and she fumbled it out of her purse. Barry.

Hello, Beautiful. She smiled her first smile since morning. *Call me later!*

•

When the bell finally signaled the end of the school day, Monica locked the door of her compartment and headed home. She wanted cake. And ice cream. And milkshakes and pasta and cookies.

Catching herself in her thoughts, she sighed. That was the old, unhealthy Monica talking. She tried to clear such cravings from her mind, to think positive, healthy thoughts, as Meg Keenan had advised. At last, the cravings subsided. Even so, she was glad there wasn't a grocery store within walking distance.

Home at last, she scooped Ginger up in her arms and hugged her. Ginger rubbed her whiskers against Monica's face, purring like mad.

"At least someone's happy to see me." She stroked the cat's ears for a long moment, then set her down and went to make a banana smoothie.

She'd just taken her first sip when the phone rang.

"Hi, Barry."

"How'd it go?"

"I want cake."

"Uh-oh."

"It was horrible. They stuck me in a broom closet to tutor no one while Miley Cyrus taught my classes."

"You're kidding."

Her voice caught. "I don't think I want to go back tomorrow. I don't think I ever want to go back again."

He was quiet for a moment. "Well, I can't say I blame you. What would you like to do instead? For a job?"

"I don't know."

"We could always use another cashier at the store."

"No. I don't know."

"Maybe the church needs a secretary."

"I don't know, Barry."

"I'll be by after work. We'll talk more about it then, okay?"

"Okay."

"Hang in there, honey. It will get better. I promise."

•

Later that night, soaking in the tub, she had the curious sensation that her life was unraveling. Coming apart. She'd always thought she was a decent teacher. Not particularly fun, but fair.

Darlene clearly enjoyed the students. And they enjoyed her, fed off her energy. Thrived. In the past couple of years, Monica had grown tired and burned out. The job had become a paycheck.

She thought of the woman at the prayer meeting, and about what she'd said about God having a purpose for every human being. If teaching was what God had called her to do, then why did she feel so dissatisfied? Maybe it was never God's plan at all. Maybe she'd run haphazardly down a career path and then halfheartedly asked God to bless her plans.

She thought of the other church service, so many years ago, that had driven her entire life and career plans. She'd thought this was what she wanted, but maybe she'd just wanted to be like Lydia, beautiful and beloved.

Maybe she never really wanted to be a teacher at all.

Chapter Twelve

Monica had started applying to colleges in the middle of her senior year. Since Geneva and Penny did not own one, she'd gone to the library and used their computer to research the best colleges to earn a teaching degree. She looked up universities from New York to California and everywhere in between, dreaming of getting as far away from Baxter as possible. But in April, when a letter arrived from Risingville College, just a half hour away, she was ecstatic.

"I got accepted!" She shrieked. "I'm going to go to Risingville College!"

"That's wonderful, honey!" Penny gave her a hug. "A college girl. Can you imagine it, Geneva?"

"Seems like only yesterday you were in the first grade. We're so proud of you, Monica," Geneva beamed.

Her stellar grades had earned her a full academic scholarship. She would have to take out a student loan for her housing. The school year would start in September. She could hardly wait.

Her home-school graduation was a small affair held in the church basement. The church ladies had decorated it with pink and white streamers and Penny had made a cake in the shape of a diploma. She received cards with twenty-dollar bills tucked inside, a watch, and a sterling silver pen set. It wasn't until later, at home, that the girls presented her with their card.

"We didn't give you a gift at the party because you have a choice to make," Geneva told her. "Penny and I will either pay for you to live in the dorm, your freshman year, or we'll buy you a car to go back and forth. Think it over and let us know which you'd prefer."

She hadn't even considered living at home. "I can let you know right now. I want to live in the dorm!"

"That's fine," she said, but Monica noticed the look of disappointment that flashed for a moment in Geneva's eyes.

"Unless you'd rather I stayed home."

"Of course you'll live in the dorm!" Penny said, a bit too enthusiastically. "That's the best part of college. It'll be like a four-year slumber party!"

The summer before college was the longest of Monica's life. The girls had sold the chickens and the goats the year before, and Penny had scaled back the vegetable garden to a single row of corn, a row of beans, and one of tomatoes. Even so, there was always work to be done. At sixty-five, Geneva seemed to be slowing down. She worked in the store just Fridays and Saturdays that summer, and seemed to need the rest of the week to recover.

Monica had stepped into her role, doing the bulk of the ordering and stocking the shelves, while Penny did the baking and ran the cash register. Business was better than she could ever remember, which was why the snippet of overheard conversation she heard stopped her in her tracks.

It was a late July evening and the girls were sitting on the front porch. It had rained heavily that afternoon, and Monica had taken a pitcher to the rain barrel on the side of the house, hoping to collect enough rain water to wash her hair. Fresh rain water made it so much softer. She'd filled the pitcher, and was heading around to the front of the house when Geneva spoke.

"I'm starting to forget things," she said. "This is the same way it happened with mother."

"It's probably just the heat," Penny said. "It's been brutal this summer."

"It's not the heat, Penny."

She heard the creak of the porch swing. What was Geneva talking about?

"I hate to think of what's coming. Remembering what father went through … I can't bear the thought of putting you through that. "

"Hey, you've taken care of me all my life. It's only fair I should take care of you now."

"I think we should close the store."

Monica nearly cried out. Close the store? What was Geneva saying?

"No, Geneva," Penny sighed. "Let's not do that."

"When Monica leaves, most of it will fall on your shoulders. Surely you can see I'm not able to keep up with things like I used to. We should sell it now, while it's still worth something."

"The store was our dream. It's who we are."

"It's who we were, Penny. I've done some calculating. We'd have plenty enough to live on, if we were careful."

Penny laughed. "When have we ever been anything but careful?"

Silence fell between them, the air heavy with the croaking of frogs and the hum of cicadas. Then Penny spoke again. "Let's wait awhile and see how it goes. If it proves to be too much, then we'll sell it."

Monica turned and hurried back across the yard, her stomach aching and her mind overflowing with questions. What was wrong with Geneva? And what had been wrong with Geneva's mother? She'd been told the woman had died in her sleep, but had never cared to learn the particulars. Memories came to her in lightning flashes. Geneva stopping at the gate on her way from the store, short of breath. Asking Monica to bring her cold glasses of water. Forgetting conversations they'd had the day before, then going to lie down, saying she felt lightheaded. How could she have been so self-absorbed as to not know something was wrong?

She started doing extra cleaning around the house, and cooking the evening meals, saying she was practicing for being out on her own. The first week in August, she and the girls headed to Risingville for a long-awaited tour of the campus, but by then the fun had gone out of it.

The campus was lovely—a cluster of hundred-year-old brick buildings covered in ivy. They toured the classroom buildings, the cafeteria, and the student center. Then the library and the football stadium. They saved the freshman dorms for last.

From the outside, Connors Hall looked like an upscale

apartment complex; a four-story structure of bricks and gleaming windows. Each suite consisted of a living room with deep pile carpet and real leather furniture, a kitchenette, two bedrooms and two bathrooms.

Monica walked through the rooms, savoring the sensations of luxury and freedom. She saw it all so clearly. Evenings of studying at the oversized desk in her bedroom, sprawled out in the living room enjoying late night movies with the friends she would finally make, fixing meals in her very own kitchen, walking across to the student center for lively discussions and games of ping-pong. She wanted this. Needed this. She indulged in her fantasies for a moment longer, and then let them slip through her fingers and disappear. She was needed at home.

"I'm so jealous!" Penny exclaimed, as they drove back to Baxter. "You're going to have so much fun in college!"

"Just don't forget, you're also there to learn," Geneva said, but with a smile.

That evening, they sat together on the porch, enjoying the first cool breezes of the day.

"You're awfully quiet, Monica," Geneva observed. "Is there something bothering you?"

She pulled in a breath and fought to keep the lie from showing in her voice. "Not really. It's just … I've been thinking about it, and I think I'd rather live here than in the dorms after all."

•

Her freshman year of college was a blur that she spent on overload, barely sleeping, and never socializing. Her classes were much more challenging than she'd expected, and her studies took up most of her spare time throughout the week. On weekends, she worked in the store.

By the time she started her sophomore year, Geneva was working just Saturday mornings, mainly stocking the shelves, which Monica and Penny would have to quickly rearrange when she'd left. Her memory loss had become alarming. It took Geneva hours to get up and around in the mornings, but when Monica asked about her health, she just smiled and said it was old age creeping in. But she was only sixty-six. Monica knew women in their seventies who were more energetic.

She ended her fourth semester on the Dean's List and Geneva and Penny took her to dinner at the Riverview, a lovely old hotel in Boswell Center that had been converted into a restaurant, to celebrate. They sat at a glass-topped table on the patio and watched the river chortle past as they savored juicy steaks and baked potatoes smothered in sour cream. It was one of the nicest evenings Monica could remember.

"We have a small gift for you, Monica," Geneva said, handing her a square, silver box. She opened it and her breath caught. "This is beautiful!" She removed the delicate silver chain and fingered the sparkling diamond solitaire pendant.

"That belonged to our mother." Penny and Geneva exchanged tearful glances. "We want you to have it."

"I love it," she said, tears filling her eyes at the extravagance of their gift. "Thank you so much."

The evening tired Geneva out, and when they returned home, she gave Monica a kiss on the cheek. "I think I'll go on up to bed early."

"Thank you for the wonderful dinner, Geneva. And for the necklace."

"It was my pleasure and privilege, child. Good night."

A dark and horrible fear had lived for years in a back corner of Monica's mind. The fear that Penny would sink into the depths of depression one time too many, and seek a permanent solution to her pain. Never once had she entertained that fear for Geneva.

The next morning she was in the kitchen making breakfast when Penny padded in, yawning.

"Morning, Penny."

"Good morning. Goodness, looks like we all overslept. We'll have to get a move on if we're going to make it to church this morning. Isn't Geneva up yet?"

"I haven't seen anything of her," Monica said, setting a plate of bacon on the table.

"I'd better go and wake her, then. Be right back."

She cracked six eggs into the fry pan and popped four slices of toast into the toaster. She poured three glasses of orange juice and set Geneva's vitamins beside her plate. She grabbed the spatula from the drawer and had just flipped the first egg when a deep, throaty wailing sent her hurrying up the stairs. She stood in the doorway of Geneva's bedroom, still clutching the spatula.

"What is it?" she asked, though she already knew.

Penny sat on the bed, cradling her sister's lifeless body.

No, no, no. Oh, God, Geneva, no!

An empty pill bottle lay on the floor next to an overturned water glass. There was no note. No explanation. No goodbye. Geneva. Solid, sensible, self-reliant, wonderful Geneva was just … gone.

Chapter Thirteen

$\mathcal{I}$t was the last Saturday in May, and Monica and Barry were walking dogs. Mimi the hand specialist was pleased with her progress, had said she was gaining more strength and mobility with every session. She encouraged Monica to keep working her hand, to keep building strength. Even so, Barry chose a senior Bassett hound named Toby for her to walk.

"He's gentle, and low energy. He won't jerk the leash, or try to walk you," he said.

For himself, he selected an enormous bullmastiff named Agnes.

"What a gorgeous day," she commented, as they strolled along West Avenue. "Is it supposed to be like this all weekend?"

"That depends on which weather station you watch," he chuckled. "But yeah, I think it looks pretty decent across the board. Which reminds me, we haven't talked about Memorial Day yet."

"I'll probably run over to Baxter."

"To decorate your aunts' graves?"

"Among other things, yes."

"Mind if I tag along?"

"I've been cleared to drive now, so you don't have to."

"I'd like to."

"Okay. I was thinking I'd leave around ten."

After a few blocks they came to a small, weedy park with rusting hot dog grills and outdated playground equipment. Without a moment's hesitation, Agnes plodded through the open gates.

"This is where she likes to pee," Barry explained.

When both of the dogs had done their business, Agnes led the group to a bench beneath a shady tree. Barry opened his backpack and produced four cold bottles of water. After handing one of them to Monica, he pulled out two plastic bowls and filled them with water for the dogs. When she'd emptied her bowl, Agnes rested her head on Barry's knee and gazed lovingly into his face.

"Barry, that dog adores you. Look how she's looking at you."

He grinned and rubbed the dog's ears. "I've been walking Aggie for almost four months. Most people are afraid of her, but I know she's just a big baby, aren't you, girl?"

Aggie wagged her tail.

"She's a gorgeous dog. And very well behaved. How does a dog like that end up at the pound, anyway?"

"Story is, her family moved and left her behind, chained to a fence in the back yard. She was disowned, just like me. I'd love to give her a home, if I could. I just don't know how I'd hide her from my landlord."

It was the first time Barry had mentioned his family, and she knew she must tread carefully. "Do you want to talk about that? Your family disowning you?"

"Nah. It was after … you know."

"Okay."

"Should I pack us a picnic lunch for Monday?" he asked. "I could grab a watermelon from the store, and maybe a rotisserie chicken."

"I'd love that."

"Is there even any place in Baxter to have a picnic?" he teased.

"I know the perfect place. Bring some strawberries, too."

Since her return home from St. Cecilia's, Monica had been existing mostly on fruit. She'd never before appreciated the succulent richness of plums, peaches and apricots. Now she couldn't get enough of them. Between following the meal plans Meg had sent home with her, and her daily walks, she'd dropped down to two-hundred and seventy-two pounds. She'd thought when she reached two-hundred she might apply again for a spot on a mission team in Costa Rica. But now she wasn't sure if she still wanted to go. The team hadn't wanted her when she was overweight, whereas Barry seemed to want her just as she was. Maybe she should stay, see how it all turned out.

•

On Monday morning she directed Barry through the small village of Baxter to Shady Grove Cemetery. He parked the car and they retrieved the flower arrangements Monica had put together from the back seat. For Geneva, she'd created a basket spilling over with baby's breath and pale pink miniature roses, and for Penny, a basket of bold red painted daisies.

She found their graves and brushed the dried grass from Geneva's headstone, then went after the dust and dirt with a bottle of stone cleaner and a cloth. Satisfied that Geneva's stone was as clean as she could make it, she moved on to Penny's.

"They died just two years apart?" Barry asked, reading the stones.

"Yep."

"Penny died young. Only fifty-five."

He gave her a questioning glance.

"Penny never recovered from Geneva's death," she told him, setting the basket of flowers in place beside Geneva's grave. "She just didn't know how to exist without her sister."

"She committed suicide?" he asked softly.

"They both did."

She gave Penny's stone a final swipe with her cloth and set the daisies beside it.

"I know you said your mother died when you were small, and that's why the girls raised you. Were they your only family?"

"My father and I lost touch years ago. We heard that he and his second wife got divorced, but I don't know if he stayed in Pittsburgh or not. He didn't come to either of the girls' funerals." She stood and brushed the dirt from her knees. "I have a half-sister that I haven't seen since she was three years old. She's probably twenty by now."

"Do you ever think of trying to find them?"

"No. Are you ready to go?"
"Sure. Where to now?"
"A place called Memory Lane."

•

She felt the familiar tug at her heartstrings as Barry pulled into the driveway. The store seemed to stare at her, its windows like sad, empty eyes. Two white rocking chairs sat, forlorn, on the porch. The tin roof was streaked with rust, and the snappy red and white sign above the door had over the years faded to pink, its lettering barely visible now. Two Gals General Store.

"So this is it, huh? This is where you worked, growing up?"

"It was much cuter then. The girls always had baskets of flowers on the porch. The windows were so clean you could see the road reflected in them for miles."

He drove slowly past the store and down the long driveway until the house came into view.

"Wow. Nice place."

"It used to be. You can park here." He pulled to the side of the house and cut the engine. Monica climbed from the car and looked around her, surveying the barn, the gardens, the chicken coop. The grass was weeks overdue for cutting, and the house desperately needed paint. A couple of spindles had come loose from the porch, and one of the upstairs shutters hung crookedly. Even so, the sight of the house warmed her through. A gentle breeze lifted her hair and seemed to whisper in her ear … Welcome home.

She stepped up onto the porch and reached for the doorknob.

"Are you sure you should do that?" Barry asked from the yard.

She turned to glance at him in surprise. "Do what?"

"Try to get in? I mean, I know it's abandoned, but even so, there are laws against that."

"I own this house, Barry."

"Oh. I didn't realize …"

She took out her key ring, and finding the small, gold key, turned it in the lock. "The girls left the farm to me when they died. When I got the job at Risingville Middle School, I sold all but two acres and rented out the house. The last tenant moved out in March. With everything that happened, this is the first chance I've had to come out and see to things."

She stepped inside, and it was as if the house physically embraced her. The air was thick with a closed-up, musty odor, and she saw with dismay that the last tenants not been kind to the house. There were holes punched in the walls, stains in the area rugs, unwanted toys and clothing strewn across the floors.

As she gave Barry a tour of the downstairs, he commented on the original wood moldings, the hardwood cherry floors, and the floor-to-ceiling cupboards. All Monica seemed to see were the girls, glimpses of them in every room. She saw Geneva in her sewing room, her head bent over her latest dress patterns. Penny in the kitchen, pulling loaves of bread from the oven. She could almost hear her cheerful singing reverberating from the walls. Tears sprang to her eyes and she wiped them away. Barry hugged her.

"It's hard, isn't it?"

"Yeah."

"Let's go outside."

They retrieved their picnic lunch from the car and carried it to the porch. He'd brought a rotisserie chicken, still warm, containers of grapes, watermelon, and strawberries.

"This is wonderful, Barry. Thank you."

"My pleasure." He settled onto the porch swing with a plate of chicken. "This is a great house, Monica."

"It's gonna need a lot of prettying up before I can rent it out again." She sighed. "Maybe I should just sell it and be done with it."

"That would be a shame, though, your childhood home. It's a beautiful piece of property. Very peaceful."

"Maybe I'll move back in, then. It would only be a half hour drive to the school. If I decide to go back."

"I'm not sure I like that idea," he said, around a mouthful of chicken. "I wouldn't see you as much."

"It's only a half-hour, Barry, not the other side of the moon." She pulled apart a cluster of grapes, popped one in her mouth.

"And besides, I'm only kidding. I don't want to move back to Baxter."

But as she gazed out at the gardens, with the scent of lilacs heavy in the air, memories came to her on the gentle breeze of happy times spent here with the girls. It lifted her hair, and whispered to her heart that she was home.

Chapter Fourteen

$\mathscr{A}$ part of Monica had known that Penny would take her own life, had always known it. In the two years that followed Geneva's death, she stood helplessly aside, watching as Penny slowly disappeared. Penny continued to run the store and tend her gardens, but it was obvious she took no pleasure in the things she'd so enjoyed. So Monica waited, ever on the alert for a phone call, a note. Though her suicide was not a shock, it was devastating. Hadn't Penny promised Monica she'd always be there, in her corner? And yet she swallowed the bottle of pills, sealing the deal by slashing both wrists, leaving Monica with another shattered promise, another jagged shard of herself that could never be repaired.

A month after Penny's funeral Monica met with Del Schwartz, the girls' attorney, for the reading of their will. The girls had left her everything; the store, the farm, a savings account with a few thousand dollars. It was July, the summer she graduated from college. The house was empty now, except for the echo of Penny's sorrow. She'd never felt more alone in her life. And so she formulated a plan of escape.

She contacted the mission about a possible spot on their Costa Rican team. She enrolled in the online courses they suggested, and applied to take the written exam. After that, all that was left was the physical, which she was told would consist of a fifteen-minute doctor's appointment. If things went well, she would be in Costa Rica by September. Costa Rica, where there would be no painful memories, no awkward family history.

Del Schwartz tapped the papers into a tidy stack and handed

them to her. "Do you have any questions for me, Monica?"

"How soon can I sell the property?"

He removed his glasses and gazed at her for long moments. "The property is yours to do with whatever you wish. I understand why selling it might seem the best option right now, but I'd advise you to give it some time. It's best not to make big decision so soon after the loss of a loved one. You may change your mind later and wish you'd held onto it. If you don't want to stay here in Baxter, you might consider renting the house out. The property is paid for, you own it outright. It would be a nice investment property for you, down the road."

"I'll think about that. Thank you."

After leaving the attorney's office, she walked two blocks to Chandler Realty. She would need money upfront for her mission trip. And while Mr. Schwartz had a point about the house being an investment, she certainly didn't need or want the responsibility of a fifteen-acre farm. With a stroke of a pen, she listed all but two acres for sale and continued with her plans, but as Geneva like to say, even the best laid plans had their flaws.

Failing the physical exam threw into a tailspin. If not Costa Rica, then what?

The void inside of her that opened as a deep, dark hole with the loss of her mother was now a gaping chasm. The only thing that seemed to fill it was food. She ate constantly, ballooning from two-hundred-fifty pounds to three-hundred, three-hundred to three-hundred-twenty-five.

She stopped attending church, because obviously Lydia had been wrong, all those years ago. Obviously God couldn't use her.

In mid-October she received a phone call from Risingville Middle School. The ELA teacher they'd hired had not worked out. They wanted to give Monica a second interview. Two weeks later, she moved the things she wanted to keep from the house into the store and padlocked the door. Then she rented out the house, and walked away from life as she knew it.

Chapter Fifteen

"*I*s your heart broken today, beloved?" Pastor Ryan asked.

Monica tensed. What kind of church service was this Barry had brought her to? She hadn't been in her pew twenty minutes and already Pastor Ryan had seen inside her soul.

"Psalm one-hundred, forty-seven, verse three says, He heals the brokenhearted and binds up their wounds. But what does that mean for you? What does it mean for me?"

He stepped from behind the lectern and circled around until he stood in front of it.

"If you've ever had a broken arm, or leg, you know the pain. You know that once the cast comes off, the injury is still tender, the limb still needs to relearn how to do its job."

She nodded. Wasn't that the truth?

"That's the way it is with a broken heart. And just like with a broken bone, ignoring the pain won't make it go away. It will only make it worse. Brokenness needs attention, healing. Healing we can't provide for ourselves. In fact, the only true healing is that which comes from the Great Physician Himself."

"Preach it, Brother," someone behind her said.

"Your heart may have been broken for years. Immobilized. Unable to love itself. Unable to love others. And that's a sad thing, because love is what Christianity is all about. It's what the Lord was all about, when He walked this earth. When your heart has been severely broken, beloved, the only way to move forward is on your knees."

"Amen and amen, Pastor."

"Jesus knew what it meant to be broken. In the book of Isaiah, chapter fifty-three and verse five we're told that He was pierced for our transgressions. He was crushed for our iniquities. The punishment that brought us peace was on Him, and by His wounds we are healed.

"The King of Kings. Broken. For you. And for me.

"He heals the brokenhearted and binds up their wounds.

"When he walked this earth, so many came to him with hurts, hoping that if only they could touch the hem of his robe, if only his shadow would fall across them, they might find comfort. Beloved, seek his shadow today. Come to the shadow of his wings. For it is only there that you will find healing for all the broken places in your life. If you're broken, beloved, come to the cross. Let him make you whole."

The message hit her. Hard. When the congregation started to sing, soft and sweet, she stood beside Barry, tears coursing down her cheeks. She wasn't sure what it all meant. But she knew that the pastor had been speaking to her. She'd been broken her whole life. If there was healing available at Pastor Ryan's alter, she wanted it. She needed it.

She slipped out of the pew and made her way, trembling, to the front of the church. And then Barry was beside her, his warm hand on her shoulder. Praying for her. With her. Others came then, Phyllis and Doug Gleason. The woman with Chronic Busy-ness Syndrome. They made a circle around her, a circle of prayer. She'd never felt more loved.

They stayed at the altar until the last hymn was sung and the service ended. Barry gave her a hug, and she left a black-mascara smudge on his shirt.

"My face must be a mess," she said.

"You've never been more beautiful."

They stayed for coffee hour, and several members of the congregation came and introduced themselves to her. It was strange, foreign to her, to feel so completely accepted.

"Some of the ladies get together on Tuesday nights for Bible Study," said Chronic Busyness, whose name she'd learned was Cheryl-Lynn. "We'd love to have you join us this week."

"I'd really like that," she said. "And I'll be sure keep it in mind for some time, but I'm going to be out of town for a while."

Barry's expression was stricken.

"Oh, well that's fine. We'll leave the invitation open, how's that?"

It wasn't until he dropped her off that afternoon that he mentioned the conversation.

"So what's this I hear about you leaving town?"

"I was going to tell you. I'm going to go back to the farm for a while."

He fiddled with his keys. "How long's a while?"

She shrugged. "A few weeks. However long it takes."

"Okay."

"I need to make some decisions. Not to mention some repairs."

"Want some help? I mean, I'm no Chip Gaines, but I know how to handle a bucket of spackling."

She grinned. "I thought you'd never ask.

His expression remained somber. "How soon will you go?"

"Tomorrow morning."

He fiddled with his keys some more. "I could come out after work for a couple of hours."

"If you want to."

He faced her. "Do you want me to, Monica? Somehow I'm feeling like this is goodbye."

"Of course it's not goodbye. I can't walk away from you. You're my best friend. The only friend I have."

"Well, that's a start, isn't it?" He kissed her then, slowly and tenderly. And she knew in her heart it was not goodbye, and never would be.

•

She set her alarm for six a.m. and packed her suitcases, along with two boxes of essential items, into the car. Then she coaxed Ginger into her cat carrier and headed to the farm. The morning was cool and sunny, adding to the feeling of optimism she'd carried with her from church the day before.

In the house, she set her suitcases in the living room. She unpacked her coffee maker and mugs, her blender, dishes and silverware while Ginger went off to explore the rooms. With a pot of coffee perking, she walked through the house, assessing. It wasn't long before she was overwhelmed. Every room needed work. And she hadn't even been upstairs yet.

"I don't know where to start," she whispered.

He glance rested on the incredible blue sky outside the window, the soft swish of the breeze in the hundred-year-old sugar maple. She'd never asked God for guidance before. Maybe that was why her life was in the shambles it was in right now.

"God, I don't know where to start. Not with this house. Not with my life. This seemed like an ending point ten years ago. But now it feels like a new start. Can you … Would you show me what to do?"

She waited quietly for a few moments, but discerned no answer.

Well for heaven's sakes, what did you expect? An audible voice? She pulled in a breath, let it out. *That's right. Breathe. Take it one day, one room at a time.*

Thankfully, the work needed was mostly cosmetic. She'd start with the living room.

Pouring herself a cup of coffee, she sat at the wobbly card table in the kitchen and began to make a list. Paint. Spackling. Wallpaper stripper. Area rugs, curtains, candles to remove that awful, musty odor.

With her list made, she felt better. She set Ginger up in the sewing room with her litter pan and food, and then drove to the bank to withdraw some money from her savings account. Thank heavens she still had most of the money from the sale of the land. She had a feeling she was going to need it.

She was in the bank, standing in an impossibly long line, when she heard her name.

"Monica Humphrey?"

She looked up in surprise to see Sarah Scott. An older, heavier, not-a-drop-of-make-up, hair-pulled-back-in-a- messy-ponytail Sarah Scott.

"Sarah Scott?"

"It's Lambert now. I married Pete. Gosh, it's so good to see you!" She gave Monica a quick hug. "I was so sorry about Penny. I'd have come to her funeral, but I was in labor. Everybody in town still misses the store. So, are you back?"

"For a while. I've got to do some work at the house."

"I always loved that house. Hey, if you need any help with the lawn—mowing and weed eating and such, I have a fourteen-year-old boy who needs something to do this summer besides playing video games."

"You have a fourteen-year-old son?"

She laughed. "And a twelve-year-old and a ten-year-old. We'll have to have lunch sometime soon, and get caught up."

"I'd like that."

"Great! Here," she scribbled her cell number on the back of a bank receipt, gave Monica another quick hug, and was gone.

•

Monica drove to Boswell Center to the hardware store. She went down her list point by point, filling her cart with paint brushes, drop cloths, and spackling. She bought two gallons of stain blocking primer, and another two gallons of off-white paint. After leaving there, she stopped at the grocery store and bought coffee, fruits, and all of the ingredients for chicken soup. She'd make Barry dinner, she decided.

She had the soup in the crock pot, dinner rolls warming in the oven, when his car pulled in the driveway. Walking across the yard, she saw someone sitting in the passenger seat.

Strange. Who had he brought with him?

Drawing closer, she peered through the windshield. She cried out in surprise as Barry stepped from the car.

"You brought Agnes?"

"Before you say anything, let me explain."

"This better be good."

"Her time is running out at the shelter, Monica. She's on the list to be euthanized next month. I couldn't let that happen. She's too nice a girl. I thought maybe she could stay here until I can find her a home. I'll pay for her food, everything she needs. And plus, I'd feel better about you living out here with Aggie for protection."

She glanced at the dog, who waited patiently in the car.

"So … what do you think? Can she stay?"

"Barry Goodrich, I think … I think you are the sweetest,

most sensitive man I've ever known." She threw her arms around him. Agnes barked. "Of course she can stay. As long as she's nice to Ginger."

"Thank you."

Barry opened the car door and Agnes bounded out. She raced around the yard, jumping, as if for joy, and they laughed at her antics.

"Are you ready for coffee?" she asked.

She poured two cups and they settled on the porch swing.

"So," Barry said, taking a swallow of coffee." "What's our plan, do we know?"

"Short term, I want to start with the living room. We've got to spackle in the holes, strip off the old, stained wall paper, paint, and put up some curtains. After that, most every room will at least need painting. Outside we'll need new porch spindles and shutters. That should take us the whole summer."

"And long-term?"

She pulled in a breath, then let it out, along with the words that up until then she'd only said in her head.

"I want to reopen the store."

Chapter Sixteen

Ten days later, Monica and Sarah Lambert sat on the porch, enjoying ice cold glasses of sweet tea. Across the yard, Agnes was busy chasing butterflies. Sarah had brought her riding mower, and her oldest son, Justin, was cutting the lawn while her other sons, Jaxon and Jace, pulled weeds in the garden. The two women were taking a well-deserved break. The living room was finished.

Sarah had shown up at the farm the day after Monica moved back home, offering a fruit and cheese platter. "I'm sorry it's just fruit. I thought about baking you something, but I didn't have time. But anyway, I wanted to officially welcome you back to Baxter."

"Fruit is perfect, Sarah. I'm dieting, and I don't want baked goods in the house."

"I'm right there with you, sister. Anyway … can I come in?"

She'd shown Sarah into the living room, where she'd spent the entire morning stripping off one half of a sheet of the old, faded wallpaper. The exertion caused her wrist to throb, and her progress was painfully slow.

"Taking this down, it almost seems like a sacrilege," she confessed. "I think the girls are fighting me."

"Oh, I think they'd be glad to see this old paper go, the shape it's in now." Sarah lightly ran her hand over a cabbage rose, long since faded from pink to gray. Her glance moved across the crown molding, which some long-ago tenant had painted brown. "This woodwork is absolutely to die for."

Monica sighed. "I never gave anyone permission to paint it. I suppose that will all have to be stripped now, too."

"Maybe not."

"Yes it will. It's hideous."

"In that shade of mud brown, yes, it is."

"But …?"

Sarah grinned. "Some women are addicted to soap operas. For me, it's home renovation programs. I have more ideas than I have rooms in my house. I think it would be gorgeous if you painted the walls off white and the trim charcoal gray. Grays are the latest thing. They're Farmhouse-y."

"Well, it is a farm house."

"To be honest, Monica, I'm a little jealous. I love our home, but it's a ho-hum ranch- style house. I'd love to have something like this to sink my teeth into."

As easily as that, Sarah was on board. She removed three strips of paper for every one of Monica's, and within three days, the old cabbage rose wallpaper was a memory.

On Thursday they started painting the walls, and on Saturday, the moldings. On Monday they made a trip to Cleveland and Sarah helped her select a cracked pepper area rug, black iron floor lamps, turquoise throw pillows for pops of color, and sheer, dove- gray curtains.

"What are you going to do for furniture?" she asked.

"I gave notice to my landlord in Risingville. We're moving my stuff this weekend. I have a cream colored sofa and recliner that will work. Plus I still have some of the girls' furniture in the store."

On Tuesday evening, they'd employed Sarah's husband Pete, and her three sons to help them lug the furniture over from the store; end tables, Geneva's grandmother's buffet, an enormous armoire that Sarah said would be perfect repurposed as a TV cabinet.

"Look at this cool old trunk." Sarah pointed to an upright steamer trunk tucked away in the corner. "This would make an amazing coffee table."

"You think so?" Monica asked doubtfully.

"I know so." She fingered the small padlock that held it shut. "What's in here, anyway?"

"I don't know. I couldn't find a key to open it."

"That's not much of a lock," Pete said. "I have a pair of bolt cutters in the truck. They should do the trick."

He went outside and retrieved them. Within seconds, the lock lay on the floor. He and Sarah looked expectantly at Monica. "Do you suppose it's full of cash? The family savings?"

Monica laughed. "Not likely." Opening the trunk, she saw that it contained common household items: yellowed dishtowels and doilies, pillow cases, a packet of letters. "Looks like someone's hope chest," she said.

"Oh. Well that's nice, too," Pete said, barely concealing his disappointment.

Monica felt excited. She knew so little of her family history. She hoped the contents of the trunk would help her put some of the pieces of the past together. "Let's take it to the house with the other furniture," she told him. "I'll sort it out later."

On Wednesday morning, Sarah was in her glory, setting the furniture in place. They hung the new curtains and rolled out the area rug and set vases of cut flowers on the end tables. Standing back, Monica could not believe the transformation that had occurred.

"Sarah, you should go into interior design."

"Nah," she said humbly, but Monica could tell the comment pleased her. "So what's next?"

"Sweet tea."

Monica poured two tall glasses and they settled on the front porch with them.

"I can't thank you enough for your help, Sarah. I'd still be stripping wallpaper, if not for you."

"I really needed this, Monica," Sarah said. "I needed something for myself. Something to make me feel … like I'm not just a wife and the mom of three boys."

"Hold that thought."

Sarah took a long swallow from her glass. "What do you mean?"

"Between you and me, I may have a job for you in the not too distant future. In the store."

"Are you serious? You're going to reopen Two Gals?"

"Barry is doing a market analysis, to see if it's even feasible. If it is, then yes."

"That would be so great. For the town and for you. I have

so many good memories of that place. Of the girls."

"Me, too."

"And one or two not so good ones." She chuckled. "Do you remember that time we trimmed the horse's tail? I don't know what we were thinking. I'd never seen Penny so angry."

"Oh gosh, we wanted to use the hair to make wigs for our dolls."

"Penny told us the pony's tail was its only protection against biting insects. That we'd left the poor thing defenseless. I cried for a week."

Monica chuckled. "Me, too."

"I had such good times here with you and the girls when we were kids." She added quietly, "I wasn't very nice to you when we got older, was I?"

Monica waved the words away. "Forget it."

"I've always felt bad about that. You were the nicest girl in our class. And we were all so horrid to you. I'm really sorry."

The words were like a healing balm to Monica's soul. They found their way deep inside her heart, sought out a decades-old hurt, and began to soothe it.

"We're friends now. That's all that matters."

•

On Saturday morning Barry steered a rented box truck into the driveway, Monica following in her car behind him.

He stepped from the moving van and stretched. "Well, I guess it's official now. Are you happy?"

"Happy, yes. But scared, too. I hope I did the right thing."

He gathered her up in a hug. "It's a big step for you. But why pay Joel Saunders six hundred dollars a month to rent eight hundred square feet when you own a fabulous home like this?"

Within moments, Sarah and her boys showed up to help. As they unloaded the boxes from the truck, Sarah became a whirlwind of activity.

"Let's get your kitchen unpacked first," she said. "Boys, stack all of the boxes marked kitchen in here. Everything else can go in the dining room for now."

Within a half hour the truck was empty. "I'm going to go and return the truck," Barry said, giving Monica a quick kiss. "I'll be back in about an hour."

Sarah stared after him. "Where did you find him?"

Monica smiled. "At the supermarket, actually."

"Monica, he's wonderful. You guys are like, soulmates. Promise me you're going to hang on to him."

She smiled. She had every intention of doing so.

The women were arranging the pantry when Barry returned with two large pizzas and a Mediterranean salad for Monica. Sarah and her boys dug into the pizza while Monica nibbled at her salad.

"I so admire your self-control," Sarah said. "I can't seem to shed these twenty post-pregnancy pounds I've been carrying for the last ten years."

Monica's glance moved over her friend's figure. She looked curvy and lovely in cut-off jeans and a T-shirt. Monica would have loved to have had Sarah's weight problem. According to the doctor's charts she should weigh between one hundred forty and one hundred sixty pounds. She was down to two hundred sixty-six. Fifty-six pounds down, a hundred and six to go. Even so, she was starting to feel better, starting to hate herself less. And that was mostly due to the praise and encouragement Barry lavished on her. She watched him joking with Sarah's boys—a splotch of tomato sauce smeared endearingly on his chin, and wondered what on earth he could possibly see in her.

•

Within a couple of hours, Monica's kitchen was in order. The dishes were stacked in the cupboards, each pot and pan in its proper place. When Sarah and the boys left, she and Barry sat at the kitchen table.

"Your friend is like a tornado," Barry said. "Except instead of creating chaos, she whips everything in her path into shape."

Monica smiled. "Exhausting, isn't she?"

"I'm glad you've got a friend here, though. I mean, in addition to Ginger and Agnes." He scratched the dog behind the ears. "Oh, before I forget, I got you a housewarming gift. Wait right here." He went out to his car and returned with a Keurig and a case of caramel cappuccino coffee pods.

"Barry, this is so sweet. Thank you!" She set up the machine and instantly brewed two frothy cups of cappuccino. "This is amazing. I'm going to be so spoiled."

"I like to spoil you."

They sipped their drinks in companionable silence for a moment.

"So … are you making any progress with the market analysis?" she asked.

"Actually I'm about done with it."

Her stomach squeezed. "And?"

"I think you can make a go of it, if you sell the right product. It's all about supply and demand. And I think I've hit on the perfect demand for Baxter."

She watched his face, waiting.

"The nearest grocery store is in Boswell Center. Then you have the two supermarkets in Risingville, of course, and another in Owensville. All within thirty miles of Baxter. Those would be your competition, if you opened a mini grocer's. Baxter already has an established bakery, and there's gas mart just outside of town where people can get milk, bread, and cigarettes without driving a half hour. Their appeal is their convenience, surely not their prices." He sighed. "I know the girls ran a general store for years and made a living from it, but from what you've told me, they struggled, even back then. I'm just not sure groceries are the way to go this time."

Her heart sank. "So I shouldn't do it?"

"No, that's not what I'm saying. You just have to provide a product that people in Baxter need and want."

"What are you thinking?"

"Pizza."

"Pizza?"

"There are no pizza places closer than thirty-five minutes from here, and none that deliver to Baxter. And if they did, it wouldn't be hot and fresh by the time it arrived. The town has a population of eleven-hundred people, give or take. That's your target group. Pizza is fairly cheap to make. You'd have to invest in some equipment initially, ovens and warmers and such. You'd have to reconfigure the building, add a kitchen, maybe a few tables for those who want to dine in. You could offer sandwiches and homemade salads, potato and macaroni, as side dishes, and put in a soda fountain. I think you could make a killing here, Monica."

After the initial surprise wore off, Monica felt a glimmer of excitement. She'd envisioned a general store, like the girls had run, with fresh produce and home-baked goods. But she knew how hard Penny and Geneva had worked to keep Two Gals going, how many months they'd struggled to pay their bills. Why not pizza? She'd use only the freshest ingredients, offer sandwiches made with homemade breads—white and whole wheat and sourdough.

God, is this it? Is this the answer?

"But doesn't the gas station outside of town have pizza?"

"I bought a slice last week. It's not worth eating."

She laughed. "I hadn't thought of pizza, but it makes sense. It really makes sense for Baxter."

"The boys today were my test market. A sort of experiment. You saw for yourself how they devoured it. Pizza is still king in these parts."

"Ahh, so there was a method to your madness."

"You'd have to hire a minimum of five people, depending on your hours. Counter help, and definitely someone to do deliveries. And a manager."

"I was hoping that could be you. I was hoping you'd want to come into this with me, Barry. Not just as a manager. As a partner."

He gave her a look that pierced her soul. An earnest, longing look.

"I want to be your partner," he said softly, taking her hand in his. "A full partner in every sense. I've been feeling left out of your life since you moved here. Like you're moving ahead without me. I know it's crazy, but it scares me. I—" He sighed, gave her hand a squeeze. "I want the everyday stuff we used to share. Not just Sundays and an hour or two during the week. I want it all. I want to marry you, Monica."

She was thunderstruck. Dumbstruck. They were the words

she wanted most to hear, and the words she least expected. She stared at her hands, which now trembled in her lap, and tried to process all that Barry had said. Finally she lifted her gaze to his.

"I don't know what to say."

His hands covered hers, stilled their trembling. "Say yes."

"I want to. I'm just … not sure."

"What can I say, Monica? What can I do that I haven't already done to prove that I love you?"

"I know you do." Tears gathered in her eyes. "But I don't know why."

"Do I need a specific reason? Is it that hard for you to believe that a man could love you just because he does?"

"Yes," she whispered.

He dropped his arm around her and pulled her close to him. For long moments, he said nothing.

"Okay. To be honest, at first I was attracted to you because you reminded me a little bit of Mandy, my ex-wife. You walked into the store, and the sunlight was behind you, and my heart just about stopped. I though … I thought she'd come back. I'd prayed for that for such a long time. I thought God had finally answered my prayer. And he had, just not in the way I expected.

"Over time, you and I started talking—about Ginger, and about books we'd read, movies we'd seen, about so many things. And I realized you were so much more than Mandy ever was. I never once felt self-conscious with you, never felt judged for my past because you accepted me as I was. You accepted me, Monica. And I loved you for that." He gently stroked her hair. "And the more I got to know you, the more I loved you. Do you … could you grow to love me, too?"

"I love you now, Barry."

And it was true. She could pinpoint the exact moment she'd first loved him. Lifted onto a stretcher, wheeled out of the entrance of the Stop-N-Shop, she'd looked back and seen him, Barry, her beloved Barry, his hand holding her red purse, his eyes holding such deep concern. She'd known she could trust him with her belongings, known it without a doubt. But to trust him with her heart …?

"Can I think about this for a while?"

"Of course. Take all the time you need." His voice held gentleness, but his eyes, his bottomless brown eyes that held nothing back from her, showed disappointment.

Chapter Seventeen

June 3, 1963

$\mathcal{I}$t was so good to hear your voice today, dearest Geneva.

I took to heart what you said about Baxter, and the fact that you don't have a private phone line at the farm kept me from saying all that is in my heart. Even so, I hope I did not give the town gossips too much to wag their foolish tongues about today!

I want to marry you. If you think I don't mean that, you are wrong.

I'm sorry your mother is so unwell, and I do understand why you had to go home. It must be confusing and terrifying for your little sister, her own mother not knowing who she is. I understand, and that you would sacrifice your job, your life, for your family makes me love you even more, but please, dearest Geneva, don't keep our lives on hold for too long. Now that I have known a life with you in it, life without you is torture.

I can't bear the office. I can't bear the empty desk where you should be sitting. I can't bear that I don't have the luxury of seeing your smile, hearing your voice, whenever I want to; which is all of the time. I am obsessed with you, in love with you. It may be selfish, but I want you here!

I will finally be sitting for my exam at the end of summer. After that, I fully expect to move up from mail clerk to accounting clerk, and eventually, to be made a full partner. But my fondest wish is to be your partner. Then my dreams will have come true. Hold me in your heart, while we are apart, as I will hold you in mine.

Counting the moments until we are together again,
Douglas

June 3, 1963

Douglas called me today. The sound of his voice was like a refreshing breeze on a scorching summer afternoon. It reassured me. It reminded me that I am more than just a farm girl in a backwards town. I have another life in Cleveland—a secretarial certificate, a man who loves me. I must hold onto the truth of that, on the difficult days. Like today.

Mother had a bad day today. Poor Father is at the end of his rope, I can see that. It frightens me, how quickly it's happening, how much farther down this dark road Mother is now than she was even at Christmas time. It seems so unfair. She is only fifty-six. Doctor Parker warned us it would be this way, but still, I am unprepared. I am brokenhearted for us all.

The main thing is to try and keep it from Penny as much as possible. She is an emotional girl in the best of circumstances, and at nine, she is far too young to understand this—gentle, sweet Mother becoming this woman we do not know.

So for now, I will stay in Baxter, where I am so desperately needed, though my heart longs for Cleveland, and for Douglas, the love of my life. We are meant to be together, I am as sure of that as I have ever been sure of anything …

Chapter Eighteen

That morning, on their way to the hardware store, Sarah had asked again about the old trunk. "Have you had time to empty the steamer trunk yet, Monica? I'm dying to get started on restoring it."

It wasn't that she hadn't had time. She'd thought about the trunk nearly every day since discovering it. She'd opened it more than once, and began sorting through the items. Something, some vague feeling that she was trespassing, always made her put them back. But that evening, when Sarah left, Monica removed the household items from the trunk and studied them—the dish towels and the pillowcases, the cloth napkins, the cook books and the patchwork quilt. And hidden away in a side pocket, the silver engagement ring.

Her breath caught as she cautiously opened the blue velvet box. As she held the diamond up to the light, a dozen sparkling prisms danced across her hand as questions filled her mind. Who did these things belong to? Who had worn this lovely ring? There were two leather-bound journals tucked amid the treasures, and she carried the first of them to the porch, knowing somehow, that it held the answers.

Dusk had become a time of quiet reflection for Monica since she'd moved back to the farm. Alone, in the first soft moments of the day, she opened the first of the journals.

A glance at the first page revealed Geneva's neat, tidy script and Monica felt a pang of loneliness for her. She read slowly, digesting the pages one at a time. It was painful and fascinating, discovering the young woman Geneva had been.

Spanning five years, the journal began on Geneva's

nineteenth birthday. Monica read of her great aunt's exhilarating escape from Baxter and the family farm to attend a secretarial school in Cleveland, and then, of her struggle to find employment in her chosen field.

For the first year after she'd graduated, she'd worked two jobs in order to hold onto her small, rented room; two days a week as a clerk at a drug store on Lake Shore Boulevard, and five days sorting and washing sheets and towels in a hotel laundry. The work in the laundry had been tiring and backbreaking, but she refused to give up and go home. Finally, after another year, she'd secured a secretarial job in an accounting office downtown, where she'd met and fallen in love with a mail clerk named Douglas Foster.

Monica read the entire journal, along with the letters tucked inside it. She read of Geneva's mother's swift decline into dementia at age fifty-six the summer Geneva was twenty-tree, and the love letters Douglas had sent her. When it was too dark to read any more, she closed the journal and leaned her head back against the swing. She had never heard Geneva mention the name of Douglas Foster. What had gone wrong for the young couple? They had both been so sure of their love.

She gazed up at the sky and thought about life. Geneva's, as well as her own.

The June days were falling away, like petals pulled from a summer daisy. Soon she would have to make a decision about her job at the middle school. Among other things.

In the two weeks that had followed Barry's proposal, a heaviness had settled between them. They'd rented a dumpster and emptied out the store, and Barry had drawn up cautious plans for remodeling it. He'd sketched a kitchen in the back with pizza ovens and a cooler, a lunch counter in the front, and a sandwich station. He'd gotten estimates for having the work done, and they'd hired a contractor. They'd spoken no more about his proposal, but it was always there between them.

The day before, the second Sunday after his proposal, they had lunch together at the farm.

"The contractors will be starting the work tomorrow, can you believe it?" she asked.

He sighed. "I just wish I wasn't leaving for Cincinnati in the morning. It seems like lousy timing."

"Can't you get out of it?"

He laughed softly. "Well, not really, since I'm going to be facilitating some of the training sessions."

"That's what you get for being such a good manager. But when you get back from your conferences next week, the work on the building should be well underway. It will actually look like a business, rather than an empty building."

"That's when the real work will begin—buying our equipment, painting the walls. It all seems so surreal."

"You still want to go through with it though, right?"

He kissed her hand. "Of course I want to go through with it."

She breathed an inward sigh of relief. Alone at night, she was filled with fear about the venture. It was Barry's confidence that made it seem conceivable, made it seem right.

"Sarah and I are going to start the bedroom this week, while the contractors are working in the store. I'd like your opinion on paint colors."

"Why? You did fine with the living room."

"Because I want you to like what I pick out." She spread the color chips out on the table in front of him. "Do you like any of these?"

His hand caressed her back. "I like you."

"How about the cream?"

"It's very creamy."

"Barry, I'm serious."

"Okay." He picked up the paint colors and studied them and selected a shade called Bleached Denim. "I like this blue. If it were my bedroom, I'd want that."

"Okay, then we'll paint it blue."

He gave her a questioning glance. She ignored it, certain he could hear the thudding of her heart. It was the closest she'd come to saying yes, to admitting they had a future together in the house, in the bedroom.

His kiss goodbye was tender that night, and she knew that his heart had understood every word she couldn't say …

•

He'd called from Cincinnati twice, so far. Yesterday, to let her know he'd arrived. And today, just to say he loved her.

She glanced up at the moon, who sitting in his quiet sky had seen a hundred billion lifetimes come and go. A hundred billion loves.

A memory of Geneva surfaced.

The girls had shown up at her father's row house in Pittsburgh two hours after Monica's abruptly ended phone call. Her father had been livid. He'd accused them of brainwashing his daughter, of turning her against him.

Geneva had faced him calmly. "Look at yourself, Will, ranting and raving like a madman. It's no wonder the child is afraid."

He'd calmed slightly. "She has no reason to be afraid."

"But she is," Geneva said. "She's afraid here. She wants to come home with us, home to the farm."

"Let her speak for herself." He'd turned to Monica, then. "Is that what you want? Speak up!"

Something told her the moment was monumental. She burst into tears, unable to answer.

"Take her then," he said, shoving her toward the girls. "Take her and go. And don't ever come back here."

She'd cried all the way home, but in truth, she felt safer in that car, tucked in between the girls, than ever before in her life. Safe with Geneva and her stern, stubborn love.

But in the end, Geneva had willingly left her.

Both of the girls had.

A gentle breeze danced across her face as an age old fear whispered to her heart that love could not always be trusted.

Chapter Nineteen

A college professor had once told Monica she would be an excellent teacher because she was able to think things through and quickly assess what needed to be done. In her career she supposed that was true. But when it came to Barry, she couldn't think things through. She couldn't seem to think at all. She could not even decide on a new dress for his homecoming tomorrow.

"Ooh, look at this one!" Sarah held up a strappy cotton dress in a bold floral print. Monica had always preferred dresses in muted colors, not wanting to call attention to her body. But she had to admit, Sarah's taste in clothes far exceeded hers. The dress was beyond cute.

"I don't know, Sarah. Don't you think it's kind of loud?"

"I think it's beautiful and I think you'll look beautiful wearing it." She handed Monica the dress. "We're not leaving here until you try something on. In case you haven't noticed, all of your clothes are hanging on you these days. How much weight have you lost, anyway?"

"Sixty-nine pounds."

"Wow. That's amazing. I don't know where you get your self-control. I have precisely zero any more when it comes to food."

Monica could not account for it herself. She was down to two-hundred fifty-three pounds, the least she'd weighed in years. All of her life she'd struggled to lose weight, starving herself, and then binging and gaining back twice what she'd lost. But this time was different. This time she had Barry to encourage her every step of the way. Remembering that the reason for the shopping trip was to find something she could look halfway nice in for his homecoming, she took the dress from Sarah and carried it into the dressing room.

It fit like a dream. She turned first one way and then the other, loving the way the skirt fell softly below her knees, and the way the slender straps crossed at the neckline. For the first time in years, she felt beautiful. Would Barry think so? Thoughts of him washed over her like sunbeams. Lord, how she missed him.

As she carefully removed the dress a small shadow intruded and she felt the icy fingers of fear grip her heart. He had asked her a monumental question. Sooner or later he would want an answer. What was this strange terror inside that kept her from giving him one?

Later that afternoon, she hung her new dress in the closet and walked down to the store. Agnes raced ahead in pursuit of chipmunks. Stepping onto the porch, she slid her key in the lock. Her stomach squeezed and she drew a deep breath. She hadn't been in all week to see what the contractors were doing, for the same reason she'd avoided reading Geneva's second journal. She was afraid that what she might discover would be painful. Steeling herself, she pushed open the door and stepped inside.

The newly sheet rocked back wall had been partitioned off for a kitchen. Stepping through the archway, she gazed at the empty spaces which she supposed were for sinks, ovens, and coolers. Barry had shown her the layout, explained to her just how it would be, but for the life of her, she couldn't picture a functioning kitchen in the empty space. She hoped Barry would be pleased with the work.

She stood in the middle of the store, ambushed by memories; women selecting produce and fresh baked bread, asking Geneva's advice on canning and freezing. Men hoping for a glimpse of Penny's smile. She could almost feel the hum of activity and it fanned the flames of excitement in her heart. It would be nice to have people in here again.

A counter hugged the inside of the front wall; a future sandwich making station. Opposite that she could see the beginnings of a lunch counter. She smiled, picturing busy people preparing and serving food, chatting with the regulars.

The last of her anxiety melted away and she hugged herself. It would all be all right. Barry would see to it. She couldn't wait for him to see it.

Outside, Agnes barked, scattering her thoughts. Peering out the window, she saw that a car had pulled up in front of the store. It was an older model sedan, a Chrysler or an Olds, badly in need of washing.

What was it doing, idling out there like that?

She opened the front door and the car sped away.

"You ran them off, didn't you? Good girl," she said, stroking Agnes' head as the dust settled around them.

•

The next morning, Monica was up early. She'd found a recipe online for butternut squash soup, and she was anxious to get it started and in the crock pot, where it could simmer until Barry arrived. With dinner rolls from the bakery and a fresh garden salad, it would be the perfect summer supper. At least she hoped so.

When she'd made the soup and poured it into the crock pot, she tidied up the house and went upstairs to take a bath. Along with the dress, Sarah had insisted she buy herself some cosmetics. She'd never worn much makeup, but after she'd brushed on the plum eye shadow and a splash of mascara and added a hint of pale pink lipstick, she studied her reflection in the mirror and was pleased with the results. She experimented with her hair, and finally pulled it up in a messy knot, letting a few curling strands fall loose around her face. At four o'clock, just as she'd stepped into her new dress, she heard Agnes barking downstairs. It was the joyful woofing sound the dog reserved for Barry's visits. Smiling, Monica went downstairs to let him in.

The stunned admiration on his face when she opened the door told her all she needed to know. The dress, the makeup and hairstyle—she'd chosen wisely.

"Hello, gorgeous." He folded her into his arms and held her. The bouquet of roses he'd brought tickled the back of her neck, but she was reluctant to move from his embrace.

They'd spoken on the phone numerous times since he'd been away, but still she felt as if they'd been apart for weeks, instead of days.

"How was your conference?"

"Not bad. Except that I missed you every minute of every day."

He pulled away from her and held her at arm's length. "Why do you look so different?"

"I don't know. Is that a bad thing?"

"No, definitely not." He kissed her. "Definitely not."

"I made dinner. Would you like to eat first, or walk down and see the store?"

"Let's go and see what they've done."

They walked to the end of the driveway, holding hands. The summer afternoon was soft with the scent of honeysuckle and the chirping of crickets. She reminded herself to slow down, to savor the feel of Barry's hand in hers, the sheer wonder of being with him again.

Inside, he inspected every inch of the building. "It looks good," he finally said.

"Tell me again where everything's going to be."

He explained again about the kitchen and the sandwich station, the lunch counter and the soda fountains. "I visited a couple of places while I was in Cincinnati, hoping to get some ideas."

"And did you?"

"You bet. Take a look at this." He produced his phone, flipped to the photos he'd taken, and handed it to her.

Her breath caught as she took in the restaurant's whitewashed brick walls, the slate gray trim and the strings of black pendant lights that hung above the counter. A chalk board lunch menu dominated an entire side wall. "I love it."

"I thought we could scatter some pub tables in the dining room, and use black wrought iron stools, like they did. The whole place had a sort of hometown/uptown feel about it.

"I love it," she said again.

He pulled her close. "I love you."

•

Back at the house, she put dinner on the table.

"This is quite a spread," he said.

"I wanted to welcome you back properly." She ladled some of the soup into their bowls. "I even made desert."

He grinned. "Strawberry gelatin?"

"Cheesecake."

"Get out of here."

"It's a low-fat recipe."

"I can't wait." He tasted his soup. "Interesting."

"Do you hate it?"

"Actually, I don't."

"Have a dinner roll. Why are you staring at me?"

"I can't help it. You look amazing, Monica. Is that a new dress?"

"Yes."

"And you're wearing eye makeup."

"Uh huh."

"And you're hair's different."

"Are you done taking inventory?" She tried to sound annoyed, but secretly, his comments pleased her.

"Not even close."

They talked about Cincinnati and his conference, and their plans for the store. It wasn't until after dinner, as they carried their coffee to the porch that the talk turned serious.

"I have something to discuss with you, Monica."

Her stomach squeezed. "All right."

"Management has asked me to help start up a new store in Cincinnati. If I accept the offer, I'll be gone for about six weeks."

Her earlier happiness evaporated. "What did you tell them?"

"I haven't given them an answer yet."

The evening quiet settled around them.

"Leaving you again is the last thing I want to do. But it will be at least a month before we can open the pizzeria. They're offering me twice my salary, a company car to drive, plus a very generous stipend. That money would buy us a brand new pizza oven, and probably the brick wall, too. But if you don't want me to go, I won't."

"Barry, I can't make that decision for you."

"I know, but I want your input. We're partners, aren't we?"

His unanswered proposal lay between them like a chasm.

"When would you have to leave?"

"Next week."

"So soon?" Everything inside her fought against the idea. But realistically, she knew it made sense. There was no way the restaurant would be ready to open within the next month. And though she had tucked away the money from the sale of the acreage all those years ago, she knew how quickly it would evaporate once the business got underway. But mostly, she knew that it was important to Barry that he contribute financially to the business. That he be a partner.

"They want to get the store up and running as soon as possible. The sooner I leave, the sooner I can come back."

"Okay. You're right."

"I can come back for a long weekend here and there. And you could always come out."

"I know. It'll be fine."

"If you're sure, I'll tell them I accept."

When they'd finished their coffee, he asked about the bedroom. "Did you decide on a color?"

"Yes, I did," she said. "Blue."

"An excellent choice."

"Would you like to see it?"

He followed her up the stairs and down the hallway to the master bedroom that had been Geneva's, and before that, Geneva's parents'. She thought the room was stunning—both strong and romantic with its gray-blue walls and white trim, with white eyelet for the curtains and bed cover. She'd brought up the bouquet he'd bought her, and the red roses were stunning on the white table beside the bed. She stepped aside, watching for his reaction.

"Wow, this looks very nice. I wouldn't have thought of the accent wall, but it works."

"Sarah saw it on one of her decorating shows."

He glanced out the oversized window opposite the bed, and then into her eyes. "I could see myself waking up to this. Rolling hills, farmland. You."

Her gaze dropped to the floor. Her heart pounded. The chasm between them grew deeper, wider. He was waiting for a response and she couldn't give him one.

"Come here," he said quietly.

She went to him and he folded her in his arms and kissed her. The first kiss melted into a second, and then a third, and after that everything around her faded into the background, and there was only Barry's hands and lips and whispered words and a sweeping desire like nothing she'd felt before.

He led her to the bed and they sat together, kissing, caressing, and the desire became a tidal wave, carrying her away. But not completely.

"No," she whispered, pulling away from him.

"Monica, why?"

"I'm not ready for you to see me yet."

"I love you. I love every bit of you."

"Can you wait until I can love myself? Or at least like myself?"

He lovingly traced a finger across her cheek. "What am I going to do with you?"

She took his hand, moved it to her lips, and kissed his fingers. "Wait for me," she said quietly.

•

That night, when Barry had gone home, she opened Geneva's second journal. A newspaper clipping, yellowed with age, fluttered to the floor.

Chapter Twenty

Death Notices

January 7, 1964

$\mathcal{L}$oretta "Babe" Humphrey nee Galliger, beloved wife of Thomas Humphrey; loving mother of Geneva Humphrey and Beatrice Humphrey; cherished sister, sister-in-law, aunt, and cousin; passed away unexpectedly on January 5. Born in 1906 in Baxter, "Babe" was a 1924 Graduate of Boswell Center High School in Boswell Center and a lifelong resident of Baxter. She devoted her life to helping run the family farm, and raising her children. She was a church organist and longtime member of Baxter First Presbyterian Church. "Babe" loved music and gardening. Funeral Services will be held Wednesday, January 9, 10:00 at Baxter First Presbyterian, 7100 Brown Church Road, Baxter, OH.

January 7, 1964

Thomas Humphrey, devoted husband of Loretta, nee Galliger; loving father of Geneva Humphrey and Beatrice Humphrey; beloved brother, uncle and friend, passed away unexpectedly on January 5. Thomas was a 1924 Graduate of Boswell Center High School in Boswell Center and a lifelong resident of Baxter. Farming, Fishing, and Family were his life. Funeral Services will be held Wednesday, January 9, 10:00 at Baxter First Presbyterian Church, 7100 Brown Church Road,

Baxter, OH.

January 5, 1964

My Darling Geneva,
The only regret I have in all of this is the pain I know it will cause you and Penny, my cherished daughters, so I will try and explain it to you the best I can and hope that somehow you will be able to understand.

I made your mother a promise three years ago, when this whole, nightmarish mess started, when she began to lose her memory. Were it not for that promise, I would gladly have carried on the best I could with her care. You know I would have, don't you? It was not cowardice on my part, but very great love. When she received the diagnosis, your mother made me swear that when the time came that the illness stole her dignity, I would gently lead her from this life. And I have done that. Geneva, you yourself could see what her quality of life had become. No soul should have to live the way she has for the past few months, and especially not so dear a one as Babe.

Just to be clear, she did not and would not have asked me to go with her. That was a promise and a choice I made for myself.

When the dust has settled from all of this, I know you will be concerned about money. There's no need. You can sell off some of the acreage from the farm and live quite comfortably. The house is paid for, so there's no need to worry about keeping a roof over your head.

I have long struggled with how to tell you this, darling, and words and courage failed me. There is a sizeable trust fund in place for you and Beatrice. I have left all of the paperwork on my desk for you. Take it to our accountant, Maurice Taylor, when you feel able and he will tell you how to proceed. It was set up by the Brighton's when Beatrice was born. I know this news will shock you, and quite probably make you angry, but please accept their money Geneva. Your mother and I felt they needed to pay for what their son did to you, what he did to all of us. I know you will think it over and do the right thing. I pray that you can find it in your heart to forgive us, for we love both of you girls unutterably.

Always,

Daddy

Chapter Twenty-One

$\mathcal{T}$ears blurred the page in front of Monica's eyes and she refolded the letter and tucked it back inside the journal. Every member of the family had resorted to suicide.

Every. Single. One of them.

She remembered she'd asked Penny about Babe and Thomas once, when they'd gone to decorate their graves. Penny had told her that she and Geneva's parents had died together, in their sleep. Merely a child, Monica had presumed that Babe and Thomas were old. She'd never dreamed they'd had a suicide pact. Was it any wonder Geneva and Penny had both taken their lives?

So many things seemed clearer now, but so many others had become cloudy.

The trust fund, started the day Penny was born. What could it mean?

Nothing good, and nothing Monica wanted to believe.

Presumably the answers were on the pages she held in her hands, but she couldn't take in any more right now. Didn't want to take in any more. She wanted to call Barry. To tell him about this sad and horrible thing she'd discovered.

Retrieving her cell phone from her pocket, she put in the call. Within seconds, his calm, comforting voice washed over her.

"Hey, pretty lady. What's up?"

"I miss you."

"You just saw me an hour ago."

"I know."

"You okay?"

"I don't know. I … Yeah, I guess so."

"What is it, sweetheart?"

She didn't know where to begin. She didn't really even want to share the discovery any more, she realized, she just wanted to hear his voice and feel reassured.

"It's going to be all right, isn't it? The pizzeria. Us?"

"It's going to be great."

"I found a letter. Thomas and Babe, the girls' parents, they committed suicide. She was sick, Babe was. He did it out of love. He didn't want her to have to go into eternity all alone."

"Wow. That's pretty sad."

"Yeah."

"Do you want me to come back over?"

"No. I just wanted to tell you."

"I'm glad you did."

"Me, too."

"Are you sure you don't want me to come back over?"

"I'm sure."

"Okay. I love you."

"I love you, too. Good night."

•

Fortified, she once again opened the journal.

January 14, 1964

I would not have thought it possible that my life could get any darker. I am not trying to be brave or strong any more. I am just trying to hold on.

Mother and Daddy's funeral was quite lovely, really. Surprisingly, that is not the bad part of all of this. The whole town turned out, and I got the sense it wasn't purely out of curiosity. Both of them were so well liked, that was evident in the memories that were shared.

Douglas came down from Cleveland. Now I wish he had not.

I was so happy to see him, I felt so strengthened by his presence at my side. After the funeral meal, in the late afternoon, we came back to the farm and I made Penny go upstairs for a nap. She looked so tired, so distraught. Douglas and I sat at the kitchen table and talked about the suicide. That much, he knew.

He asked about my plans, and I could not give him an answer. It is far too soon, and there is too much to be decided. And then the unthinkable happened. He knelt beside me and slid an engagement ring on my finger. A beautiful silver band with a sparkling diamond that caught the sun in a shower of glittering prisms. A glorious declaration of his love. Oh, how I wish he had left it at that. I wish he had let me enjoy and savor that moment, instead of pushing me.

"I don't want to seem insensitive," he said. "But there's no reason we can't be together now."

I hadn't told him everything … hadn't found the words or the courage. I didn't know whether he would feel the same, once he knew the truth.

"Douglas …"

"We can be married in my parent's church as soon as next month," he said, as if everything were all settled. "What shall we do with your sister? Have you got any family that can take her in?"

"Really, Douglas. You can't expect me to—"

The door creaked opened just then, and I have never seen a man's face grow so pale. I glanced behind me, and there stood Penny with mother's butcher knife gripped in both hands. She lunged toward Douglas, her beautiful face twisted in rage.

"Get out! Get out!" she shrieked again and again.

Poor Douglas scrambled away on his hands and knees, knocking over a chair in his hurry to get away. It took all I had to hold Penny back. She is a slender child, but her strength was fueled by hysteria. And isn't it perfect that Lottie Hastings chose that very moment to show up at the farm with a casserole? She was decent about it, I must say. She helped me to calm Penny down, and agreed that anyone could see the child was terrified. She'd lost so much already, and felt in danger of losing her home. And me.

Even so, I'm sure the news of what she witnessed has spread clear across the county by now.

Douglas nearly smashed into her car in his rush to get out of the driveway.

I have not heard from him in four days.

January 15, 1964

Geneva,

It has taken me quite some time to recover from the shocking events of last week, and to think through how to proceed with our relationship. I still love you and I still want to marry you. We can still move ahead with our plans. There is nothing standing in our way now except your sister.

I must admit, her violent behavior was astounding. I no longer think you should place her with a family member, as I first suggested. I think you should look toward having her institutionalized, for the safety of everyone involved. You should know that I considered driving straight to the police station when I left, and reporting Penny's attempt to do me physical harm. I didn't do that out of respect and concern for you, dearest. I did not want to make things more difficult for you than they already are.

I realize the child is your sister, and that your family history together and your affection for her clouds your judgment, but you must think it through, Geneva. You and I can have no future together with such a violent, unpredictable child in it. It would be dangerous for you, and for me, and especially for our future children.

Please think carefully about all I have said. I await your decision and pray it will be a wise one.

Always,
Douglas

January 18, 1964

Douglas has made up his mind, that could not be more clear. He wants a life with me only if it is according to his plan. But everything has changed. I cannot return to Cleveland right now. I cannot, in good conscience, take Penny away from this farm. She needs the familiarity and the stability of it. In any case, Douglas wants no part of a life with Penny in it. He fears she will be a danger to our future children. How could I tell him she is the child of my past? Either way, our romance is finished. He is not the man I thought he was. I have written and told him as much, told him to come and collect his diamond ring.

Penny and I will stay in Baxter, consequences be damned. As for the town, let them talk. I am beyond caring. No one believes for a moment the lie my family has lived for the past ten years. Oh, they believe I went to Pittsburgh to stay with Aunt Bess and Uncle Arthur. Yes, that much they believe. But no one believes the reason I went was to help Aunt Bess with the cooking and cleaning in her last months of pregnancy, or the beautifully crafted lie that the child who returned to Baxter with me, the redheaded child mother and dad adopted, is the daughter of daddy's beloved sister-in-law, who died in childbirth.

Any fool could see the child is Wayne Brighton's daughter.

The Brighton's power and influence will make the town pretend to believe it. For a while. I hope to God for long enough that I can find the courage to tell Penny the truth, a softened version of it, before someone else does.

I am not afraid for her to know that I am her mother. But what shall I say when she asks about her father? Will I be truthful? Tell her he is a heartless, despicable human being who forced himself on a thirteen-year-old girl, and then left her bloodied and broken in the weeds along the road and drove off without a backward glance? No. I cannot tell her the truth. But then … what can I tell her?

Even a month ago, I would have returned the Brighton's money. I would have felt twice violated. It would have felt like prostitution. But as I said, everything has changed. I will accept the trust fund and use it to buy Penny and myself a future. The future Wayne Brighton stole from me, his parents will now purchase in full. I will make an appointment with the accountant in the morning. So much to think about, when all I want is to crawl into bed and sleep. Forever. But I have my daughter to think of now …

Monica laid the journal in her lap, feeling numb.

Everything she knew, or thought she knew about the girls had changed and she realized she hadn't really known the two women at all. She wept for them both, and for the sacrifices Geneva had been forced to make. No, the sacrifices she'd chosen to make for love.

And she wept for her courage, a new admiration for Geneva swelling in her heart.

A fleeting memory from years ago surfaced. Padding down the hallway one evening, she'd noticed a light on in Penny's room. She'd glanced in. Penny sat at her vanity while Geneva brushed her hair. Neither of them spoke. Monica remembered being struck by how loving the act seemed. When she'd finished, Geneva set the hairbrush on the vanity and placed her hands on Penny's shoulders. Reflected in the mirror, Monica saw a smile that radiated pure love pass between the two sisters. Mother and daughter, she now knew.

She reread a section of the entry to be sure she had it straight. Her grandparents, Bess and Arthur Humphrey, had taken young, pregnant Geneva in. Was that why, years later, the girls had taken Monica in? Bess and Arthur's son, William's, child? Out of a sense of debt or obligation?

But no. The girls had wanted her. If she knew nothing else on that overcast June evening, she knew that Geneva and Penny had loved her. And love was about sacrifice. And it required courage. And even when it was hard, love was worth it.

In that moment, she could see it all so clearly, her past and future aligned. Her future here, on the family land, with Barry. And she knew that they would make it, because she possessed that same kind of reckless love. That reckless, courageous, sacrificial Humphrey love.

Chapter Twenty-Two

*O*n Friday afternoon, a week after Barry left for Cincinnati, Monica decided to have her hair highlighted. She was having a late lunch after her monthly therapy appointment with Mimi the hand specialist when a sign in front of a salon across the street caught her eye. Life is too short to have boring hair! Grand Opening Special: *Highlights and lowlights — $45. Walk- Ins Welcome!*

She swept her hand back through her tresses. There was no doubt her honey colored curls were her best feature, but lately she'd been feeling like the shoulder length cut she'd worn since high school was outdated. The sign was right. Her hair was boring.

Stepping into the salon, she was greeted by a girl in a tight white dress and a pair of boots that crept to her thighs. The girl looked young enough to be one of her students, and all at once Monica felt a hundred years old.

"What can we do for you today, hon?"

"I noticed your sign out front. I'm thinking about getting some highlights."

"Great! Let's get started!" The girl swept her into a chair. A few moments later a second stylist, who looked only slightly older than the first one, appeared.

"Hi, I'm Tiffany. So we're going to do some highlights today, right? You're gonna love it!" She immediately plunged her hands into Monica's hair. "Yeah, this definitely needs some kick. What were you thinking?"

"I have no idea." Monica's glance swept over Tiffany's long, pink-and-white striped hair. Good Lord, she looked like a candy cane. Maybe this was a mistake.

"Nothing too drastic."

"How about something that will compliment this gorgeous color, but give it a little bit of an edge?" She reached into a drawer at her station and produced a color chart. She pointed to a photo of a model with subtle highlights that looked like a mixture of butter and honey.

"I like this one for you."

Monica had to admit, Tiffany had a good eye. If she could look even half as good in those colors as the model, it would be well worth the money.

"I like it, too."

"It will look super with your fair complexion and blue eyes. Sort of a sun-kissed look. Why don't we shorten it up a bit, too?"

Throwing caution to the winds, Monica sat back and allowed Tiffany to work her magic. It was unlike her to be impulsive, to make a move she hadn't thought through to the last detail. But that was going to change. It was time to stop playing it safe. She was going to visit Barry in Cincinnati in two weeks and she wanted to look fabulous when she gave him the news.

She was going to accept his proposal.

The smile that was in her heart spread across her face. Now that she'd made up her mind, the wonderful life she and Barry were going to share was all she could think about. She'd asked Sarah to help her plan the perfect wedding, and as usual, Sarah had dug into the project with both hands. If all of Sarah's plans came together, it was going to be beautiful. Never mind that she only had a few guests on her list. This day would be for her. Her and Barry.

On the night before he left, she'd poured out her heart to him; told him about the journals and the letters, the diamond ring and the secrets. She'd stopped short of accepting his marriage proposal. But it wasn't out of fear this time. She wanted the circumstances to be right.

They'd planned for her to visit for a long weekend after he'd been there three weeks, to give him time to settle in and learn the 'lay of the land' he said. He wanted to show her the city, and take her to the pizzeria he'd photographed. She would lose a few more pounds, she decided, and have something done with her hair. And then, after the romantic dinner he was sure to plan, she would accept his proposal. She'd buy a camisole of some sort, or a pretty nightgown. And she'd let the evening go where it would.

The thought of it set her tummy to fluttering.

An hour and a half later she left the salon with a short, messy, sun-kissed bob. She felt chic and stylish, and couldn't help smiling as she caught her reflection in a store window. She and Sarah had been using the exercise equipment in Sarah's basement gym every day for the past two weeks, and she was feeling more toned and healthy. She'd lost another three pounds this week. Seventy-two gone, one hundred more to go. It was a long-range goal, and maybe an unattainable one, but if she worked hard, maybe she could shed another five pounds before her trip.

In another rare, impulsive moment, she turned down Euclid Avenue. As she crawled past her old rental house, she saw that the lilies Barry planted were flourishing. Flourishing here as she never had. So many tears she'd shed here, so many endless lonely days and nights she'd endured. She felt like a different person now. Had it only been three months since the accident? It seemed a lifetime ago.

The new, braver Monica returned home an hour later and drafted a letter of resignation to the middle school, then addressed it to Layla's attention. Tomorrow she would buy a stamp and put it in the mail. Feeling like a hundred-pound barbell had been lifted from her shoulders, she changed into her comfy sweat pants and walked down the driveway to the store. Letting herself in, she saw that the contractors were nearly finished. The back room had been fitted with shelving and shiny steel sinks and countertops. She could plainly see now where the ovens and coolers would go.

Out front, the sandwich station, also gleaming stainless steel, was fitted with compartments for meats, cheeses and condiments. The lunch counter was a long island with black wainscoting on the bottom, its butcher block top a dark, rustic walnut. It was coming together beautifully. When the first round of renovations was complete, she'd get estimates on brick facing for the walls. Then they'd paint the trim and buy their equipment, apply for a business license, a food service license, a certificate of occupancy. So much to think about, and she was looking forward to every bit of it. Her eyes swept lovingly across the building and she hugged herself. Her restaurant. Hers and Barry's.

By the time she arrived home, dusk had fallen. The day's heat was trapped inside the old house, so she poured an iced tea and carried Geneva's journal outside to the porch. Turning on the porch light, she settled into the swing.

So far she'd read through four months' worth of entries, from the funeral, through the girls' first long winter without Thomas and Babe, and into the spring.

April 10, 1964

I've taken a part-time secretarial position at Penny's school. It's not so much for the money, as that I want to be where I can keep an eye on her. I know it's only been a few months since the funerals, but I would think the sadness would have eased for her by now, at least a little. Most children are resilient, but not my Penny. She cries every day, and most days it's all I can do to get her out of bed in the morning. It's as if she's enveloped in a thick, heavy blanket and doesn't want to throw it off. I phoned Doctor Stevens and made an appointment for her to talk with him. He is new in town and specializes in mental issues. Most people in town think his practice is quackery, but I'm willing to take a chance on anything that might help Penny. I honestly don't know where else to turn.

A well-meaning teacher of hers thinks the girl simply has the blues. I might be tempted, as she advised me, to just give it time and let her work it out in her own way. But there have always been whispers around town that there are mental disturbances in the Brighton's family history. I remember once hearing about a relative of theirs who was given shock treatments. I pray to God that nothing awful has been passed down to my child …

April 22, 1964

Doctor Stevens has concluded that Penny suffers from melancholia. He has prescribed a new drug, which he explained is a tricyclic antidepressant drug. In any case, it seems to be working. He also suggested we engage in some sort of positive hobby together, so we joined the church choir. Penny didn't want to go at first, and I admit, I strong-armed her. She needs to have something positive to do with her time. And regularly attending church services won't hurt either one of us a bit.

April 30, 1964

Mother's garden is the first thing Penny has shown interest in for months. When the catalogues came in the mail, I set them in a box for trash, as I always do. How surprising to—

•

Agnes heard the car before Monica saw its headlights sweep the driveway. She produced a threatening growl low in her throat, making Monica glance up from the journal. Seconds later, a dirt-encrusted sedan rolled slowly toward the house. Fear fluttered in Monica's heart. As it drew closer, she could see it was the same car she'd seen before, outside the store. When the car came to a stop, Agnes leapt from the porch and raced toward it, barking ferociously.

The driver's side window came down, and a male voice rasped, "Can you please call off your dog?"

In the commotion, Monica could barely hear him. "Agnes, sit!"

The dog obeyed reluctantly, the low growl once again rumbling in her throat.

"Is it safe to get out?" the man asked.

"What do you want?"

"I just want to talk to you, if that's all right."

"Who are you?"

"Monica, girl, have some sense! Don't you even recognize

your own father?"

Chapter Twenty-Three

In the kitchen, Will Humphrey settled himself at the table, while Agnes kept a wary eye on him from across the room. It was strange and awkward, Monica thought. She'd pictured a dozen scenarios in which she saw her father again, but none of them played out like this.

"Can I get you a glass of iced tea?" she asked.

"Please."

She poured the tea, added ice cubes and lemon, and set it before him. His hands shook slightly as he picked it up. She had not seen her father in eighteen years, and those years had not been kind to him. His graying hair was unclean, his cheeks, sunken. He'd developed a lazy eye, which gave his face a slightly lopsided look. At sixty, he looked fully ten years older than he was.

"If you don't look like your mother," he commented, his pale eyes sweeping across her face.

Her blonde-haired, blue-eyed mother, perpetually twenty-eight years old in Monica's memory, was younger when she died than Monica was now. It was a strangely sobering thought, and one that Monica did not care to entertain.

"What did you want to talk to me about, Dad?"

"I came to bring you some news," he said, setting his glass on the table. "Your sister, Juliet. She died of a drug overdose. Been six weeks ago, now."

The news left her stunned. She tried to reconcile this information with the image of the little blonde girl she'd last seen playing with her dolls in the living room of the row house in Pittsburgh.

"I'm sorry to hear that."

"Me on the road so much, she got in with bad sort of crowd back when she was a teenager. Started drinking and taking pills. She was clean for almost three years. Then her worthless boyfriend dragged her back into it. He's dead, too."

She regarded him thoughtfully, no idea how to respond.

"I was always afraid it would come to this, with her."

"I'm sorry. I truly am."

He nodded and reclaimed his glass, took another swallow of tea, said nothing.

"You came by here once before," she prompted. "I saw your car. Down by the store."

He nodded.

"Why didn't you come in?"

His gaze met hers, fell away. "I was afraid."

"Afraid? Of me?"

"Of what you might say. To what I want to ask you."

She braced herself. What could he possibly want of her after all these years? Money?

He sighed. "Juliet had a child. Social Services brought her to me, gave me temporary custody, after …"

So it was about money. For the child.

"I can help you out, Dad."

His expression turned hopeful. "I'm really hoping so. I know it's a lot to ask."

"How much do you need?"

"Need?" His hopeful expression morphed to one of anger. "I don't want your money, girl. I want you to raise the child!"

At his change in tone, Agnes growled. The astonishing request rendered Monica momentarily speechless. "Raise the child? No, I'm sorry. I can't do that."

He stared at her. "Can't? Or won't?"

"I don't know anything about raising a child."

"Sure you do. You're a school teacher, ain't ya?"

She wondered fleetingly how he knew that. "I teach Middle School English. Twelve and thirteen-year-olds. I don't know anything about caring for a baby."

"She's not so much of a baby. Juliet had her at sixteen. Just one of many brilliant choices that girl made. Elsa is five years old. About the age you were when the girls took you from me."

Her anger flared. *You mean when you gave me away!*

"I thought it might be a second chance, raising my granddaughter. But I was kidding myself. I can't take care of her. Any more than I could take care of you."

The question she'd ached to ask for more than twenty-five years tumbled out before she could stop it. "Why couldn't you take care of me?"

His eyes dropped to his hands and his tone softened. "I'm a drunk, Monica. I was a drunk then, and I'm a drunk now. I guess you were too young to realize that."

She sank into her chair, desperate to clear her head, to think it through. "What about Juliet's mother? Can't she take her?"

His bitter laughter caused Agnes to growl again. "I'd sooner leave the child under a bridge. Listen, Elsa won't be much trouble. She's barely even spoke two words since … since the night they brought her to me. Would you be willing to at least meet her?"

"I don't think that would be—"

She broke off when the front door opened and a little girl walked in.

"Grandad?" she asked, in a tiny voice.

"I thought I told you to wait in the car, girlie."

"It's dark."

Monica stared at the child, dumbstruck. Underneath the dirty, teat-streaked face, Elsa was the picture of herself at age five. Whimpering softly, Agnes inched closer.

The girl's steady gaze went from Monica to Agnes and back again.

"Hello, Elsa. I'm your Aunt Monica. Would you like a cookie?" Not answering, the child swiped at her tears with her sleeve. Unable to resist, Agnes rose from her blanket, went to the girl, and gently nuzzled her.

"This is Agnes," Monica told her. "Don't be afraid. She won't hurt you."

But already Elsa's arms were encircling the oversized dog, her tear-stained face pressed into her fur. Conflicting emotions swirled in Monica's heart. She ached to provide the child with a warm bath and a soft bed for the night, to give herself time to think this through. But if she offered that, her father was likely to leave and not come back. And then what? She turned back to him. "This is a lot to think about."

"I know."

"Where are you even living now?"

"Still in Pittsburgh, technically. But Social Services says I have to have some repairs made on my house. It's not fit for a child. We've been staying in a motel near here for a couple of weeks. I thought if you could just meet her …"

If I could just meet her – what? I'd take her off your hands? She sighed, deeply troubled. "Give me your phone number. I'll call you in a few days."

•

History was repeating itself. It was incredible. Incredibly terrifying.

Monica sat at the table long after her father's taillights had disappeared down the driveway. Agnes could not stop looking out the window, crying, pining for the little girl. Ginger sat in Monica's lap, and she absently stroked the cat's fur.

History …

She remembered so clearly the night the girls had brought her here. A motherless child of six, she'd felt overwhelmingly sad, but unconditionally loved. Safe. The magic of the farm had healed all of her broken places. And now her sister's child was in that same broken place, and Monica had turned her away.

Tears slid from her eyes and down her face. Just this morning, she'd been excitedly planning her new life. Now her life was so topsy-turvy she couldn't think straight.

But it didn't have to be. She didn't have to take the child in. She could hardly be expected to change her whole life for the child of a sister she never even knew. She could let her father go his way. She could proceed with all her lovely plans.

Elsa's little face, her little tear-stained face, rose up in her memory to haunt her.

"God," she whispered. "I need your help. What should I do?"

She went to the sink, dumped out her tea, poured a glass of water and returned to the table. Her father was right about one thing, he was not fit to raise a little girl. And it wasn't about whatever repairs his house needed, though she could well imagine. She could plainly see she was his last hope. He was probably in some seedy motel room hitting the bottle right now. And Elsa was probably crying herself to sleep in a dirty bed, feeling unloved and unwanted. If she didn't step up, it was only a matter of time before Social Services stepped back in. Elsa would end up in foster care.

No. She couldn't, wouldn't, let that happen. Whatever else the child was or was not, she was a Humphrey.

The silence around her was deafening, as if the house held its breath, waiting for her decision. She massaged her aching head, trying to think it through.

"I don't know what to do," she whispered again. Agnes turned from the window, whined, gazed out at the driveway.

Oh, but you do know what to do.

The child was clearly traumatized. The farm's sweet magic might not even be enough this time. Elsa probably needed a therapist.

Okay, not a big deal. The Yellow Pages are filled with listings. It would be a simple matter of choosing one.

She'd have to enroll her in school. Not in backwards Boswell Center, where she herself had endured so much pain and bullying.

But where? Risingville?

She glanced at her resignation letter, which she'd penned with such confidence just hours before. She'd have to show that she had stable employment, health insurance. If she took the child in, she'd have to continue on at the school, a least for a while.

And what about the restaurant? And most importantly … what about Barry?

Surely Barry would understand this. Wouldn't he?

Panic rose in her breast and she pushed it down. She saw again Elsa's face, buried in Agnes' neck, the only means the child had of concealing her sorrow and fear, and then she felt the restaurant slipping through her hands.

There was no question of what the right thing was. Elsa was clearly scared to death of her grandfather. Her niece needed her, just as she'd needed the girls all those years ago. She'd once had grand dreams of traveling to Costa Rica, of being used by God to make a difference in the lives of children. And now the voice of truth whispered across her heart, as clearly as if the words were spoken aloud. This child was to be her mission field. This child was her Costa Rica.

She picked up the resignation letter, wadded it into a tight ball, and dropped it in the wastebasket.

Glancing at the clock, she saw that it was 10:15. Late, but the urgency she felt told her it could not wait until morning. With trembling hands, she picked up the scrap of paper beside her phone and punched in the number she'd scribbled.

Her call was answered immediately.

"Hello?"

"Dad?"

"Monica?"

"Dad, I've changed my mind. Please—" her voice cracked. "Please bring Elsa back."

Chapter Twenty-Four

*M*onica awoke at seven a.m. after all of two hours of sleep.
It was late when she tucked Elsa into bed in her old room, and then she and her father had talked late into the night. They considered all of their options, and what was best for the child. Now, with her head feeling as if it were full of cotton, she poured a cup of coffee and flipped through one of Geneva's old recipe books. At last she found the page she was looking for: *Penny's Fabulous Chocolate Chip Pancakes.*

She'd made cookies for Sarah's boys last week and was sure she still had half a bag of chocolate chips. The girls had always made the pancakes for Monica on special occasions. It had come to her, around three a.m. that it would be a nice tradition to start with Elsa.

After a second cup of coffee she assembled all of the ingredients and warmed up the griddle. She'd hoped to spend the morning showing Elsa around the farm; pointing out the apple trees, perfect for climbing, and the pond where she and Penny had spent hours fishing, so many years ago, but the sky outside her window threatened rain. She'd have to think of something else to entice the child to stay. She'd just flipped the last pancake into the warming bowl when her father appeared in the kitchen, looking as worn out as she felt.

"How did you sleep?" she asked.

"I didn't. Much. Got any more of that coffee?"

"Help yourself." She gestured toward the coffeemaker.

He prepared a cup, sloshed in some milk, and sat down at the table. She set a plate of pancakes in front of him. Picking up a fork, he dug in.

"I think you should call Social Services first thing this morning and tell them what's going on," he said around a mouthful of food.

"I agree. But I still think we should talk to Elsa first, let her feel like she has a choice in this."

"She doesn't, though."

"That's how I'd like to handle this." She stopped before saying she knew all too well what it was like to feel small and powerless over her own destiny.

"What if she says she don't want to stay?"

"Then we'll cross that bridge if we come to it."

He pulled a business card from his pants pocket and set it by the sugar bowl. "Here's the number for the social worker."

"I don't know if we'll get ahold of anyone on a Saturday. It might have to wait until Monday."

"That ain't what the woman said." And edge crept into his voice. "She said I could call her any time, day or night."

Lured by the smell of breakfast, Elsa wandered into the kitchen with Agnes close on her heels. Monica smiled at her.

"Good morning, Elsa."

Elsa said nothing, her gaze drifting from Monica to the stack of pancakes.

"Have a seat, hon. Are you hungry?"

Eyes still on the pancakes, she nodded. Monica forked two onto a plate and cut them into bite-sized pieces. Her father shoved the syrup and butter across the table.

"Eat up, girlie."

The child ate slowly, almost cautiously, Agnes planted at her side.

Monica pulled in a silent breath. "Elsa, your grandpa and I would like to talk with you about something."

Elsa's pale blue eyes, so much like Monica's, filled with concern. Shooing Agnes away, Monica squatted beside her and brushed her tangled hair from her eyes. Had her father washed the child's hair, even once?

"We've been talking about it, and we thought it might be nice for you to stay here for a while, with me and Agnes. Grandad and I thought you might like to try living in the country. You'd have a nice big yard to play in, and your own room. Of course Grandad can come and visit you whenever he wants to. What do you think? Would you like to give it a try?"

Elsa's eyes crashed to her lap. Once again Monica got the strange sensation the house was holding its breath. She tucked Elsa's hair behind her ears.

"You can think about it for a little while, if you want to."

Elsa said nothing.

"Looks like we might get some rain this morning," Monica said, too brightly.

Elsa's gaze went to Agnes, then dropped again to her lap. When she finally spoke, it was barely a whisper.

"I will."

Monica glanced at her father, and then at the child. "Will what, honey?"

"Stay here with Agnes."

Monica, her father, and the house let out a collective breath.

"Wonderful! After breakfast we'll go upstairs and get you a bath, and then if it doesn't rain, Agnes and I will show you around the farm."

•

With the breakfast dishes washed, Monica ran the tub for Elsa's bath. She found an ancient bottle of bath bubbles, leftover from one tenant or another, in the back of the linen closet. She added two capfuls to the water. While the tub filled, she went in search of her father. She found him on the porch, smoking a cigarette.

"Did you think to bring Elsa's clothes?"

"I've got her things in the car. I'll bring them in shortly."

"Okay, good. I'm going to put her in the tub now. Just leave them outside the bathroom door."

"Monica."

She turned back, eyebrows raised.

"I called the social worker just now. They're sending someone out."

Her stomach tightened. "All right."

"This is a good thing you're doing," he mumbled, "for your sister's child, and for me. I appreciate it."

"She's family," she said simply.

After helping Elsa into the old, claw-footed tub, she washed the girl's tangled hair and added conditioner.

"Do you have a favorite song, Elsa? I always like to sing when I'm in the bath tub."

"No."

"I know one I bet you'll like." She began to sing the *Head and Shoulders* song. To her amazement, the second time through, Elsa softly sang along.

"Eyes and ears and mouth and nose, head and shoulders knees and toes."

Hearing the rumble of exhaust, she parted the blinds and saw her father's car barreling out of the driveway.

"What? Are you kidding me?"

Elsa stopped singing, alarmed.

"It's okay, baby." She smiled. "You wash those knees and toes for me, all right? I'll be right back."

Downstairs, she saw that her father had parked two cardboard boxes in the living room. Opening the flaps, she discovered that they contained Elsa's clothing.

"Vanished without a trace," she murmured. "How typical."

She'd half expected him to do something like this, but even so, she was shaken. She'd counted on her father being there when the social worker arrived.

So now what?

Not knowing where to turn, she grabbed her cell phone and called Sarah.

"Hello-oo?"

"Hey. Can you come over?"

"Sure. Is everything okay?"

"I don't know. I mean yeah, everything's fine."

"Okay, let me finish loading the dishwasher and I'll be right up."

"Thanks. And can you bring some toys? Like, coloring books and puzzles and things?"

"Toys? Monica, you're killing me, here."

"I'm killing myself, too."

"What's this about?"

"You'll see."

When she'd brushed the tangles from Elsa's hair and dressed her in a relatively clean pair of shorts and a tee shirt, she parked her in the living room with Agnes and turned on cartoons. She was waiting on the porch when Sarah arrived.

"Okay, I've got coloring books, Hot Wheels, and all the Legos you can handle," she said, juggling a box of toys. "Now talk to me."

Monica pulled in a breath. "My father showed up here yesterday with my half-sister's daughter. Juliet died of a drug overdose six weeks ago. They gave my dad temporary guardianship, but he can't take care of the child. So right now I've got a five-year-old little girl in the living room and a social worker on the way, and I have no idea what to do."

"Wow."

"Yeah."

"All right, first things first. Do you want to raise her?"

"Yes, I do."

"How does Barry feel?"

Her stomach squeezed. "I haven't told him yet. It all came about so quickly."

"You told me but you haven't told Barry?" The look of astonishment on Sarah's face rankled her. Her throat went tight and tears threatened.

"This is hard for me, okay?"

"I know it is. I'm sorry." She gave Monica a hug. "So where is she?"

"She's inside with Agnes. Do you want to meet her?"

"Of course I want to meet her."

Inside, she called Elsa into the kitchen.

"This is my friend, Sarah. Look, she brought you some toys."

Elsa looked hopefully at the box of toys but made no move to take them. Sarah squatted beside the girl.

"Hello, Elsa."

"Hi," she whispered.

"These are things my boys don't play with any more, but I hope you'll find some things you like. Shall we take a look?" Without waiting for an answer, Sarah opened the box and spread the contents out on the floor. Elsa considered each item before cautiously reaching for a box of Legos.

"I like these," she said softly.

"I'm glad. Just don't let Agnes get ahold of them, okay Tootsie, or they'll end up puppy chow."

Elsa smiled. "She's not a puppy."

"No, she's not. She's a big girl, just like you." Sarah hugged her and smoothed back her hair. "Look at those pretty blonde curls. I always wanted a little girl, but I don't know how to make them. I have three boys."

"What are their names?"

"Justin is the oldest, then there's Jace, and Jaxon is my baby. He's ten years old."

"That's not a baby."

"I know, but to me he'll always be my baby. Even when he's a hundred years old."

Monica watched the exchange with a sinking heart. Sarah had gotten more words out of the child in five minutes than she had all morning. She knew nothing about how to relate to a little girl. Nothing. Tears threatened again.

It was all too much—her father's sudden appearance turning her life upside down, this child, this beautiful child that she had no idea how to raise. She wanted so badly to give Elsa the same gift the girls had given her, but who was she kidding? Maybe she should let Sarah apply for guardianship instead.

Tears she could not hold back flooded her eyes. She turned to the window and furiously blinked them back. Sarah and Elsa sorted through the pile of toys, oblivious.

"I'm going to have my own room," Elsa said.

"You are? Can I see it?"

Monica dabbed at her eyes with a napkin. Pulling in a breath, she turned from the window and smiled. "Yes, let's take Sarah upstairs and show her your room."

She and Sarah had spent many hours in the room, as young girls, listening to music and looking through pop star and fashion magazines. It had always seemed to Monica a sanctuary. But now, seeing it through Sarah's eyes, the yellow-flowered wallpaper looked dingy, the throw rugs and bed spread she'd brought down from the attic looked worn and frayed. Monica saw her friend's eyes take in all of these things. The room was no more adequate than she was.

"What a sweet little room!" Sarah exclaimed.

"This was Aunt Monica's room when she was my age," Elsa told her solemnly.

"Yes, I know it was. It's the perfect room for a little girl. But I feel like we should paint it, unless you like it just the way it is?"

The child looked at her feet and shrugged.

"When I was a little girl I had to share a room with my older sister. Her favorite color was blue, but I always wanted a pink bedroom. I bet you do, too."

Elsa nodded.

"We'll go to the store this week and you can pick out a paint color," Monica promised. "Any color you want."

"Okay."

"And some new curtains, and a bedspread," Sarah added. "And maybe even a Barbie doll."

With Elsa happily playing with her new toys, Sarah and Monica returned to the kitchen.

"She's absolutely precious," Sarah said.

"She is, isn't she?"

"What time is the social worker coming?"

"I don't know. My father put in a call this morning and they said they'd send someone out. Then he conveniently disappeared. Lord, Sarah, I have no idea what to say to them."

"It's going to be fine."

"Do you think they'll take her away?"

"No, I don't. You're Elsa's closest family member, aside from her grandfather, who just abandoned her. These case workers are notoriously overworked. They'll probably be thankful not to have to find a temporary home for her on such short notice."

"I hope you're right."

"Pete and I did foster care for a while, so I know what they look for. The main thing they'll be concerned with is what's best for Elsa. You have a nice, safe home. You're financially and emotionally stable. Those are two big things right there. They'll look into your background, and probably Barry's too. I'm sure you have nothing to worry about."

The last statement made her stomach queasy. She hadn't considered that they might check into Barry's background. She thought of his jail time ten years before. Would that have any bearing on this?

•

The Social worker, a young, pretty blonde, showed up at two o'clock. If she was perturbed about making an emergency visit on a Saturday, she didn't show it.

"I'm Melanie Braggs," she said, offering her hand. "And you must be Monica?"

"Yes. Thank you for coming," Monica said, shaking her hand. "Can I get you a cup of coffee?"

"No, thanks, but I'd love a glass of water."

Melanie sat at the table and Monica placed the water in front of her.

"So, tell me what's going on. Your father said he was turning Elsa over to you?"

Monica sat woodenly across from her, her carefully organized thoughts all at once scattered. "My father is very ill. He brought Elsa to me hoping I'd be willing to care for her in his place."

"And are you?"

"Yes. I am."

"Okay. The situation is unfortunate, but not all that unusual. Grandparents wanting to take in their grandchildren and discovering that for one reason or another, they're just not able to. We see it sometimes. It's best to place a child with family whenever possible."

Her nonjudgmental tone put Monica at ease.

"Are you employed, Monica?"

"I'm an English teacher at Risingville Middle School."

"Good. How long have you worked there?"

"Eight years."

"Excellent. And have you got any resources in the way of child care, if you should need it?"

Monica glanced at Sarah, who nodded encouragingly. "She's sitting right next to you. This is my friend and neighbor,

Sarah Lambert."

"It's nice to meet you, Sarah."

"You, too."

Melanie's eyes swept across the kitchen. "And it's just you here, no partner?"

"I'm single."

"Are there any boyfriends, or any other significant adults that will be in the home?"

Her mouth went dry. "It's just me."

She saw a look of surprise cross Sarah's face and averted her gaze.

"How's your health, Monica? All good?"

"My health is fine."

"Okay. I'd like to talk privately with Elsa for a bit, then maybe you can show me around."

•

After shutting Agnes in the pantry, she showed Melanie to Elsa's room. With the two of them behind closed doors, Monica returned to the kitchen. She let out a breath.

"Relax," Sarah said. "You did fine."

Thirty minutes later Melanie returned. "Elsa says she wants to stay here."

"Good, then."

"Tell me about the dog."

"Agnes is a rescue, a big baby. My cat likes to chew on her ears and play with her tail and she's fine with that. She hasn't got a mean bone in her body."

"I'm glad to hear that. Elsa is certainly attached to her."

After a tour of the house and farm, they congregated at Melanie's SUV. "You have a lovely home here, Ms. Humphrey."

"Thank you."

"In the interest of not disrupting Elsa again, I'm going to recommend that guardianship be transferred from your father to you, but the final determination will be made by the judge. You'll have to file a petition with the court, and we'll need your father to send a document asking for the transfer also. As I said, we like to place children with family members if at all possible. We'll do an investigation into your background and finances. If everything checks out, the court will set a date for a hearing in Pittsburgh. If we file it as an emergency petition, that should happen fairly soon. There will be a second hearing here, in Ohio, to transfer guardianship from state to state. That usually takes about ninety days." She retrieved a packet of papers from her vehicle and handed them to Monica. "I brought the forms along with me. If we can fill them out now, I'll take them with me and get them filed first thing Monday morning."

•

With Pete working late, Sarah collected her boys and the six of them went out for pizza and a movie. By eight o'clock, Elsa was fast asleep in her room.

Carrying her phone to the porch, Monica saw that she had three missed calls from Barry. She gathered her courage and returned them.

"Hey, lady, where have you been all day? I was getting ready to get in the car and drive out there."

"It's been pretty crazy."

"Yeah? Tell me about it."

She pulled in a quiet breath. "Believe it or not, my father showed up here."

"You're kidding."

"No, I'm not. It was pretty shocking, actually. I haven't seen him since I was fourteen years old. He looks like an old man."

"Wow. What did he want?"

She hesitated. "I'll tell you about it later. He didn't stay long."

"Are you okay, though?"

"Yeah, I'm okay. Tell me about your day."

They chatted for another twenty minutes. She ended the call with so much left unsaid. In all of the hours of conversation they'd shared, she and Barry had never once discussed children. Monica loved Elsa at first sight. She wanted the child, wanted her more than she wanted to breathe. And if Barry didn't feel the same way, she didn't want to know. Not tonight.

Chapter Twenty-Five

*M*onica awoke the next morning with a renewed sense of purpose. She was not like Sarah, a natural born mother, but that was okay. She would make mistakes, but she would learn from them. She'd had two very good mentors. She would raise Elsa the way the girls had raised her.

After setting up the ironing board, she went to the living room and looked through Elsa's boxes of clothing again. Finding only one dress, she carried it back to the kitchen. In shades of black, it was the most dismal children's garment she had ever seen. Even so, it was in better shape than most of the other things Elsa had brought. She'd definitely have to take the child shopping soon.

She glanced up when Elsa walked in, sleepily rubbing her eyes.

"Up so soon? I was going to let you sleep another hour."

Elsa watched her intently. "That's my fun'ral dress."

"Your what?"

"Grandad bought me it for Mommy's fun'ral."

Ahh. That certainly explained a few things. "I didn't see any other dresses in your box. Will it bother you to wear it just one more time?"

She thought about it for a moment, then shook her head.

"I thought we might go to church today."

"What for?"

She remembered asking a similar question, at Elsa's age. She answered the girl now as Geneva had answered her then. "Because it would make God happy. We want to make God happy, don't we?"

She nodded and Monica smiled. "Good girl. Now, what would you like for breakfast? I have toast and eggs, or maybe you'd like oatmeal?"

"I like Coca Shapes."

Monica cringed. No way would she feed the child chocolate for breakfast. "I don't have any Coca Shapes, sweetie. Tell you what, why don't you have some toast and jelly for today, and after church we'll go to the store and see what we can find that you might like, how will that be?"

"Okay."

She seated herself at the table and Monica prepared the toast, thanking God that she'd gotten over the first hurdle of the day.

•

She hadn't been inside the Presbyterian Church since Penny's funeral and found it comforting and disconcerting at the same time. The gleaming old pipe organ and the stained glass windows were like old friends, but the red velvet pews had been reupholstered in gold and she noted with a stab of regret that the church no longer had a formal choir. Glancing around, it occurred to her that there were no longer enough congregants to justify a formal choir. She knew hardly anyone there, and of the few she recognized, none seemed to know her.

Pastor Cuthbert had long since retired and a woman pastor now stood in the pulpit. Another big change. Even so, the familiar hymns and prayers brought her a sense of wellbeing. As a child, Monica had often been restless and fidgety during service, but Elsa seemed to drink in every word the pastor said. Such a serious girl, Monica thought. Turning her attention back to the sermon, she paid close attention, wanting to be able to answer any questions the child might ask her later.

•

After church, she treated Elsa to lunch at a hamburger place. She ordered herself a garden salad, and Elsa a burger and fries.

When the waitress brought their lunch, Elsa stared at Monica's plate in surprise. "You're only having lettuce?"

"I like lettuce."

"Don't you like French fries?"

"I used to."

"Why don't you now?"

"Because they make you fat."

"You're not so fat."

Now it was Monica's turn to be surprised. "You don't think so?"

"You're fatter than mommy, but not fat like Mrs. Cravens."

"And who is Mrs. Cravens?"

She shrugged. "She watches me sometimes. Mostly she sleeps. She smells bad."

Monica hid a smile. The child's honesty was delightful.

After lunch they stopped at the Gold Mart, where Elsa selected a gallon of hot pink paint for her room. Geneva would roll in her grave, but tucking the paint in her shopping cart, Monica could almost feel Penny's smile of approval.

In the girls section, she bought Elsa a pastel striped dress, two shorts sets, and a pair of sandals. They were heading to the checkout line when she remembered the doll.

"We were going to get you a Barbie doll. I almost forgot."

Perusing the toy aisle, Elsa agonized over two dolls: a bikini clad blonde and a brunette in a red velvet evening gown. Seeing her dilemma, Monica took the dolls from her hands.

"Let's get them both."

Elsa rewarded her with a bright smile, and Monica melted on the spot. She'd made it over the second hurdle.

Their last stop was the supermarket. Elsa's short list of favorites included boxed macaroni and cheese, microwavable French toast sticks, and chicken nuggets. Monica cringed as she placed the items in the cart with her own fruits and vegetables.

With drug addicted parents, the poor child had probably been left to fend for herself more often than not. Convenience foods were obviously all she knew of cuisine. That was going to change. She'd let it slide for now, but she'd make it a priority to introduce her niece to a more healthful way of eating.

•

With Elsa tucked into bed that evening, Monica carried her phone to the porch. She would call Barry, right now, before she lost her nerve, and tell him everything. She was organizing her thoughts when her phone rang. She glanced at the screen and her anger ignited. Dad. She thought about letting the call go to voice mail, but at the last minute, she answered it.

"Monica?"

"What do you need, Dad?"

"Did that social worker ever come?"

"Yes, she did."

"What did she say?"

"If you had stayed around, you would know, wouldn't you?"

His silence hummed across the line.

Monica pulled in a breath. "She said we have to file some papers. And then wait for a court date."

"I might want to see Elsa. To say goodbye."

"Maybe you should have thought of that yesterday. You couldn't get out of here fast enough."

"I'm sorry about that."

She rubbed her eyes, suddenly weary. "You can come see her any time you want. I told you that."

"I'm thinking maybe I made a mistake."

At that, she tensed. "What mistake?"

"Maybe I still want her."

"You've got to be kidding!"

"I don't have to sign anything, you know. I already have custody. I just need to fix up the house and a couple of other things. I was told I might even be able to get grants from the state. You know, to help me out."

"You're not getting her back. It's out of the question."

"Maybe we can work something out."

"Like what?"

"I won't get the grants if I don't keep Elsa."

"And?"

"The girls left you pretty well set, didn't they? A nice house, probably a chunk of change to go with it. They didn't leave me anything, their own nephew. Doesn't seem right."

"So what are you saying? You want me to give you money?"

"Just a little here and there. Just to make up for what those bitches did, taking you from me. They owed me."

She was flabbergasted. Infuriated. "In the first place, the girls gave me a home because you couldn't—or wouldn't. You were the one that owed them. And secondly, I can't believe you're making this about money." Realizing she was shouting, she lowered her voice. "This is about a little girl's life, Dad. Your own granddaughter."

"They told me they were going to send some papers in the mail. I'm just saying, a little spending money might persuade me to sign them. Just think about it."

"Goodbye, Dad."

She disconnected the call, all at once feeling physically ill. He was a heartless, despicable man. How did he sleep at night? She pulled in a few deep breaths, trying to calm herself. If push came to shove, she would tell the judge everything. About his drinking problem. His explosive temper. Not to mention the fact that he abandoned not only his granddaughter, but his own daughter, as a little girl. She would hold nothing back. She would protect Elsa as the girls had protected her. Or spend her last breath trying.

•

She was still shaking, a bundle of nerves and rage, when her phone rang again. Barry. Her dear, sweet Barry. Her man. How she needed his strength and gentle guidance right now. How she ached to pour this mess out before him and have him sort through it with her and help her make sense of it. She ached to tell him everything.

But not now. Not like this. Not before she'd had time to organize it and think how to present it to him. The well thought out words and sentences she'd had in her mind were gone now. Her father's astonishing request had scattered them to the winds. She wasn't ready. Wasn't at all ready.

She let the call go to voicemail.

•

The next morning they emptied out Elsa's bedroom and scrubbed the walls with pine cleaner. Sarah showed up at noon and they began painting. As the walls slowly transformed from faded yellow to shocking pink, Monica got the uncanny sense that her life, like her old bedroom, was being renewed. Elsa managed to get more paint on herself than the wall, but what did it matter? They were creating memories.

Geneva would have put the child in the tub and scrubbed her back into apple pie order. Penny would have laughed and said she liked the hot pink highlights in Elsa's hair. Monica saw the happiness on the child's face and struggled to find a balance. In the end, she allowed Elsa to continue painting until the first coat was drying on the walls, and then took her to the bathroom and wiped down her skin and hair with a soapy washcloth. She would be neither too stern, nor too lenient, she decided. She would try to be the best of both of the girls.

Washed clean, she sent Elsa outside to play with Agnes while she and Sarah enjoyed a coffee break. With the coffee brewed, Monica glanced out the window and saw that the little girl and the enormous dog were happily tossing a ball around the yard.

"You're doing a fabulous job," Sarah commented. "She's come out of her shell so much in only a couple of days."

"It's the farm. It has that effect on children," Monica answered, stirring a spoonful of milk into her coffee. "That, and I think she was afraid of my father."

"No, it's not just the farm, it's you. The way you love and care for her, it just comes pouring out of you."

"Thanks."

Sarah stirred a spoonful of sugar into her coffee. "Have you told Barry about her yet?"

"No."

"But why not?"

Though asked gently, the question put her on the defense. "I just ... I don't know."

"What are you afraid of?"

She wished she knew. Her unnamed fears had her in a vice

grip. If she could only name them, she might be able to break their terrible hold. Barry was the best man she knew. He was kind, understanding, and patient. So what was she afraid of?

"I noticed you didn't tell the social worker you had a boyfriend," Sarah prompted.

"Barry got in some trouble a while back. Like ten years ago. I didn't know if it would matter to them, if it would hurt my custody case. So I kept quiet about it."

"What kind of trouble could Barry possibly have gotten in?"

She told Sarah about the accident, the jail time, and Barry's ruined life.

"But that was years ago. He's proven himself to be a solid citizen. I'm sure none of that would matter now. "

"I suppose not."

That sat quietly for a long moment, and then finally, Monica acknowledged her fears. "What if … He might not want this."

"He might not. But Monica, he might. Barry loves you. Don't you think you should give him a chance to tell you what he does want?"

"I know I should."

Sarah's hand covered hers. "He may embrace Elsa and love her just as much as you do. And he may not. But I think you owe it to him, and to yourself, to be honest with him."

•

That evening, Monica put Elsa to bed in a sleeping bag beside her own bed. Though the paint in her room was dry, she worried about the lingering fumes.

"Can Agnes sleep in here with us?" Elsa asked hopefully. Monica smiled. "I suppose so. As long as she doesn't get it in her noggin to try and get in my bed."

"I won't let her."

"Okay. I'll send her in."

With a kiss on the forehead, she opened the door and Agnes bounded in.

"You go right to sleep, now. We've got another big day of painting tomorrow."

"I will," Elsa said, snuggling next to the dog.

Collecting her phone and her courage, she went outside and called Barry. He answered on the first ring, his voice a soothing balm to her senses.

"Hey, pretty lady."

"Hey. How was your day? "

"My last two days were pretty long," he said. "I tried to call you last night."

"I'm sorry. I went to bed early."

"Did you have a good day?"

"Yeah. I went to church yesterday."

"I'm glad."

"I went to the church I grew up in. It's changed a lot, but in some ways, it's just the same."

He paused, then, "Why don't you tell me what's wrong?"

Her heart squeezed. "What do you mean?"

"You haven't seemed like yourself lately."

It was time to tell him. Past time. But she couldn't.

"I haven't been feeling that well."

"Is there anything I can do?"

Her eyes filled with tears and she fought to keep them from her voice. "Just, please …"

"What is it, sweetheart?"

Her voice broke. "Please don't stop loving me."

"Not loving you is not even an option, Monica." He sighed. "I shouldn't have left. It's upset you and filled you with all of these crazy doubts. I'm going to tell them I can't do this."

Terror gripped her. She needed time, space. "No, don't do that. It's only for a few more weeks. I'll be okay."

"We'll be together next weekend. And after that, you won't have another doubt. I promise."

The words pushed her over the edge and into her fears. The fist squeezed tight around her, and for a long moment, she was spiraling downward, unable to breathe.

Chapter Twenty-Six

*O*n Saturday afternoon, Monica, Sarah and Elsa stood in the little girl's newly remodeled bedroom. The hot pink paint Elsa chose had been toned down with glittery white heart decals. Gently scrolling letters above the bed spelled out the word "Dream," complemented by pink-and-white striped curtains and a matching comforter. As a crowning touch, Sarah had seen a filmy white canopy on one of her decorating programs and had duplicated it beautifully. The room was a little girl's paradise, fit for a princess and Elsa could not have been more pleased.

"This is a room that will grow up with you," Sarah told her. "At least for a few years."

"I'm never going to change it," Elsa insisted. "Never!"

"You may feel differently when you're a teenager." Sarah planted a kiss on top of Elsa's head. "But I'm glad you like it."

A fist of anxiety squeezed Monica's stomach. She only hoped Elsa would be here long enough to outgrow the room.

•

The next afternoon they packed a picnic lunch and carried it to the fishing hole. After Monica baited their poles, she and Elsa sat by the side of the creek while Agnes happily chased dragonflies.

"So how was children's church today? Did you like it?"

"Uh-huh."

"What did Mrs. Collins talk to you about?"

"She told us a story about this little boy who ran away. His daddy waited on the porch everyday, wishing for him to come home. Then the little boy did come home and his daddy gave him a big party."

"How nice."

Elsa gazed into the water. "I ran away once."

Monica gaped at her. "You did?"

"Just to the bus station, then the cops called Mommy. She didn't give me a party, though. She spanked me. She was mad."

"I'm sure she was just very afraid."

"She locked me in the cellar. There was a spider."

"That was …" Criminal "… scary."

"Bruce said church was for sissies. I think it's nice."

"Who is Bruce?"

"Mommy's boyfriend. But he died."

"I know."

"Mommy died, too."

She wrapped her arms around the child and pulled her close. "I'm so sorry, Elsa."

"Are you going to be my mommy now?"

The question stole her breath. "I'll never be able to replace your mommy, Elsa. But I hope you'll want to stay here with me for a long, long time."

"You and Agnes?"

"Yes, me and Agnes. And Ginger."

Elsa snuggled against her side, and her heart swelled with love. And regret for lost time. She would have loved to have been a proper aunt. How could five years have gone by, and she'd not even known this child existed?

•

On Monday morning, unable to stand the constant churning in her stomach one minute longer, Monica put in a call to Melanie Braggs.

"Monica, I'm glad you called. I actually have a note on my desk to call you this afternoon."

She waited, her pulse pounding in her ears. The aching in her stomach was unbearable.

"Hang on, let me get your case file." She heard the shuffling of papers. "Okay, looks like your background checked out beautifully, so there's no problem there. It doesn't look like your father has filed the petition, but he can bring it with him to court, if need be. They're anxious to get this settled before the school year starts. You'll be getting a certified letter, but I wanted to give you a heads up. Court is a scheduled for a week from today at ten o'clock. Can you be there?"

"Of course I'll be there."

"The judge will want to talk with Elsa, as well."

She let out a breath. "Monday at ten. We'll be there."

Ending the call, she went limp. One more week, and it would be over. Unless …

What if her father refused to sign the paperwork?

She tried to think back to her first summer on the farm. Had the girls gone through all of this to obtain guardianship of her? They must have, though she could not recall ever talking to a judge. Her father had likely just signed off on her and mailed his forms in.

Why wouldn't he do that now?

With the question came a sick realization.

He'd signed off on her guardianship because the girls had paid him, demanded money in return for … her.

And the girls had loved her enough to give it to him. He'd manipulated them, used their love for Monica against them, just as he was using Monica's love for Elsa now.

A slow burning started in her belly and worked its way through her bloodstream until it consumed her. This time he had picked the wrong woman.

Grabbing her phone, she placed a second call, praying her instincts were right.

Her father did not even bother with a greeting.

"So did you think about what I said?"

"Oh yes, I've thought about it quite a lot."

"And?"

"And if they've sent you paperwork, I suggest you sign it."

His tone became belligerent. "Or else what?"

"Or I'll tell the judge exactly what kind of guardian you really are."

Silence.

"I'm sure he'd be interested to know how you sold your own little girl to your aunts."

"You're crazy."

"I know all about it, so don't try to deny it."

"You don't know …"

"And just exactly where were you when Juliet had your granddaughter locked in a spider-infested basement? When she was left on her own to prepare her own meals … or go without eating?"

Silence.

"The way I see it, you have two choices. You can sign the papers and file them tomorrow, or you can show up in court on Monday and fight me on this. I don't think you'll win."

He hung up on her, and she sat at the table, trembling. She'd gambled everything on the hunch that he wouldn't show up in court. She hoped to God she was right.

The call left her shaken, in need of reassurance. In need of the girls. Pulling Geneva's journal from the book case, she carried it to the sofa.

April 30, 1964

Mother's garden is the first thing Penny has shown interest in in months. When the seed catalogues came in the mail, I put them in a box for trash, as I always do. How surprising to find Penny curled up in father's armchair, poring over them. She'd circled all of the plants she liked with a marker and wrote out all of their prices. She told me she would save her allowance to buy them. I told her that if she would get the garden ready, pull the weeds and turn the soil, it would prove to me that she was serious and I would buy her the plants.

The child has barely left the garden since. Her every spare moment is consumed with weeding and fertilizing and planning. Who would have thought a neglected patch of earth would be our salvation?

•

"Are you reading a storybook?"

She looked up to see Elsa watching her from the doorway. She patted the place beside her on the couch.

"Sort of. Come and sit with me."

Elsa sat, and Ginger claimed the space in the child's lap. "Will you read it to me?"

"I don't think it's anything you'd be interested in, sweetie."

"What's it about?"

"It's about a girl and how she loved her garden. Right here on the farm."

"What's a garden?"

"It's a little piece of land, or sometimes a big piece of land, where people grow flowers and vegetables and all kinds of nice things."

"Like strawberries?"

"Yes, definitely."

"I like gardens, then."

"Maybe next spring we'll put the garden back in. You could have your own little corner, plant whatever you like, how would that be?"

"Good."

"What flowers are your favorite?"

"Yellow."

"Oh, there are lots of yellow flowers we could plant. But before we can plant, we have a lot of work to do."

"Like what?"

"First we have to pull out all of the weeds. Then take a shovel and make the ground soft, so the flowers have wiggle room for their roots. And then we can plant the seeds. That's the fun part."

"Okay." She pressed her face in Ginger's fur, and Monica pushed a lock of hair behind her ear.

"You and I are going to be going to Pittsburgh next week."

Alarm registered on her face. "Why?"

"We have to talk to a man called a judge. He's going to ask you some questions about where you want to live."

"I want to live here with you."

Her heart overflowed. "It's nothing for you to worry about, okay? You just have to tell him how you feel."

•

It took three days for Monica to work up the courage to let Barry down. On Thursday afternoon, with time running out, she returned his phone call from earlier that day. The days had been circled on her calendar with hearts for three weeks; Saturday through Tuesday. Her and Barry's long weekend together in Cincinnati. And now she couldn't go.

She put in the call, her stomach coiling into tight knots as she listened to it ring.

"Hey! How's my favorite girl?"

"I'm good. How's my favorite manager?"

"More than ready for a few days off. So what's your ETA on Saturday? God, I can't wait to see you."

She broke out in a sweat and the phone trembled in her hands. "About that... It looks like I won't be able to come out this weekend after all."

"What do you mean you can't come out? Why not?"

"I have to go to Pittsburgh."

"Is this about your father?"

"More or less, yes. Some family things that have to be worked out."

"And it's going to take the whole weekend? "

"Yes. I'm so sorry."

He paused for long moments. "Okay, well what if I come there? I could go with you to Pittsburgh."

"It's going to be a zoo-ey weekend. I don't think we'd have any time to spend together."

"Monica, what's going on?"

"I just told you. My father ..."

"It's more than that, though. You've been acting really strange ever since I left. I want to know what it's about."

She thought of what Sarah had said. She owed him the truth. But now she was so far into the deception she didn't know how to get out.

"It's family matters, Barry. Please let me work this out my own way."

"Fine. If that's what you want."

His clipped tone pierced her heart. "Maybe I can come next

weekend."

"I won't have next weekend off. I asked for this weekend way in advance."

"I'm really sorry."

"Yeah, me too."

"… I love you."

"I hope that's still true."

•

Both Sarah and Melanie Braggs were present at the hearing on Monday morning. Monica sat like a stone, her stomach rolling as the judge reviewed the documents before him; her petition as well as her father's, the background report from Social Services, and Lord knew what else. She felt like he held her whole life in his age-spotted hands.

With Elsa behind closed doors with a court appointed advocate, His Honor Richard Saxton asked all of the questions she had prepared herself for.

"You're petitioning for legal guardianship of your niece, Elsa Louise Humphrey, the daughter of your deceased half-sister, in the wake of your father's recent health problems, is that correct?'

"Yes, Your Honor."

"And you are employed at …" He glanced at the documents in front of him, "Risingville Middle school as a teacher."

"That's right."

"And you own your own home, a farm in Baxter, Ohio."

"Yes."

He removed his glasses. "Describe for me your relationship with your late sister."

"I never knew her."

His eyebrows arched in surprise. "And yet you're willing to raise her child?"

"Yes, Sir."

"Can you explain that to me, Ms. Humphrey?"

She cleared her throat. "My mother died when I was six years old. That's when my family fell apart. My father was a truck driver. He spent days at a time on the road, and he wasn't able to care for me. His two aunts took me in. They gave me a home on their farm, trees to climb, a garden to tend, bread to bake. They were wonderful women."

Tears threatened and she paused to control them.

"Now my niece is also a motherless child. I consider it my duty and privilege to provide for her that same safe, loving home that was given to me. I have the means. And I have the desire."

The judge considered her words, then turned to address Melanie.

"Child Protective Services feels this is in Elsa's best interests?"

"We do, Your Honor."

"I'd like to speak with the child. We'll reconvene in twenty minutes."

When the judge left the courtroom, Monica broke down. She wept into her hands, overwhelmed and afraid.

"You did fine, hon," Melanie assured her, patting her arm.

"Heck," Sarah said. "You made me want to come live at the farm."

She fought to control herself. "What do you think he'll decide?"

"If Elsa tells him she wants to live with you, I think he'll let her."

It was less than fifteen minutes when the judge returned, holding Elsa by the hand. Seeing Monica, she ran to her and hugged her neck.

"Guess what?"

"What, sweetie?"

"You are going to be my mommy! You and Ginger and Agnes!"

•

In all, the court case took thirty-five minutes. As far as the state of Pennsylvania was concerned, Monica was now Elsa's legal guardian. With a hug, Melanie assured her the transfer to Ohio would be a mere formality.

On the way home, Sarah, Elsa and Monica stopped for

lunch to celebrate. Monica had barely eaten in a week, and walking into the diner, the lingering scents of bacon and eggs made her mouth water. She ordered a BLT salad and a cup of coffee. Life was good. Now that the court case was settled, she would call Barry this evening and tell him everything.

Sarah dropped them off at the end of the driveway and they walked, hand in hand to the house. She saw the white Impala at the same moment Elsa noticed the man.

"Who is that man sitting on our porch with Agnes?"

Monica's knees nearly buckled. "Oh Lord," she whispered. "Barry."

Chapter Twenty-Seven

She should have known he would come. Why had she not known it, prepared for it?

As she walked toward him, her lunch cartwheeled in her stomach. Pulling in a breath, she stepped onto the porch.

"Well, this is a surprise."

"You're back from Pittsburgh."

"We're just getting home."

His eyes swept over Elsa and he smiled a tight smile.

"Hello."

Flinching as if he'd struck her, she pressed her face into Monica's side. Agnes whimpered, and it dawned on Monica that the child was not just afraid of her father. She was afraid of all men.

"Elsa, why don't you take Agnes in the living room and see what you can find to watch on TV?"

Head down, Elsa scurried inside, Agnes close on her heels. Monica turned back to Barry, went to hug him.

"Hi."

He didn't hug her back, not really. His embrace was unnaturally rigid, hinting at a tethered anger.

"Who is the little girl?"

"I have a lot to tell you."

Removing himself from her embrace, he sat back down on the swing. "I'm listening."

"Her name is Elsa. She's my sister's child."

When he didn't respond, she forged ahead. "My father brought her here two weeks ago. Juliet died. Actually she and her boyfriend both died. Of a drug overdose. The County turned Elsa over to my father, but he's a drunk. I couldn't leave her with him, Barry. I … I applied for legal guardianship."

A muscle twitched in his jaw. She looked away from the heat of his stare.

"I didn't know how to tell you," she said quietly.

"What do you mean you didn't know how to tell me?"

"I had to go to Pittsburgh today, for court. The judge granted me Elsa's legal guardianship. I'll still have to appear here in Ohio, but it's pretty much all settled."

She saw a mixture of anger and disbelief on his face. Her words tumbled out, faster and faster. "So I'm going to have to return to my job at the school, at least for a few months. I had to show proof that I could provide for Elsa financially. We might have to delay opening the restaurant. Just for a while."

She fell silent.

Barry shook his head.

"Would you like to go inside and meet her properly? She's leery of men, but I'm sure she'll warm up—"

"No."

"She's a sweet little girl, Barry. She's been through so much."

"It's not about the little girl, Monica. God." He ran both hands back though his hair and pushed out a breath, clearly trying to composed himself. "It's about you not trusting me enough, after all this time, to let me be a part of this decision."

"Barry."

"It's about me being an afterthought in your life. As usual."

"That's not true."

"Isn't it? We talked on the phone every day. Every single day, and you said nothing. Not one word. You made these monumental decisions and you never said one single word!"

Underneath his clenched fists and anger, she could see how deeply she'd hurt him.

"If that's your idea of a partnership …"

"I'm sorry."

"I thought we had something special between us. Something real. Obviously I was wrong."

Tears filled her eyes. "I'm so sorry."

"I'm sorry too. I love you so much, and you …" His voice cracked. "I asked you a question a few weeks ago, and you couldn't even give me an answer. You've spent weeks making a decision that should have taken seconds."

She could not bear this moment, or the tears he she saw gathering in his eyes.

"I should have known your silence was your answer."

"I was going to give you an answer. I was going to tell you everything."

"When, Monica?"

"I was going to call you tonight."

"Tonight, after it was all a done deal."

"I was hoping you'd want to be a part of it, that you'd want to help me raise her."

"And what if I don't?"

It was the question that had kept her awake at night, that had kept her stomach churning. The question that meant she'd have to choose. Barry or Elsa. She steeled herself.

"If you don't … Then I guess I can't marry you."

The silence that crashed around them was unbearable. He regarded her for a long moment. "You're choosing her over me? A little girl you that up until two weeks ago you didn't even know existed?"

"Yes," she whispered.

He looked stunned. "Okay," he said softly. "They offered me the store in Cincinnati. Permanently. I guess I'm going to take it. Goodbye, Monica."

She did not call out as he turned and walked away, only stood on the porch, tears streaming from her eyes. She could have run after him. Saved their love. He would still forgive her, return to her, if only she asked.

For Elsa's sake, she let him go.

As he got in his company car and drove away, she felt herself breaking apart. Barry had been the one to mend her, and now, like a fragile porcelain doll swept to the floor, her glue not yet dry, she was breaking into a thousand pieces.

Chapter Twenty-Eight

July 16, 1965

It has been a year and a half now, since our lives were torn apart. It's funny, how tragedy makes you separate time into compartments: before and after. But dwelling on the past serves no purpose. What's done is done. The time to live is now.

Even so, when I think about who I used to be, I can hardly recognize myself. The things I wanted so badly in life, I no longer desire. It's true what they say. The things that don't kill you serve to make you stronger.

There's not a day that goes by that I don't think of Mother and Dad. How I miss them. I still cry every day. In that, I am no stronger. But Douglas, whom I thought I could not live without, I hardly think of any more at all.

Penny copes by filling our lives and home with flowers. She says flowers soothe the soul, and for her, I believe that's true. On the window sills in the kitchen she has placed mason jars filled with daisies. In the dining and living rooms, she has placed large, showy bouquets of sunflowers and lavender and lilies in Mother's crystal vases. In each of the bedrooms, on the night stands, a single sweetheart rose in a bottle, with baby's breath and ribbons. The arrangements are as beautiful and as unusual as Penny is.

Her garden is thriving, just as she is thriving.

I had a little produce stand built and set it up at the end of the driveway. On Fridays and Saturdays Penny sells her bouquets, along with the vegetables she grows. I thought it would merely be something constructive for her to do, and a way for her to earn some spending money. I had no idea how well the little stand would do. Next summer, Penny wants to expand her gardens and grow more flowers and vegetables, and even put in a strawberry patch. She wants to perfect her baking skills this fall, and try selling homemade bread and cookies in the stand next year. I'm amazed daily by this girl of mine. I am so proud of her.

The time to live is now. And so we go on ...

•

Monica closed the journal. The entry was profound, shocking in its relevance. The time to live was now. But how did you go on living when your heart was shattered? For the last two weeks, since her breakup with Barry, she'd felt barely alive, dragging herself out of bed and making herself function for Elsa's sake.

"How do I get through these endless days?" she asked.

And the answer whispered across her heart. *One moment at a time* ...

Despite her pain, she had tried to make Elsa's first weeks at the farm special. There were picnic lunches at the fishing hole, and evenings at the playground in the local park. With each new day, Elsa blossomed a little more, unfolding like a shy flower in the sunshine. Monica had done the right thing in bringing her here. Even if the right thing hurt like hell.

Opening the old Hoosier cabinet, she took out Penny's worn, red cook book. She ran her hands over the pages, stained with years' worth of spilled ingredients, and managed a smile. One moment at a time.

Elsa came in from the yard, where she'd been playing Frisbee with Agnes.

"What are you doing, Mama?"

The word stole her breath, and she knew she would never get used to the joy it brought her.

"I thought maybe we could make some cookies for Sarah and the boys today."

"Why?"

"Just as a way of saying thank you. She does a lot of nice things for us."

Elsa climbed into the chair next to Monica and together they flipped through the pages.

"Tell me when you see something you think they would like."

"I think they'd like chocolate chips."

"You think they would?" She smiled. "Or you think Miss Elsa would?"

"I think they would and I think I would."

•

When they'd assembled all of the ingredients, she showed Elsa how to crack the eggs and measure the sugar and flour, and finally, how to drop the cookie dough by spoonful's onto a cookie sheet.

While the cookies were baking, they played a board game Sarah had brought over the week before. The kitchen filled with the comforting scents of Monica's childhood as the moments ticked away.

With the cookies out of the oven, they put them on waxed paper to cool.

"Do we have to give all of the cookies to Sarah?" Elsa asked wistfully.

Monica took the child's face in her hands and smiled. "Oh, maybe we can keep back one or two."

Her cell phone rang, and the familiar squeeze of hope swelled in her chest. By now, she knew Barry was not going to call, knew it with a certainty in her core, but even so, the smoldering flame of hope inside her would not die. She glanced at the name displayed on the screen. Layla. Hope was replaced by disappointment. And a curious sense of unease.

"You sit tight," she told Elsa. "I'll be right back."

She carried the phone outside, where she could speak privately.

"Hello?"

"Hi, Monica, it's Layla."

"Hi, Layla."

"How's your summer going? Are you feeling back to normal?" Layla was overly friendly, overly cheerful, and Monica's sense of unease grew.

"I'm well, thank you."

"I'm glad to hear that. Hey, we're in the process of doing some reshuffling for the coming school year. I have a proposition for you."

"I'm listening."

"How would you feel about doing some small group tutoring this year?"

Closing her eyes, she massaged her temples. In the back of her mind, she'd known the call was coming, had tried to prepare herself for it. She sat down on the swing.

"Instead of teaching my classes, or in addition to?"

"I should back up. I'm sure you've noticed that we are getting more and more Spanish-speaking students every year. Some of them, the ones that speak poor English, are really struggling academically. Since you're fluent in Spanish, we thought you'd be the perfect one to work with them, to bring them up to speed."

When Monica didn't answer, she continued. "We're thinking you could meet with them three or four at a time, seeing different groups throughout the day. You'd have to get with their other teachers and coordinate your schedules, but as far as programming you'd pretty much have free reign."

She knew she didn't have to take Layla's deal. As a tenured employee there were contractual issues she could use as a loophole. But she also knew how her administration worked. She'd seen more than one teacher fall from favor at Risingville Middle School. She was aware of Layla's dirty tricks.

"I might be interested in that," she said.

"Wonderful!" Did she detect relief in Layla's voice? "Can you come in next week so we can discuss it more fully?"

They set up an appointment for the following Wednesday and Monica returned to the kitchen, a tension headache blooming behind her eyes.

•

Later that afternoon, she and Elsa packed the cookies into a basket and took them to Sarah's house. Elsa went outside to play with the boys while Sarah and Monica visited in the kitchen.

"How are you holding up?" Sarah asked.

"I'm okay."

"You don't look okay. Are you sleeping?"

"Not much."

Sarah spooned some sugar into her coffee. "I still can't believe Barry reacted that way to Elsa. He always seemed so kind and understanding. I would have thought he'd—"

"I'd rather not talk about it, Sarah."

"Right. I'm sorry."

Sarah reached for a cookie and took a bite. "I really shouldn't get started on these, but they smell amazing. And knowing my boys, this is the only one I'll get."

Monica smiled, then winced and rubbed her temples.

"Got a headache?"

"More like a thunderstorm in my brain. I got a call from my supervisor at work today."

"And …?"

"They want me to do small group tutoring next year instead of teaching my regular classes."

"Would that be a bad thing?"

She sighed. "It wouldn't be, if they're being honest about what it is."

"I don't understand."

"Let me tell you a story." She splashed some milk into her coffee and stirred. "Last spring, after my accident, I wanted to return for the last few days of the school year. I was feeling strong, and I wanted to say goodbye to the students that were moving on to high school. I wasn't in the building more than fifteen minutes before it became crystal clear they didn't want me back."

"What do you mean, they didn't want you back?"

"They'd gotten this young teacher, a kid, really, to sub in my place. They loved her and so did the kids. They said they didn't want to disrupt my classes any more than they already had been and stuck me in a little broom closet beside the boiler room to do 'tutoring.' I sat there at a rickety old desk the whole week and not a single student came to me for tutoring. If it's going to be like that, I don't think I can do it."

"That's horrible! They can't make you do it, can they?"

"Well, technically, no. And technically they can't make me leave my job if I refuse to do it. But they can make it real uncomfortable for me to stay."

She told Sarah about Evelyn Brenner, the sixty-three year old Social Studies teacher who'd been treated horribly by administration until she'd finally retired.

"First they gave her bright, airy classroom to a first-year teacher and stuck her in a room in the dank West Wing. Their next order of business was to assign her after-school detention four nights a week. And schedule her for recess duty during her lunch breaks."

Sarah looked at her, incredulous. "Why would they do all that?"

"Because she was old and they wanted her to retire. One of the Board members had a nephew with a brand new teaching degree and they wanted him to have her spot. A new teacher's salary is much lower, almost half what they were paying Evelyn. She left in tears on the first of October. The nephew has been there ever since."

"Wow." She sipped her coffee. "That's what I call dirty pool."

"I can't do it again, sit in a closet, unwanted and unneeded. But I can't not do it, either."

"Well, let's hope for your sake it's a legitimate position."

•

The following Wednesday she dropped Elsa off at Sarah's house and headed to Risingville, determined to keep an open mind. Like Geneva said, what didn't kill her would make her stronger.

The floral dress Sarah had helped her pick out a month ago was already too big on her. She'd eaten very little in the past few weeks, and had dropped down to two hundred twenty-five pounds. Ninety-eight down. Seventy-five to go. She and

Elsa would have to go shopping again before the school year started.

The smelled of old books and disinfectant greeted her as she walked into the school. In her office, Layla glanced up from her desk.

"Monica, thanks for coming in. I—" Her expression turned to one of disbelief as her glance traveled over Monica's figure. "You've lost weight."

"Yes."

"A lot of weight."

Monica smiled. "Almost a hundred pounds."

"Wow. You look fabulous."

"Thanks. It's amazing what having your mouth wired shut can do."

"Yes, I guess so." She recovered quickly, and became all business. "Here's a list of the students you'll potentially be tutoring. Most of them are sixth graders, but there are three or four older ones as well. Maybe they could be in a group together." She handed Monica the list, along with a thick stack of folders. "Here are their files. There are fourteen, so far. You'll notice most of them scored very poorly on the standardized tests. That's where we'll need your help."

Monica opened a file and glanced through it, then moved to another. "I'm surprised these kids even made it into middle school."

"That's why we need someone with your experience, Monica. I'm sure with your help they can get to where they need to be."

Monica wasn't quite as sure.

"Who would teach my classes?"

Layla hesitated. "We were thinking that since Darlene was with them last year, and she knows the ropes, we would offer it to her."

Monica knew, with a sick churning in her stomach, that the offer had already been made, the contract already signed. The meeting was not about Monica's skills and experience. It was about how to keep Darlene Dixon without Monica filing a lawsuit.

"We're thinking we could put your classroom out in the

Mobile. It would be perfectly suited to small groups."

The Mobile. The joke of the school. How often had Monica heard the banter passed across the table in the teacher's lounge? Late again? You keep it up and you'll be working in the mobile.

She was better than this, deserved better than this.

She thought of all the extra hours she'd put in, the money she'd spent out of her own pocket, the evenings and weekends given up for school activities. And what had her dedication gotten her? A dingy old classroom far removed from the rest of the school.

She was unwanted and unappreciated. But she was stuck.

She told Layla she'd like to think about it for a week or two, but really, what choice did she have? She would have to accept the offer and make the best of it. For now.

•

Her first instinct, when she was feeling low, was to eat. Her second was to seek Barry out. Since her stomach was too unsettled for the former, she drove south, in the direction of Barry's rental house, knowing she was being foolish. He would not be there. He would be staying in Cincinnati for at least three more weeks, if not permanently.

Even so, her heart propelled her to the third block of Grandview.

From a block away, she noticed a minivan in the driveway. Definitely not Barry's vehicle. Her heart raced. Slowing, she saw a play set in the side yard, and unfamiliar furniture on the porch—two wicker chairs and a love seat with red-striped cushions.

"No," she whispered.

The front door opened and two small children ran out to the yard and claimed the swings. A young redheaded woman came behind them, carrying a basket of laundry to the clothesline.

As she set down her basket and called to her laughing children, Monica let go of her last shred of hope. Barry had taken the store in Cincinnati. He was gone from his rental house. Gone from Risingville.

Gone from her life.

… *Gone.*

Chapter Twenty-Nine

"*W*aa-waaa-waa. Annie is sad. A-a-a is A. Buh-buh-buh. Billy is bad."

"Why is Billy so bad, Mama?"

"Look at the picture. It looks to me like he didn't eat his string beans."

"He gave them to the dog, though. That was nice."

Agnes thumped her tail.

Monica smiled and patted Elsa's head. "You think so, do you?"

In the weeks that followed her meeting with Layla, the last weeks of her summer vacation, Monica turned her attention toward getting Elsa ready for kindergarten. She worked with her on phonics and recognizing simple sight words, taught her the basic colors and to count from one to ten. Eager to learn, Elsa drank in the stories Monica read to her and practiced writing her letters and numbers without complaint. Monica only hoped her new students would be as compliant.

She spent her evenings going over their files, trying to get a sense of who they were and where they were academically. Of her fourteen students, only six were girls. Their records indicated learning delays, low reading scores, and behavioral issues.

Most concerning was a seventh grade girl named Valentina Rivera. Based on her file, the girl came from a horrible background. With her mother often incarcerated on drug and prostitution charges, Valentina had been shuffled from foster home to foster home since the age of seven, many of which she'd run away from. Her file was thick with truancies and write ups for inappropriate behavior, mostly sexual.

Two of the older boys, Rico Donati and Tommy Cruz, were also flagged for intervention. Both boys had appeared in Juvenile Court on charges of petty theft and vandalism. Both read at a second grade level. Monica sighed. She was going to have her hands full.

•

Driving to work on the first day of school, Monica thought how drastically her life had changed in the last few months. She'd come through a devastating injury. She'd gained a child, and found a friend she'd thought was lost. She'd shed more than one hundred pounds, and she'd found and lost the love of her life … But she would not go there this morning. Not with the sun shining down on her with the promise of a brand new, beautiful day.

After locating her new parking spot, she walked to the mobile and slid her key into the lock. She'd come in the week before and set up her classroom, making it as cheerful as possible with potted plants, motivational posters, and a reading corner stocked with what she hoped were fun and interesting books. It was going to be a tough year, but she was determined to give it her best shot. She would be a fun teacher if it killed her.

At eight fifteen her first group of seventh graders shuffled in, among them Rico, Tommy, and Valentina, wearing full makeup and very little clothing.

"Buenos Dias! Good morning, and welcome to my class. I'm Ms. Humphrey and I have a lot of fun things planned, so let's get started, yes?"

While they chose their places at the tables, she wrote on the white board in bold, blue marker: *Respeto*.

"You'll find I only have one rule in my classroom. Respect. I expect you to respect me and your classmates. And I expect you to respect yourselves. That means doing your best. It means completing the work I give you to do. If you have problems with it, respect yourself enough to ask for help."

She felt their stares on her, heavy as wool blankets.

"I won't be giving you tests. But—"

The news brought the expected cheers.

"But … You'll be using the Accelerated Reading program on your iPads. You'll be expected to pass at least two quizzes at your reading levels every week."

The word was spoken softly. Creeping to where she stood, it was almost lost amid the snickers of the other students. "Mierda."

"Tommy, have you got something to say?"

"Uhh, I go by Cruz."

"All right, thank you for letting me know that, Cruz." She leaned back against her desk. "And just so you know, the quizzes are actually not BS. If you do your assigned reading every day, you shouldn't have any trouble getting a seventy per cent score, which is what I require."

Beside Cruz, Rico groaned.

"Rico, what's on your mind?"

"Nothing."

"You sure?"

He sighed a long suffering sigh. "Yeah, no disrespect, Ms. Humphrey, but why are we gonna need this?"

"Need what?"

"All this reading."

Valentina nodded her agreement.

"That's a fair question. Let's start with the long-term. What do you plan to do when you get out of high school? For a career?"

"I'll prob'ly fix cars."

"That's a good goal. So to fix cars, won't you need to be able to read and understand repair manuals?"

"You don't gotta read for that. You just gotta watch YouTube videos."

"There's videos for everything," a boy named Dexter Maylor chimed in. "You don't have to read nothing no more."

"I see. Well, that's a shame. By not reading you're going to miss out on reading a lot of really good books."

"Bor-ring."

"Okay, so let's say you're right. Let's say that the written word has no place in modern society. Let's talk shorter term.

You do need to pass a state reading exam to get of out middle school. And—"

There was a collective groan, as she'd known there would be.

"And you need to pass at least two AR reading quizzes every week if you want to earn rewards in here."

Cruz perked up. "What kind of rewards?"

"That's something I wanted to discuss with you all. Passing eight tests a month is going to be a lot of work. What would be a decent payoff?"

"Cigarettes," Rico said. "Beer."

The two brothers in the class, Dante and Lucas, nudged each other and smiled behind their hands.

"Ahh, I was thinking more of something that won't get me fired. Like a movie day once a month, or an ice cream party. Maybe an extra fifteen minutes of recess?"

Rico shrugged. "That'll work."

She took down a shoebox she'd decorated with gray and red-striped fabric. "This is our idea box. You can write your reward suggestions on a slip of paper and put them in here, along with any other suggestions for making our classroom a great place. When each of you has completed and passed the required number of tests, we'll take out the reward suggestions and vote on them. Does that work for you guys? Valentina?"

The girl shrugged. "That might not be too bad."

Her first session went by quickly, and as the students shuffled off to their next classes, Monica let out a breath. She'd gotten over the first hurdle of the day.

Her second session consisted of mostly sixth graders. She gave them the respect spiel and a reading assessment quiz and they read round-robin from a collection of short stories. By lunch time she was ravenous. Retrieving her yogurt and granola bar from her lunch bag, she ate alone in the mobile, then spent the remaining twenty minutes of her break on a walk around the block. As she walked, her thoughts returned to Elsa. Today was her first day of school as well, and she hoped the child was doing all right.

Lester H. Phillips Elementary School had closed years before, and a brand new school had been built in Baxter. Touring the school the month before, Monica had been impressed. Ruth Rhodes Elementary was beautiful aesthetically and up-to-date academically. She'd registered Elsa for kindergarten, hoping the student body would be as welcoming as the building, and that her child would not feel as shut out as she had.

Her child ...

She glanced at her watch. It would be two hours before Sarah picked Elsa up from school. Three before Monica would hear about her day. How could she bear it?

•

When three o'clock finally arrived, she hurried to her car. The vague uneasiness she'd felt all day had built to an irrational sense of dread. Elsa was still such a fragile child. Had the other children been nice to her? She'd received a memo from Layla about a casual faculty get together for drinks at the bowling alley after school, and though she had vowed to be more outgoing and friendly with her co-workers this year, she turned the car toward home instead. It was the first day she and Elsa had spent apart since the night she came to the farm. She missed the girl terribly.

Walking in Sarah's house, thirty minutes later, she discovered Elsa sitting at the table, happily coloring a page in her coloring book. When she noticed Monica in the doorway, she abandoned her crayons and rushed into her arms.

"Hi, Mama!"

"Hi, pumpkin." Monica held her tight, savoring the sweet softness of her, the cotton candy scent of shampoo that lingered in her hair. She glanced up and saw Sarah grinning from the doorway.

"Looks like you survived."

"One day down, one-hundred-seventy-nine to go." She held Elsa at arm's length, her gaze searching the child's face for any clue. "Now tell me, how was your first day of school?"

"I loved it, Mommy."

"You did? I'm so glad."

All the way back to the farm, Elsa chattered about the toys she'd played with in her new classroom, the books and the finger paints, the friends she'd met, and her pretty new teacher, Mrs. Wiseman.

"Everyone was nice to you, then?"

"Uh-huh. Well, except for Cassie. She didn't really talk to me. She didn't talk to anyone. Mostly she just cried."

"Why did she cry?"

"She wanted to go home. The kids were being mean to her."

"What do you mean?"

"They called her mean names. Her feet are really dirty, and she smells funny."

"You didn't call her names, did you?"

"No."

"I want you to be nice to everyone, okay, Elsa? Especially Cassie. It sounds like she needs a friend."

"I will."

She smiled. "I know you will."

Monica felt a twinge of sadness for the little girl with the dirty feet. The outcast. She knew the long, hard road that little girl would walk. She had walked it herself for most of her life, feeling unwanted and unaccepted, until …

Feeling a familiar stab of pain, she reminded herself to count her blessings. She'd found a wonderful friend in Sarah. She had a beautiful child who called her "Mama," and a dog and a cat that adored her. That was more than a lot of people had. She pushed away the aching loneliness she'd lived with ever since Barry left. How could he be so thoroughly finished with her when she still loved him so much? She knew that in time, her heart would catch on to what her head had warned her of from the start. That love couldn't hold people in place.

Barry had left her, just like everyone else.

•

By end of the second week of school, Monica's classroom rules had been established, her boundaries had been tested and reinforced, and she was seeing the first faint glimmers of progress. Most of her students had taken at least one Accelerated Reading test. Many had passed. Except for Cruz. As her first class shuffled into the mobile on Friday morning,

Monica handed them each a copy of the chart she'd made.

"Bienvenidos! Happy Friday everyone. Have a seat and let's get started, shall we?"

When they were seated at their tables, she said," I looked over your progress reports last night. It looks like most of you have taken at least one reading quiz. Since many of you got passing grades, I'm assuming that means you actually read the books."

Some of the students snickered.

"Now, who can tell me how the last book you read changed you?"

They stared at her, their faces blank.

"No one?"

"What do you mean, changed us?" Valentina asked. "It's just a book. How can a book change a person?"

"Good question, Valentina." Encouraged, she launched into her lesson. "In my opinion, every book, article, and even cereal box, literally everything you read should change you in some way. It should make you see something in a different way, think about something you never thought of before. It should teach you how to do something you didn't know how to do, or even just learn a word you didn't know. If a book or article doesn't change you in some way, then you probably didn't read it right."

"You mean there's a wrong way to read?" Cruz said. "I don't get that."

"A lot of people don't. We read the right way by asking ourselves questions. And there are as many questions as there are books, articles and cereal boxes. So before you read, ask yourself … why am I curious about this subject? What am I hoping to learn by reading this? And then while you're reading, stop every once in a while and ask yourself questions about what you've read."

Rico yawned. "That sounds like too much work."

"Everything's work until you learn how to do it right."

She introduced the idea of thick and thin questions and explained the difference.

"This is where your charts come in. You'll see there are two columns, labeled thick and thin. From now on, I want you to start a chart for each thing you read. I want you to ask and answer at least one of each kind of question. We'll do some today, to give you an idea."

She picked up a two-paragraph article about sunflowers and read it to them.

"Okay, who's got a thin question for me? Dante, how about you?"

The boy shook his head.

"What color are sunflowers?" Dexter hollered out.

"Good." She wrote the question on the white board under "Thin Questions."

"Who else?"

The next question came from Cruz.

"How tall do they grow to be?"

"Excellent. Valentina, have you got one?"

"Not really."

"Think about it."

She sighed. "Do sunflowers grow out of seeds?"

"These are all great thin questions." She wrote the question on the board. "You'll notice that a lot of thin questions only have one answer, like Do sunflowers grow out of seeds? Some, like Dexter's, have more than one answer. What color are sunflowers? Thin questions can easily be answered by finding the answers in the story, because the answers are usually based on facts. Who's got a thick question for me?"

Her gaze swept across the table. "No one? Okay, I'll give you the first one. Why do we need sunflowers in the world?"

"We don't," Dexter said.

"Yes we do," Valentina shot back.

He scrunched up his face. "Why?"

"Because they're pretty."

"Thick questions are harder to answer," Monica continued, "because the answers are not necessarily found in the book or article. To answer a thick question, you have to have an opinion about it. In other words, you have to think."

"Oh, man," Cruz said. His classmates laughed.

Monica put a variety of magazine articles on the table and told them each to choose one to read and ask questions about. "You can work together on these, but I expect each of your questions and answers to be different."

Surprisingly, the lesson held their attention. As they worked, Monica took mental notes.

The way Valentina moved her chair too close to Rico's, and how she adjusted her shirt so that it hung much too low in the front. The way Dexter pretended to read his article, his cell phone held discreetly beneath the table. The way the two brothers, Dante and Lucas, sat at a table by themselves, whispering softly together, and the deep concentration on Cruz' face as he struggled to decipher a grade level article about a soccer player. Her heart swelled with an inexplicable burst of tenderness for these messed up, misunderstood children who up until now had fallen through the cracks. My class, she thought.

My kids.

At the end of class, she announced, "We'll be starting a read aloud book next week. That's when we'll really start to practice asking thick and thin questions. I'll give you each a pad of post it notes. I want you to jot down your questions as we read. We'll discuss the book and your questions during class. By the time we finish the book, your charts will be filled and you'll all be old pros at asking thick and thin questions."

"What do we gotta read?"

"I'm getting to that, Rico. If anyone has a book you'd like for us to read as a class, write it down and drop it in the suggestion box. Here a few I like." She set four books on the table. "But I'm open to your suggestions. Keep in mind that we're going to spend the next few weeks with whatever book is chosen. If you guys don't choose a book, then I will. And I don't want to hear any complaining, *comprende*?"

As they stuffed their books and papers in their backpacks, she said, "Cruz, can I talk to you for a minute?"

While the rest of the class filed out of the mobile, Cruz ambled up to her desk.

"Wassup?"

"I noticed you haven't taken any reading quizzes yet. Are you not doing your reading each night?"

"I haven't really had time."

"I really hate to see you fall behind on this. It's only fifteen minutes a day. You're not that busy, are you?"

His gaze crashed to the floor. "It ain't really that."

"What is it, then?"

A blush crept up his neck. "I can't take these books home, Ms. Humphrey." He pulled a book from his backpack and laid it on her desk. *Little Bear Makes a Friend*. "My father will knock me into next week if he sees me reading something like that."

She thought of his file, of the things she'd learned about his home life. He was a seventh son, a rough boy in a long, long line of rough boys. And she got it.

"Okay. We'll work it out. Could you come in here after lunch for fifteen minutes each day? Do your assigned reading then?"

"That might work. Can Rico come, too?"

"Sure, if he wants to."

He grinned "He don't want to take his baby books home, either."

"Have a good weekend, Cruz. I'll see you Monday morning."

"Yeah, have a good one, Ms. Humphrey."

As she watched him disappear across the parking lot she felt the swell of tenderness again and thought with shame of all the students throughout the years she'd carelessly labeled stubborn, lazy or defiant. She'd never understood before. She'd never even tried.

Chapter Thirty

In the second week of September, Monica found a crumpled party invitation in the bottom of Elsa's backpack. She'd been searching for the child's "take home" folder when a mermaid's crinkled face winked up at her. Curious, she retrieved it, smoothed out the wrinkles, and read the glittery blue words:

It's a Birthday Party!
Come help us celebrate
Saturday, September 12
1:00 – 3:00
27 Elm Street, Baxter, OH

"Elsa, what's this?"

"It's a birthday card. For Cassie's party."

"But this party is on Saturday. Why didn't you show this to me before?"

Elsa cast her eyes to the floor. "I don't know."

Monica regarded her thoughtfully. "Don't you want to go?"

"I want to, but I can't."

"Of course you can go. We'll just have to run out and get a gift quickly, like tomorrow. And I'll have to call Cassie's mother. I wish I'd known about it a little sooner."

"I've never went to a birthday party before." A tear rolled down Elsa's cheek and she bit her lip.

Monica dropped to the child's level and studied her face. "What's wrong?"

Her lips quivered. "Adelyn and Amelia said if I go to Cassie's party I can't be their friend anymore."

The confession slammed into Monica like a fist. Mean

girls. Was it really starting this early, in kindergarten? Taking a breath to control her anger, she pulled Elsa close to her. "Sweetie, listen to me. I know it's hard to understand, and I know you want to make your friends happy, but what they've told you, and what they're doing to Cassie, it's wrong. It's mean. Do you understand that?"

"Yeah."

"Just think how sad Cassie would feel if no one showed up for her party. Think how sad you would feel if we had a party and no one came."

Elsa's lip quivered again. "That would make me really sad, Mommy."

Monica smoothed a lock of hair behind Elsa's ear. "Those other girls, they are going to miss out on a lot of good things in life, but that doesn't mean you have to, right?"

Elsa wrapped her arms around Monica's neck and hugged her tight and Monica savored the sweetness of her.

"Mommy?"

"What, love?"

"Could we go and get Cassie's present today?"

She thought fleetingly of the dishes in the sink, the papers waiting to be graded. All of that could wait. She was teaching her child how to be kind.

"You bet we can."

In the toy aisle at the Gold Mart an hour later, Elsa considered her choices.

"Pick out something you would like to get if it was your birthday," Monica advised.

"Oh, this!" Elsa plucked a mermaid doll from the shelf, her eyes caressing the doll's long golden hair and sequined tail.

"I think that's a very good choice. She's beautiful."

At the end of the aisle, Elsa spied a package of three ponies with pastel manes and tails. "Oh, but I'd like this, too." She bit her lip, deciding.

"Why don't we get them both?" Monica said, placing the items in her cart.

She let Elsa select a roll of wrapping paper, pink with purple mermaids and starfish. She added two packages of curly ribbons in shimmering colors and hoped the pretty presents would make up for the ones the little girl on Elm Street was probably dreaming of, and probably would not receive.

Her anger flared again as she thought about the meanness, how early it started. Her heart broke for the outcasts, like Cassie and herself. And like Valentina.

The girl had come to her after the second week of school, all hair gel and black boots and attitude. "I want to do like Cruz and Rico and eat lunch in here," she announced.

"You're welcome to eat in here, Valentina." She hesitated. It would have been hard not to notice the way Valentina's flirty gaze continually slid to Rico. To not hear the not-so-subtle invitations the girl extended to him. "Any of the students in my class are more than welcome to join us for lunch and reading time. But this is a no flirting zone, all right? I expect you to use the time wisely."

She tossed her long, dark mane. "I get that, Ms. Humphrey."

"You're actually doing well, Valentina. You're closer to meeting your reading goal for the quarter than anyone."

"Yeah, I know. I just don't want to be in the cafeteria. The kids are jerks."

She added the last words with lowered eyes, and Monica got it. Despite her tough veneer, Valentina was as fragile as butterfly wings. In the mobile, the kids all stood on equal ground. They could be themselves without fear of being shunned because of their street address or the color of their skin. The small, hot, stuffy mobile was a haven, a safety zone where they didn't have to pay for the sins of their parents.

After she'd tucked Elsa into bed, she wrapped the presents and took a moment to admire them. Public school was a war zone. She'd learned that many years ago. She could not change it, but maybe she could change it for one child. Or two. She smiled. Or maybe seven.

•

After her last class on Friday Monica stopped in the office to check her mailbox. Due to her neglect, she found it overflowing with memos. She sorted through them, discarding some and placing others in a tidy stack.

"Hello, Monica."

She glanced up to see Brad Holmes watching her from the doorway.

"Hi, Brad."

"I didn't think you worked here anymore." He grinned. "Banished to the mobile, eh?"

She shrugged. "It's not so bad."

"I hear you've got Tommy Cruz coming in to read on his lunch break. So tell me, what's your superpower?"

I care, she thought.

"I'm bribing them with ice cream and extra recess."

"You really look great." His gaze slid over her inch by inch. "Hey, so some of us are going out for a beer, later. Like to go?"

"I can't. I have to get home."

He flashed his sexy grin. "Aww, come on. What's an hour?"

"It's sixty minutes my little girl waits for me at daycare."

His surprise registered. "I didn't know you had a daughter."

The word went through her, thrilled her. She smiled. "Well, now you do."

He folded his arms across his chest and regarded her. "Monica Humphrey, you're a woman of secrets. Sometime soon we're going to have that beer. I'd like to learn some of them."

Driving home, she wondered how it was possible that Bradley Holmes had tried to hit on her and she felt nothing. She'd been attracted to the dark-haired, thirty-something math teacher from the first day he was hired, had admired him from afar, secretly wishing he would ask her out, knowing he never would. A year ago the conversation they'd just had would have put her over the moon. Today, all she felt was the desire to be away from his probing eyes, his open admiration that had nothing whatsoever to do with who she really was.

•

On Saturday morning Sarah coaxed Elsa's unruly curls into a French braid. Agnes kept watch from her blanket in the corner while Ginger batted a hair tie around the kitchen.

"You're going to have so much fun!" Sarah chirped. "Games

and cake and ice cream. I love birthday parties. I want to hear every single detail later. Don't leave a single thing out, all right?"

"Okay."

At twelve forty-five Monica and Elsa set out. The sun shined bright in a cloudless September sky, adding to their feeling of festivity as they drove through town.

"Do you think Cassie will like her presents, Mommy?"

"I'm sure she'll love them."

"And do you think there will be chocolate cake, and games with prizes?"

"I think you're going to have a lovely time, no matter what kind of cake Cassie serves."

Twenty-seven Elm Street was in an alley that dog-legged off of Center Street—the third in a lineup of ramshackle row houses Monica never even knew existed. She slowed the car, her happiness evaporating when she saw the colorful balloons tethered to a rickety porch, where three young men sat, smoking cigarettes. Her first impulse was to quickly drive past, pretend she couldn't find the address. She couldn't possibly leave her child in that horrid place.

In the seconds it took her to decide, Elsa spotted the balloons. "There it is! Cassie said there would be balloons."

Reluctantly, Monica parked the car, retrieved the birthday presents from the back seat, and propelled Elsa up the porch steps.

One of the smokers, a twenty something man with a brown ponytail, exhaled a stream of smoke. He smiled widely.

"You here for the party?"

She forced a smile. "Yes, that's right."

"Go on inside, you're the first ones here."

The front door opened into a small, cramped living room, where folding chairs had been lined up along the wall. Her glance flicked over the purple and pink streamers that hung from the ceiling, intermingled with years old cobwebs. She fought the urge to cover her nose against the stench; a combination of mildew and fried onions.

A woman appeared, Cassie's mother, Monica assumed, not much more than a girl, herself. "Hi, are you Elsa?"

Elsa nodded.

"And you're her mother?"

Monica attempted another smile. "I'm Monica. It's nice to meet you."

"I'm Gabbie, Cassie's mom." She walked to a staircase and hollered up for her daughter, then returned to them. "Thanks for coming. You're the only one who RSVP'd, so I'm not sure how many will be here. We invited ten."

"Do you need any help? I'd be glad to stay."

"Oh. Well I actually wasn't planning on the parents staying. I don't have much room here, and my mother and sister are here to help, so …"

"Oh. Okay."

She heard the soft sound of footsteps on the stairs. Moments later, Cassie appeared, a bedraggled child in a pink tee shirt and bare feet, a tangle of red hair falling across her shoulder in a Frozen braid gone terribly wrong.

"Hi, Elsa."

"Hi, Cassie."

"Happy Birthday, Cassie," Monica said.

"Thanks." She eyed the presents longingly and Monica set them on the coffee table where ten little party bags waited cheerfully. She knew with a sad certainty that nine of them would not be opened. As much as she did not want to leave Elsa there alone, there was clearly no way around it. She planted a kiss on Elsa's forehead.

"Have fun, pumpkin. I'll see you at three o'clock, okay?"

"Okay."

With nothing left to do, she turned and forced herself to walk out the door.

She'd intended to spend the time at home, writing lesson plans, but knew now she would not be able to concentrate. She pulled from the alley and circled around to an adjacent parking lot, where she could see the row house without being noticed.

At one-fifteen, she called Sarah.

"Hey."

"Hey, what's up? Did you find the party okay?"

"I sure did."

"And …?"

"Oh Sarah, the place is horrible. The house looks like it's about to cave in."

"Uh oh."

"And it's filthy inside. I could just cry. The poor mother hung up balloons and streamers, but it obviously didn't occur to her to sweep the carpet or knock down the cob webs. Or empty the litter box. I hope to God the cake is store bought and not baked in that kitchen."

"Come over. We'll have coffee."

"I should, but …" She fought tears. "I can't. I need to be where I can see the house."

"Why?"

"It's a horrible neighborhood with no yard. What if they decide to go out and play in the street?"

"Oh, I'm sure they won't do that."

"I'm sorry. I'm being silly."

"No you're not. You're being a mother."

Fifteen minutes later, Sarah showed up with two steaming cups of coffee. Climbing in the passenger seat of Monica's car, she handed her one of the cups.

"What are you doing here?"

"I came to worry with you. So which house is it? Wait, let me guess." She squinted across the lot. "Not that blue one?"

"Afraid so."

"Oh, Lord. Motherhood is so hard sometimes."

They drank coffee. And they talked. The young men came back out on the porch to smoke. They went back inside. A patrol car cruised down the alley. And minute by agonizing minute, the two hours passed. At two fifty-five, Sarah hugged her and drove away and Monica returned to the house on Elm Street.

Gabbie opened to her knock. "Come on in, gosh, is it three already? The girls are up in Cassie's room. Hey, thanks for the great gifts. She loved them."

"It was our pleasure."

She called up the stairs, then turned back to Monica. "Thanks for bringing Elsa. Cassie hasn't made many friends in school yet. It makes it hard."

"Thanks for inviting her. This was her first party and she was so excited to come."

"If you wanted to bring Elsa to come and play sometimes, that would be great."

"Oh, well … we'll have to arrange that."

Before Gabbie could pursue the conversation further, Elsa and Cassie bounded down the stairs.

"Hi, pumpkin."

"Hi, Mommy." Monica gathered the child up in her arms and wished she could keep her there, safe from the world and all of its dangers, forever.

"Are you ready to go?"

"Yep. Bye, Cassie. Bye, Gabbie."

Out in the car, Elsa couldn't stop talking about the party.

"So did you get your chocolate cake?" Monica asked.

"Chocolate cupcakes. From the bakery. And ice cream. And I broke the piñata, and I got prizes!"

"How nice. Were there a lot of kids there?"

"No, just me. And Cassie's aunts and uncles. They got prizes too. And we played pin the stem on the pumpkin."

"It sounds like a fun day."

"It was. Cassie loved her presents, Mommy."

"I'm glad you went. I'm sure that made Cassie really happy."

"When is my birthday going to be?"

"In February."

"Maybe I'll have a party too."

"Of course you'll have a party."

Her brow furrowed. "Amelia and Emily might not come. But I can invite Cassie."

"You can invite Cassie. And Jace and Justin and Sarah." She paused. "Elsa, if those girls give you any trouble about going to Cassie's party, you can tell them Mommy made you go."

"No. I'm going to tell them I wanted to go. Cassie is my BFF now."

Monica smiled. In a month, Cassie's party would be forgotten. But she hoped the lesson learned today would stay with the child forever. Sarah was right. Motherhood was hard. It was going to stretch her, to require everything she had, and more. To make the right choices. To lead by example when the right way was the hard way. To fit all of the pieces together into a mosaic when she was still so broken, herself. But she hoped, at the end of the journey, she could stand back and look at the whole picture and see a sequined mermaid and three pastel ponies, fitted together with kindness, and know they were part of a masterpiece.

Chapter Thirty-One

$\mathscr{S}$unday was Elsa and Monica's day to bake.

On Sunday afternoons, they changed out of their church dresses, donned aprons, and scoured Penny's old cook books in search of delicious and unusual after-school snacks to take to Sarah's house for the week ahead. On the second Sunday after the birthday party, they were joined by Cassie. The night before, Elsa's friend had seemed mystified when Monica bathed her and Elsa, surprised that baths were an everyday occurrence in Elsa's world. On Sunday afternoon, as the two girls pored over mouth-watering photos of cakes, cookies and pies, Cassie seemed doubly astonished.

"You mean you make these things right here? In your own house?"

"Of course. Haven't you ever baked cookies before, Cassie?"

"No. I thought cookies came from the store."

With a twinge of sadness, Monica thought how blessed she'd been, growing up in this kitchen at Penny's side. She'd learned how to bake and how to put together a fabulous meal, but more than that, by following the girls' example, she'd learned how to be a good human being.

"Well, you're partly right. Sometimes they do come from the store. But Elsa and I like to make our own."

"It's more funner!" Elsa chirped.

"More fun," Monica corrected.

After much consideration, Cassie decided on fudge nut brownies. Monica stood back, allowing Elsa to instruct Cassie on the arts of sifting and mixing and cracking eggs. As their giggles and the scent of warm chocolate filled the kitchen, an idea came to Monica and she tucked it away to think about later.

•

On Monday morning she got to work early and checked the master schedule. After she'd compared it with her own schedule, she put in a call to Layla, asking if she could meet with her later that afternoon.

"I have a few minutes at two o'clock," Layla said, a definite edge to her tone.

"Great. A few minutes are all I need," Monica said.

When she arrived in Layla's office, later that day, her supervisor was definitely on her guard, no doubt supposing Monica was there to complain about her new position.

"So, Monica. What's on your mind?"

"I wanted to talk to you about an idea I have."

The other woman's demeanor relaxed slightly. "Okay."

"I went over the master schedule earlier and I noticed that Family and Consumer Science is only on the schedule three days a week this year."

"Right. Cutbacks, you know?"

"It looks like the FACS room is available on Tuesday mornings. I'd like to use it."

"We could probably arrange that. What do you have in mind?"

"I want to teach my seventh graders how to bake."

Her eyebrows shot up. "You're a reading teacher. You're going to teach them to bake cookies?"

"If things go the way I'm hoping they will, I'm going to teach them the value of learning how to read and follow written directions. Starting with a cookbook."

Layla regarded Monica for a long moment, her fingers steepled in front of her.

"I like it," she finally said. "In fact, I love it."

Monica smiled. "This is just the first of what I hope will be many experiments. I'm looking for ways to make reading seem relevant to them. Ways to incorporate it into their everyday lives."

"It's a fabulous idea." Layla retrieved a pen and a sticky note. "When would you like to start this experiment of yours?"

"Tomorrow."

•

For their first lesson, Monica chose a simple oatmeal cookie recipe. As her class trooped into the FACS room, she handed them each an apron and a printed recipe card.

"So, like, what are we doing?" Rico asked.

"We're making cookies," Monica told him. "But first, we're washing our hands."

With their hands washed, she split them into two groups, putting Valentina with Dante and Lucas. Cruz, Dexter and Rico made up the second group. Laughing, they put on their aprons.

"You'll see a list of ingredients on your recipe cards. You'll find everything you need on the table there. You may start now."

They moved to the table she'd set up earlier that morning with rolled oats, flour, and sugar. She'd included several dummy ingredients, and winced when Dante carried a container of celery salt back to his station.

"Dude, we don't need that," Valentina told him. "Pay attention. She's trying to trick us."

"I don't see no soda," Cruz exclaimed. "Ms. Humphrey, you didn't get everything."

"Everything's there, you just have to check the labels."

"Oh, wait." He picked up a can of baking soda and studied it. "Is this it?"

"That's the one."

"This don't look like any kind of soda I ever seen," he grumbled.

With the first test passed, Monica hid a smile.

She watched as they fumbled their way through the baking process, laughing together, helping each other. As she'd expected, Rico's group took shortcuts. She smiled again, seeing a teachable moment on the horizon. With their cookies baking in the ovens, the students got busy cleaning up the kitchen.

When the timers went off, Valentina removed four trays of golden brown, perfectly shaped cookies from her oven.

The other group's looked like bumpy white rocks.

"Brah, these are a mess," Cruz said, eyeing his cookies.

"We can't eat these," Dexter agreed. "They feel like concrete. What'd we do wrong, Ms. Humphrey?"

"Looks like you used either too much of something, or too little. Did you measure your ingredients?"

He shrugged. "Mostly."

"This is exactly why it's important to know how to read and follow directions. If you don't …" She flipped a hand toward the ruined cookies.

Dexter sighed. "Yeah, I get that. Now."

"No worries," Valentina told him. "We've got lots. We'll share."

•

The following Tuesday they advanced to a more adventurous experiment—macaroni and cheese, and a chocolate cake.

"If you read and follow the directions without taking shortcuts, you'll have yourselves a nice, homemade lunch this afternoon," Monica told them.

She stood back to observe, noting the way Rico painstakingly measured each of his ingredients this time. But what struck her most was the ease with which Valentina moved around the kitchen—shredding cheese, stirring cream sauce, tasting, adding a pinch of this, a dash of that. Like Penny, she made cooking look like art.

"You have a real flair for cooking," Monica told her. "My aunt was that way, too."

"Thanks." The girl's smile was genuine. "I don't know why, I just feel comfortable doing this."

"You're a natural."

"I've never felt like I was good at nothing before."

"You have a natural talent, that's obvious. With practice, you could be an amazing cook."

"You think?"

"I do."

With the dishes washed and the kitchen tidied, the students headed to their next classes while Monica packed up the food to take back to the mobile.

At lunch time, they dug in with gusto. "This ain't half bad, Valentina," Rico said, around a mouthful of macaroni and cheese.

"Brah, it's like … amazing," Cruz corrected. He turned to Valentina. "If you could make this every day, I might even want to marry you."

"Oh, in your dreams," she shot back, but Monica could see how much the praise pleased her.

With lunch over, Valentina lingered.

"Ms. Humphrey, you really think I could be an amazing cook some day?"

"Absolutely."

"'Cause I been thinking maybe after I graduate from school I could work in a restaurant. Maybe someday I'll even open my own."

Monica smiled. "Maybe you will."

•

By the second week in October her students were making Manicotti, the unseasonably warm weather had cooled, and autumn had arrived at the farm in a fragrant burst of chilly, apple-scented air and cascades of falling leaves.

On Saturday afternoon Monica, Elsa and Cassie raked the leaves from the enormous sugar maple in the front yard into a pile, and busily stuffed them into a pair of patched overalls and a red and orange flannel shirt.

"He's gonna be the best Punkinman ever!" Elsa exclaimed.

"The best ever!" Cassie echoed. "But who is Punkinman, anyway? Is he like Spiderman?"

"Sorta, but he doesn't have a superpower."

"Then what good is he? He doesn't even have a head."

"Tomorrow after church we're gonna go to Radcliffe Farms and pick him out a punkin head. Then we're gonna carve him a face. I already know how I want him to look…"

Their chatter was interrupted by Agnes' joyful barking.

She charged to the end of the driveway, where the mail Jeep was pulling in. Rather than stopping at the mailbox, the mail carrier, Janice Hale, pulled the Jeep to the end of the driveway and tossed Agnes a biscuit. The dog threw his treat into the air, then caught it up and trotted back to the shade of the Maple tree to eat it.

"Beautiful day," Janice said, climbing from her Jeep.

"They don't get much prettier than this," Monica agreed.

"I've got a certified letter here for you," Janice said. Retrieving one of the envelopes from her stack, she tore off the green and white flap and handed it to Monica to sign.

Monica reached for the letter, her heart skipping as she saw the return address.

State of Ohio

Boone County Courts

Her breath cut through her lungs like a knife as she signed her name. She'd known the court date was approaching. She'd received a request for documents, had sent them weeks ago. And though she'd been assured that transferring her guardianship status to Ohio was merely a formality, a shadow of fear had been her constant companion, these last few weeks.

"Have a nice day, now," Janice, said, but Monica was already walking away, clutching the envelope in her hand. On the porch, hands trembling, she pulled in a breath and tore it open.

She scanned the documents, blinking in surprise.

Notice of Guardianship — State of Ohio.

She stared at the pages, tears streaming from her eyes, then clasped them to her heart.

It was over.

Quietly, with a stroke of judge's pen, for better or for worse, she had officially become Elsa's legal guardian.

She went inside the house, carrying the letter like it was precious gold.

It was over.

The future was beginning.

"What's wrong, Mommy? Aren't you gonna help us finish the Punkinman?"

She palmed her tears from her face, dropped to a squat and

pulled her child to her. Her child.

"You and Cassie keep working on him, okay? Make him nice and fat. I'll be out to help in a few minutes."

With the girls happily back at work on the leaf man, Monica phoned Sarah to tell her the good news.

"So wait … there's no court appearance? He just signed the document?"

"Looks like."

"Monica, that's wonderful! We'll have to pick an evening this week to go out and celebrate. We'll take you both out to dinner. Anywhere you want to go. Can you believe it? I'm officially a kind of aunt!"

Monica's tears started again. "And I'm officially a kind of a mother."

After she hung up with Sarah, she carried the letter upstairs to her room and put it in her file cabinet, then closed and locked the drawer. Back in the kitchen, she poured a glass of water from the tap. Glancing out the window, she saw the two girls kneeling beside the overgrown garden, Pumpkin Man forgotten beneath the maple tree. Elsa held something in her cupped hands, and both girls were studying it intently. Curious, Monica walked outside.

Elsa jumped to her feet and streaked across the yard. "I've got something for you, Mommy," she said, bounding up the steps. "Look, we found a star!"

Monica's breath caught at the sight of the lily blossom, deep crimson with a gold star in its center. And a memory flooded over her …

•

It was May and the town's Spring Festival was just two weeks away. The choir director at her church had recommended Monica for a solo in the spring pageant. After a gut wrenching audition, the pageant director had narrowed it down to three soloists. The panel had voted. Monica had won the honor. And she was scared to death. Her hands trembled as she read the acceptance letter.

"What is it, Monica? What's wrong?" Penny hurried to her,

took the letter from her hands, and read it. A smile broke out on her face.

"But this is wonderful! Out of all the applicants, they chose you!" She threw her arms around Monica in a bear hug, then held her at arm's length and studied her.

"How come you don't look happy?"

"The whole town will be there, Penny. What if I mess it up? What if everyone laughs at me?"

"Come here." Penny propelled her outside, to the garden. She dropped to her knees and pointed to a crimson bloom on one of her daylilies. "Do you see this blossom? This is a Scarlet Lady. She's perfect and beautiful." She pinched it from the plant and handed it to Monica. "Each blossom only lasts for one day ... but oh, what a day! While it blossoms, it brings people color and scent and joy. Beauty, Monica. So much beauty."

She paused as Monica stroked the silky petals.

"Our lives are like these lily blossoms. Short, but glorious. Don't be afraid to share your gift with the world, Monica. Don't be afraid to make every moment beautiful ..."

•

"Elsa, where did you get this?"

"We found it in the garden."

In October? She took the child's hand. "Show me."

They walked together to the neglected garden. At the edge, Elsa parted the overgrown weeds to reveal Penny's beloved Scarlet Lady lilies flowering among the Timothy grass and the ragweed.

Monica cried out softly. How was it possible? The plant had to be a decade old, untended and unfertilized since Penny's death. And yet, here it was, blooming on this, of all days.

Once again, she fought tears. Her head told her it was a freak coincidence and nothing more. But her swelling heart knew. It was a sign from the girls. A sign that she'd done the right thing, the beautiful thing, and that they were pleased.

That evening, when the house was quiet, she stroked the lily's velvety petals one last time, before she pressed it between two sheets of waxed paper and tucked in inside Geneva's journal.

Chapter Thirty-Two

June 8, 1969

*P*enny got into a fight with another girl at summer school today. The reason isn't clear, much as I tried, I could not get an answer out of her, but I suspect the altercation was over a boy. Lord, help me through these teenage years of hers. They are difficult with the best of girls. But Penny … Penny is such a high-strung child, a tumultuous child, her moods as changeable as the summer skies. As always, after the upset, she went straight to her garden.

What was Mother's garden is now Penny's. The plot of land has always been her salvation. It calms her, somehow. It stabilizes her. She finds so much joy in growing her flowers and her vegetables, and for that, I am deeply thankful.

The produce stand continues to thrive. People have begun to place orders for our pastries. Some weeks we can hardly fill them all. Women drive clear from Risingville to buy Penny's bouquets for their parties. The tomatoes and cucumbers and things she coaxes from the ground are often spoken for before they are grown. Our sourdough bread and our homemade preserves have become something of a local legend. Who would have dreamed it?

I've decided I am going to open a little store. The outbuilding at the end of the driveway is still in fairly good shape. The work needed to update it would be minimal. We will start small, open it on weekends and see how it goes, and proceed from there.

In the long-term, I'm afraid Penny is much too unpredictable to hold a job. She is by turns explosive, and melancholy. I cannot see her being successful working as a bank teller, or a school teacher, or even as a housekeeper.

There are days when the child is so sorrowful she can barely get out of bed. A little general store might be the answer to my prayers. Penny is thrilled at the thought of it. Of course, she has no idea the work it will involve. Still, I think, with proper planning, we could make a go of it, Penny and me. Two small gals with a big dream.

I've made an appointment to speak with our accountant in the morning. I will take some of the trust money that was given to me and we will open a store.

We will build a legacy.

Chapter Thirty-Three

$\mathcal{O}$n the last Monday in October, Monica arrived at work early. Her students had mastered all of the cooking projects she'd assigned them, and she was ready for them to move on to a new challenge. She'd found some simple woodworking patterns online and was anxious to show them to Miriam Connelly, the FACS teacher, and get her thoughts.

Together, they selected a beginner's skill bird feeder pattern. Miriam had agreed to come in the next week and give the students a tutorial on using the tools. Having taught basic woodcrafts as part of the Consumer Science program for nearly twenty years without a single mishap, she assured Monica her students would do just fine.

With a half-hour before the start of the school day, she stopped in the office to check her mailbox. As usual, it overflowed.

"So a little birdie told me you're going to introduce the Sensational Six to woodworking."

She looked up to see Brad watching her from the doorway.

"Word travels fast."

"Lucas and Dante using power tools." He winced. "You're a brave lady."

"I'm sure it will be fine."

"Hey, some of us are getting together to watch the game at Mick's on Sunday. I wanted to personally invite you, if you can get a babysitter."

Mick's Sixth Avenue Sports Bar was a popular hangout among the Risingville staff. She'd been there once, in her first year at the school, and had never wanted to go back. She was searching for a polite way to turn down Brad's offer when she felt her phone vibrating in her purse.

Immediately, her thoughts flew to Elsa, imagining concussions, broken arms, and worse. She supposed the constant worry went along with being the guardian of a small child, although the girls had worried about her even when she was in college. She could not imagine a time when she would not worry about Elsa.

"I don't know. Let me think about it, okay?"

Gathering her mail, she brushed past him.

"Okay." He grinned. "But just be prepared, I'm going to ask you again tomorrow."

She fled the office with a wave over her shoulder. Outside, she fumbled her phone out of her purse and shot a hurried glanced at the screen.

Missed call from Barry.

She stood, stunned, clutching the phone. It was as if she'd shifted gears while speeding down the highway at seventy miles per hour. She was wrecked. Immobilized. Incapacitated. Slowly, she slid the phone back in her purse and walked to the mobile.

Her morning class filed into the room, laughing and jostling, a kaleidoscope of bright clothing and off-color jokes. For once, she did not correct them. As she discussed adjectives and pronouns, she noticed Rico sneaking a game on his iPad under the table and she did not call him out. The class took turns reading from *Of Mice and Men.* They asked what she supposed were excellent questions, and she answered them. But when they'd moved on to their next classes, she could not remember a word she'd said.

Missed call from Barry …

Anxiety raged in her stomach all afternoon. Beyond the sick churning, she could not identify exactly what she felt. The pain of losing him had dulled in the past few weeks, and was no longer the sharp, jagged ache it had been before. She was not sure what it was now, was not sure how to feel. And so she waited.

After school she worked with Elsa on her letters and colors. She prepared a dinner of baked chicken and rice. She bathed

Elsa and read her a story and tucked her into bed. She drank a glass of wine. And later, when she felt calm and Elsa was safely off to sleep, Agnes curled up at her feet, she returned Barry's call.

"Monica, hello!"

His voice was like soothing honey pouring over the chapped places in her heart.

"Hello, Barry. I noticed I missed a call from you earlier."

"You did. Thanks for calling me back. How are you?"

"I'm good, actually."

"Great."

A bottomless silence fell between them, and she waited.

"Hey, the thing is, I'm going to be in town over the weekend. I was hoping we could have a cappuccino together, for old time's sake?"

"I'd like that," she said.

But if that was true, why did she feel so much anger, so much dread?

"Great. So how about I meet you in the park Saturday? Say two o'clock?"

"I'll look forward to it."

As she hung up the phone, she wasn't at all sure she'd told him the truth.

•

Five days had never passed so slowly.

Monica went through the motions in her classroom, detached and unable to concentrate, her emotions swinging like a pendulum. Elation. Surely Barry wanted to reconcile. What else could he want? She would be reclaiming her partner, her friend, her love.

But at home in the evenings she was acutely aware of the routines that she and Elsa moved through: schoolwork, dinner, bath, story, bedtime, and waves of anxiety rolled in her stomach. What would it be like to have Barry here to share in Elsa's upbringing? And would it be fair to Elsa, introducing a man into the equation so soon? Did Barry even want that?

But he must. What else could he want after all these weeks?

And then her anger flared again. Barry hadn't wanted any part of the child, he'd said as much. She honestly didn't know whether she could get past that.

On Thursday when she picked Elsa up after school, Sarah extended her usual invitation for coffee. This time, Monica accepted. She settled herself at Sarah's table and accepted the steaming mug she offered. She added cream and sweetener, stirred slowly.

"Sarah, can you watch Elsa for a couple hours on Saturday?"

"Of course. What's up?"

She pulled in a breath, let it go. "I'm having coffee with Barry."

Sarah's coffee cup stopped midway to her lips. "You're kidding."

"He called me on Monday."

"Wow."

"I don't know how I feel about seeing him again. I'm a mess."

"I knew something was bothering you. You haven't been yourself at all the last couple of days."

"I'm torn between wanting to see him and wanting to tear his head off." She took a swallow of coffee. "What do I even wear?"

"You wear a pair of black leggings and a sweater. The pale violet one that brings out the blue in your eyes. And your black boots."

"I don't want to seem …"

"You won't." Sarah's cup found its way to her lips and she took a sip. "Besides, you can't help it if you're beautiful."

Monica laughed softly. "I'm not beautiful. I'm a mess."

"What do you think he wants?"

"I wish I knew."

"I wonder if he wants to get back together."

"I don't know."

"If he does want you to take him back … will you?"

She sighed. "I don't know, Sarah. A part of me still loves him. Very much. Another part of me hates him."

"That's normal, considering … But don't be too quick to take him back. Don't make it too easy for him." She took another swallow of coffee. "Just saying."

•

On Saturday Monica drove to Risingville, certain of only one thing. Her life was about to change. One way or another, this day would end and she would be different because of it.

Like a late autumn gift, the day was sunny and mild. The trees lifted bare branches to the brilliant blue sky and a scattering of surviving wildflowers bloomed beside the highway in a dazzling display of purple and gold. She took note of everything, memorizing the moment, knowing that when she passed this way again, everything would be different. All of the questions that had tortured her for weeks would be answered.

Was she ready for the truth?

Barry was already in the park when she arrived. His lone car sat beneath the maple tree she'd once thought of as theirs. Hands trembling on the wheel, she pulled into the spot beside him. A cluster of windswept leaves fluttered around him as he stepped from his car. Her breath caught. He was just an ordinary man in a navy blue windbreaker and a baseball cap, and yet ...

He grinned at her, and the familiarity of him melted her insides.

"Monica." He folded her into his arms in a brief hug, then stood back to look at her. "Thanks so much for coming. Wow, you sure look good."

"So do you."

"Let me get the coffees. Is it too chilly to sit at the table?"

Not waiting for an answer, he reached into his car and retrieved two cups of cappuccino. They took their paces at the table, and he pulled back the tabs on the coffees and handed her one. "I fixed it just the way you like it," he said, grinning again.

She'd spoken thousands of silent words to him that week, but just then, "Thank you," was all she could think to say.

"So. You look like you've lost all the weight you wanted to, huh?"

"I still have a ways to go." She shrugged. "Or not."

According to the doctor's charts, she was still almost fifty pounds away from her ideal weight. But she was in no hurry to get there. She was comfortable with herself, disciplined enough to allow little splurges now and then without falling back into her old binging habits. She no longer needed food to fill the void inside her. She had Elsa and Sarah and fourteen wonderful students in a stuffy, rundown mobile classroom.

She no longer had a void.

"How's the job going?" she asked.

"Good. Real good." He stirred his coffee, then set the plastic stir stick on the table. "I'm assuming you're still at the middle school?"

"Yes. For now, anyway."

An awkward silence fell between them, growing as they sipped their drinks, both avoiding what needed to be said. Finally Barry reached across the table for her hand.

"Monica, I want ... I need to ask your forgiveness."

With the words the pressure between them was relieved. She felt like she could breathe again. But still, she remained silent.

"I'm not comfortable with the way we left things. Or the feeling that there's something bad between us. I was selfish, and I'll admit it, jealous. Of a five-year-old. I'm not proud of that."

Sarah's words came back to her. *Don't make it too easy for him* ...

But still, she met him halfway.

"I was partly to blame. I should have been honest with you about what was happening. It was wrong of me to spring it on you after the fact. But I do accept your apology."

"Thank you." He released her hand. "It's haunted me, knowing that I hurt you. The feeling that I'd made an enemy. Especially of someone so dear to me. I couldn't move forward with that on my conscience."

Move forward? She pulled in a breath.

"I'm fine, Barry, I really am. And we're fine. I hope you know how much I appreciate all you did for me after the accident. You helped me more than you could know."

"It means a lot to hear you say that."

She played with her Styrofoam cup. "It's funny, at the time I felt like it was the worst thing that could have happened to me. The whole ordeal with my jaw and wrist, the hospital ... and it became the catalyst for the best thing."

He smiled. "How so?"

"It forced me to change. I don't think I ever would have otherwise. I'd be sitting alone in my house watching TV and getting bigger by the day. I have a beautiful life now, a life I love." She added softly, "I have Elsa."

"The little girl. How is she?"

"She's wonderful. She's come so far in such a short amount of time."

"I'm glad to hear that." He took another swallow of coffee, gazed out at the park beyond her. "In a way, this experience was a catalyst for me too. It made me change. It made me move out of a city where I've always felt judged, stymied. My life is better, away from here. I no longer feel I have to look over my shoulder, pay for mistakes I've already paid for a hundred times over. I feel ... I don't know. Free."

Suddenly, it dawned on her that this was not about reconciling—not in the way she'd thought it would be. It was about something else entirely. The knowing gripped her, and she braced herself.

"I'm getting married, Monica."

Shock waves slammed through her and she felt something shift deep inside. She was stunned and deeply saddened, but somehow, not devastated.

"You are?"

"I know it's soon. Probably too soon, but, honestly, nothing's ever felt more right."

"Tell me."

"I met her at the church I've been going to. Her name is Randi. She's a little younger than me, twenty-seven to be exact. She's cute and petite, and she has this unbelievable mop of brown, curly hair."

He laughed softly and she forced a smile.

"She's had it rough. Life dealt her a tough hand and she coped with it by using prescription drugs and alcohol. But she's seven months clean and sober as of last week. She's stronger than she thinks she is. And she has the kind of faith that could move a semi."

He retrieved his phone from his pocket, flipped through his pictures, and proudly showed her Randi's photo. The young woman with the frizzy curls and shy smile looked anything but strong to Monica. And all at once she understood.

"I'm happy for you, Barry."

"Thank you. I'm glad to hear you say that."

She stood, walked to his side of the table, and kissed his cheek. "Thank you for telling me. I hope you and Randi have a great life."

And then she walked away.

•

She'd been right earlier. She drove back home, different than when she'd left. She wiped away a last stray tear of sadness for what might have been. She'd come to the park fully expecting to leave with an engagement ring on her finger. She should have been crushed. Instead she was relieved. She studied the feeling from every angle, trying to understand it.

Barry was the kind of man who needed someone to fix. She was not that person any longer. She was well and strong, able to stand on her own. She had been for quite some time, she just hadn't known it. But Barry had. And once he'd recognized that, the relationship no longer worked for him.

Barry had been a lifeboat in the raging sea of her life. But as she'd slowly kept swimming, slowly grown stronger, she'd begun to resent his smothering help. For a time, she'd thought she needed him, had confused that need with love. But she didn't need a man in order to be complete. Geneva had raised a child alone, and so could Monica.

•

She was anxious to retrieve Elsa, hold her close to her heart and savor her. But as she entered Baxter Township, the store drew her like a magnet. Parking the car out front, she took a long, hard look at it. The wide porch, the oversized window, the sign above the door, faded but still visible. *Two Gals General Store.*

The girls' legacy.

Stepping inside, she experienced it all again. Penny's infectious laughter, her copper hair glinting in the sun as she flirted with the customers.

Geneva sitting at a desk in the corner, glasses perched on the end of her nose, head bent over her bookwork.

Customers eagerly buying up their home baked breads and snickerdoodles.

She saw herself, a young girl placing jars of apple butter and peach preserves so carefully on the shelves. Her store. Hers and Penny's and Geneva's.

And she saw something else. And she knew with a certainty that Barry had been wrong.

The empty spaces in the kitchen out back. Not pizza ovens. Confection ovens.

The large open space out front. Not pub tables. Display cabinets for baked goods, flower arrangements, produce and preserves.

The empty walls. Not exposed brick, but Sarah's lovely paintings. And shelves filled with handcrafts from local artisans.

She saw it clearly, and her excitement grew. Next spring they would till up the garden, plant strawberries, melons and tomatoes. They would plant rows of zinnias and sunflowers. They would serve simple lunches, homemade soups and sandwiches. Perhaps she could arrange a work study program for Valentina. Perhaps there were other kids who needed the store too.

She would reopen Two Gals, make it as it had been, only better.

A long while later she locked the door and stood on the porch, drinking in the gently rolling hillside that cradled the farm. She'd come back here to find herself, and had discovered a life filled with possibilities. A life of sacrifices and hardships, but also a life of beauty and joy. She was ready to live it—all of it.

Life had broken her, but in the midst of her brokenness she'd found true healing. Whatever else came her way, she would face it without fear. She was strong. She was able.

She was a Humphrey.

Chapter Thirty-Four

May 2, 1970
Sixth Period English Class
Mother's Day Essay
Penny Humphrey

My Mother
By Penny Humphrey

If I had to describe my mother in one word, the word would be "beautiful." Not the kind of beautiful that makes people look at you on the street. That's the outward kind. My mother has dark hair and brown eyes, and she keeps her figure nice and trim. But even so, she is not the outward kind of beautiful. She is beautiful in a sensible kind of way that makes people feel safe and loved.

My mother's hands are beautiful because they are always busy doing what needs to be done. When Mrs. Donovan fell and broke her shoulder, my mother was the first person to arrive at her house with a chicken casserole and a bucket full of cleaning rags and furniture polish. When the organist at our church came down with the flu, my mother quietly sat down and played without even being asked. At home, her hands are busy baking bread and washing dishes and making beds. Because that is what is needed.

She takes care of things.

Mostly me.

Sometimes I feel like a bag of dirty laundry. I bring her my messy thoughts, my stained ego, my wrinkled attitudes, like a basketful of dirty socks and blouses and skirts. And mother sorts it all out and tidies it up and puts it all back together into nice, neat stacks.

A lot of mothers would have given me away. I know that. She gave up a lot for me, but she never makes me feel like I am a burden. She makes me feel like I am loved. From her, I have learned that love is about giving things up so you can get better things in return. I don't always act like it, but my mother means everything to me. I don't know what I would do without her.

I hope I never have to find out.

The End

www.ingramcontent.com/pod-product-compliance
Lightning Source LLC
Chambersburg PA
CBHW070928260626
47162CB00007B/2838